KEEPER OF SECRETS

DAY ONE

a novel by

JOHN DUNSON

ALPHARETTA, GEORGIA

KEEPER
OF
SECRETS

DAY ONE

Published by
Black & White Publishing Group
P.O. Box 4123
Alpharetta, Georgia 30023-4123

For information regarding special discounts for bulk purchases, please contact
Special Sales at: 1.770.557.0301.

Printed in the United States of America

1st printing tradepaperback 2004
10 9 8 7 6 5 4 3 2 1
Jacket design by Marion Designs
Book design by Burtch Hunter Design LLC

Library of Congress Cataloging-in-Publication Data
Dunson, John.
    Keeper of secrets, day one / John Dunson. --1st ed.

    p. cm. -- (24-hour series ; Book one)
    LCCN 2001118968
    ISBN 0-9714420-1-0

    1. Politics, Practical--Fiction. 2. Atlanta (Ga.)--Fiction.
3. Political fiction. I. Title.

PS3554.U4985K44 2002   813'.6
                                                  QBI01-701162

For Sarah, Devan, and Julie

Kristin,

Thanks for your support.

Hope you enjoy.

John

ACKNOWLEDGMENTS

First, let me say thanks to HIM for making this all possible. Without YOU there would be no ME.

Through this process, I've learned that it takes a whole lot of people to publish a novel. I've also learned a thing or two about myself. And you know what? From conception to completion, I wouldn't have changed a thing.

To Sarah, Devan, and Julie, I thank you. It's because of you that I do what I do. I love you more than words can say.

To my parents, my sisters, and my nephews, I thank you. Your support didn't and doesn't go unnoticed or unappreciated. I love you guys.

To my number one fan and editor, Amy Mason, I thank you. If I could make you co-author of this project, I would. Your counsel, words, suggestions, and guidance have made me and this project, BETTER. I wish all writers could be so lucky to have one of you. You are the best. By the way, I changed my mind; I think you do want it.

To my advance readers: Nandi Beede, DeDe Brown, Shelly Call, Toni Campbell, Kevin Cannon, Duane Covert, Wayne Cromartie, Cheryl Dickerson, Chris Dorsey, Jeffri Epps, Dorothy Ferguson, Susan Gerdvil, Jill Haskins, Holly Hoeppner, Danny Jackson, Audrey Jeffries, Kristina Kamman, Amy Levin, Kim Nejad, Lloyd Owens, Karri Parks, Peggy Rubin, Bill & Karen Shelton, Cheryl Sneed, Michelle Starks, James Stovall, Tish Thomas-Dickens, Erin Towns, Julee Vanhorse, Arlinda Vaughn, and Gretchen Watkins, I thank you. This project wouldn't be what it is without your input and suggestions.

To Team John, I thank you. Let's conquer the world.

To Burtch Hunter. You helped me create a quality product. Thank you for taking my vision and running with it. You are the best.

To James Alexander III (Jimbo), Amy Mason (Goldie Locks), Michael McCray (Osiris), and Vesna Codougan (Duggie), I thank you. Because of your belief in me, my dream came true. Let's sell some books.

And lastly, to YOU, the READER, I thank you. You took a chance on an unknown, and for that I am forever grateful. I promise to always give you my best. Until we meet face to face, take this as a token of my appreciation.

Peace and love,
John Dunson

KEEPER
OF
SECRETS

DAY ONE

PROLOGUE

SOMETIMES GOOD PEO-
PLE ...

```
        MIAMI,   FL
     A DOCTOR'S OFFICE
SUNDAY,   DECEMBER  12ᵀᴴ,  8:02
            P.M.
```

THE BLACK Chevy Suburban stopped at the corner of Third and Habersham, right next to the tracks. The doctor's office was located on Habersham, a half a block up on the right. It was a nondescript brick edifice that could easily be mistaken for an abandoned office building. One could drive by it and not give it a second thought. He had watched Senator Paul Barrett enter through the private entrance twenty minutes earlier. Since then there had been no new arrivals.

The detonation device rested peacefully in his hands. For the last ten minutes, it had provided him with an immense sense of power. He looked at it, smiled, then placed it back on the dashboard. At the same time, he casually glanced at the

Suburban's clock, which had been set a few minutes fast so that everyone and everything would be in place.

Because he wanted the only sound to be the approach of the hourly commuter train, he reached over and turned off the radio. His timing was perfect; the train could be heard in the distance. He wasn't surprised it was running five minutes late. He had anticipated this.

The thunderous vibrations the commuter train generated as it passed caused his glasses to shift. Without hesitation, he removed them and placed them back in their case. The glasses had already served their purpose for the evening and from that moment on could only serve as a hindrance.

He picked up the night-vision goggles from the floorboard, placed them to his eyes, and again scanned his surroundings. Satisfied, he stepped out of the Suburban and into the darkness.

From behind him, he heard the meow of a cat, followed by the patter of paws breaking through what sounded like days of accumulated trash. He turned toward the direction of the sound and zeroed in on the big, white creature scurrying across the street. The cat appeared to be chasing after some invisible object, leaving him to wonder whether it could be a metaphor for things to come.

Dressed in black jeans, a black long sleeve T-shirt, black boots and a black skullcap, he fit the image of a fashionable criminal. That is, if one had to label him. He had never cared too much for labels. Labels represented nothing more than a person's inability to think outside the box.

Labels were easy to digest.

God forbid you were a little different, as he was. He was an educated man. A holder of several advanced degrees. A computer engineer by training; soon to be a partner in an upstart telecommunications firm. But just like any other man, he had principles.

He stood for a few minutes taking in the Miami breeze. On any other night, hanging out on South Beach picking up women would have been welcome. But not tonight, not right now.

Tonight was business, then pleasure.

He knew this act would be considered barbaric by some, but that didn't matter to him. He had long since learned that sometimes it took extreme acts to prove a point. For him, this was all about R-E-S-P-E-C-T. Plain and simple.

Barrett's refusal to give it.

His refusal to be denied it.

He checked the surroundings for the third time, then stepped back inside the Suburban. Through tinted windows, he could see the Golden Dragon carryout less than eighty yards up the street. Aside from the owners of the establishment, the place was deserted. And they would be leaving in fifteen minutes.

Again he looked at his watch.

It was time.

The shock waves this incident would ignite gave him chills. He bared his teeth in a sneer that could have passed for a smile. This murder would be perfect, or at least as perfect as it could be.

Oh, the irony of the situation.

Barrett, too, would die violently.

Everything had come full circle. Every detail planned. Every scenario accounted for. Senator Paul Barrett's murder would be instant and spectacular. The message? Delivered. Barrett? Punished. Vindication? Sweet.

That's all he wanted. Just the satisfaction of knowing that Senator Paul Barrett would leave this world with a bang. A BIG BANG!

———◄○►———

While he programmed the detonation device, he thought about his parents. He missed them. Four years later, it was still like yesterday. The pain, still raw. He doubted it would ever leave, only hoped that over time it would lessen.

His eyes moved cautiously from the alley to the clinic back to Third Street. He wondered what Barrett was doing at that very moment inside the building, unaware of death's loud footsteps. More than likely, Barrett would be talking on the phone to an underling.

Wouldn't they be surprised when the phone went dead? Wouldn't they be even more surprised when Barrett was discovered dead? Better yet, how were they going to explain his death? What sensational lies would they conjure up?

Having these questions answered was almost more than he could stand. But since he had waited four years for some form of retribution, waiting a little longer would be a piece of cake. He pulled on his soul patch and thought about the scandalous relationship that had brought him there. For the past year his cousin, Rick, had been having physical relations with Senator Barrett's wife. And though this had been a relationship he did not condone, its benefits were immeasurable.

Barrett's wife couldn't be trusted. He had been certain of this from day one. He had learned long ago never to underestimate a woman scorned, especially a politician's wife. Erin Barrett had done nothing to quench his suspicion. To the contrary, she had only reinforced it by providing damaging, detailed information. The kind only a woman out to destroy a man would give.

But there had been a development that he hadn't anticipated. Rick had become attached to her, presenting the high probability of a major problem. Over the past few months, Rick had become distant and distracted. Rick had also started to attract a lot of attention -- not a good thing in their current line of business. After this night, he would have to sever the business relationship with Rick. Trouble was on the horizon if he didn't.

———◦———

The red beam of light flashed from the dark alley. Spanky moved the SUV to the adjacent curb. Before it had come to a complete halt, Rick and Fat Toney emerged from the darkness and jumped into the rear seats. Not thirty seconds later, the lights from a sedan cornered the block and pulled up next to the private entrance.

"Looks like we have company." Spanky nodded toward the Town Car.

"Who is it?" An out of breath Fat Toney asked.

"I can't tell, but I suspect it is one of Barrett's men. They're probably checking to see if everything is all right." Spanky offered this information as if he knew it as fact.

"I thought you said Barrett was coming to Miami alone?"

"Hell, Stu, he did come alone. You saw him get off the plane just like I did."

"Then who's in the Town Car, Rick?"

"How in the hell am I supposed to know, Stuart? I'm sittin' right here with you!"

There had been tension between the two of them for weeks. Sooner or later, it would come to a head.

"Man, Rick, if you weren't my cousin."

"What? If I wasn't your cousin, what?" Rick was almost in the front seat of the Suburban.

"I tell you, ain't nothing like family love. Can't you just feel the love?" Spanky joked.

"Shut up, Spanky!" Rick yelled.

It was obvious to all that Rick didn't want to be there.

"Man, don't get mad at me because you screwed up. I ain't your cousin and you know I don't play that shit!" Spanky shot

Rick a stare that could have melted steel.

"Look, someone is getting out the car!" Fat Toney pointed toward the private entrance.

The driver exited the vehicle. At the same time, the back door opened and out stepped a young female. As if on cue, in the private doorway of the clinic Senator Paul Barrett appeared.

Barrett walked to the car and kissed the passenger on the forehead. He then turned and said a few words to the driver. The driver awkwardly turned to the passenger as if she wanted to say something, but before she could, Barrett motioned for her to leave. The driver did as instructed and within seconds, had pulled off.

After the Town Car disappeared, Barrett stood at the entrance and continued to talk to the young lady. There appeared to be apprehension on her part, but Barrett seemed to be persuading her. Three minutes later, Barrett ushered her into the building.

"What was that about?" Fat Toney asked.

"Rick, I thought Barrett was coming to Miami on business?"

"Stuart, that's what I was told."

"Well obviously, Rick, you were lied to."

The Suburban was silent, which provided him with the opportunity to think. He had promised himself that there would be no innocent bystanders, but he also knew that there would never be another opportunity like this.

"Always take advantage of an opportunity." His father's words resonated in his head.

He thought about the young lady. Was she now no more than a mere footnote in history?

Possibly.

Probably.

She was only a little older than his sister.

His sister.

"Always look out for your sister." His mother's words battled with his father's.

"Stop it! Stop it! Stop it!" His inner voice demanded.

He tuned everything out. This decision impacted him more than anyone else. NO! This one act would not make him a bad person. YES! He was still a good person. This one event would not define him. He would not allow it to.

With eyes closed, he remembered the talks with his grandmother. Nana had always given him such good advice, such sound advice. What was it that Nana used to say? Was it something about good people sometimes doing bad things? That's what this was, right? A good person doing a bad thing. Nana would know the answer to that. She had always protected him from bad things. He wondered whether Nana was in heaven protecting him now. He so desperately needed to know that she was.

Spanky interrupted the silence by tapping him on the arm and leaning close as if he had a secret.

"Stuart, check it out. I think it is now safe to assume that Barrett's wife knew he was messing around. We can probably even take it a step further and say that it wasn't the first time. Now from my experience, most women, who are married to public figures, know that some messing around comes with the territory. But regardless of that fact, the ego can only take so much."

"So you think Mrs. Barrett was trying to get back at the senator by sleeping with Rick?" Fat Toney asked like a student who had finally caught up with the rest of his classmates.

Spanky nodded.

"Stuart, don't you find it too coincidental that of all the men in Atlanta, Mrs. Barrett chose Rick? Not to knock Rick's game, but they don't run in the same circles. On the surface, it doesn't make sense. Unless she had other motives."

"Like what?"

"Like this," Spanky replied, gesturing to their surroundings.

"Make your case, Spanky."

"All right, Stuart, I'll do just that. Georgia Tech, if your woman fucks around on you, what are you going to do?"

"Simple, I'm gonna go fuck someone else. That's a given," Fat Toney replied.

"Exactly. And Stuart, you would do the same thing, right?"

"Yeah. So what does any of that have to do with this, Spank?"

Spanky raised his hand to temper his friend.

"Stu, I don't believe most women would respond that way and frankly, neither would I."

"You a lie, Spanky! We've all heard you brag many times about sleeping with friends of former girlfriends," yelled Rick.

Spanky turned in Rick's direction and smiled. "Yes, you have. But, gentleman, each and every one of those times served a purpose."

"Yeah, revenge." Rick was tired of Spanky's amateur psychology.

"No, that's what you and most men do. Revenge fucking I call it. I think differently. Rarely, if ever, do I engage in such pettiness. It suits no purpose other than momentary satisfaction. Yeah sure, you're thinking about hurting that other person and occasionally you do. But at the end of the day, revenge fucking has little benefit."

"Okay, Dr. Phil. What kind of fucking do you do?" Rick snapped. Spanky was beyond full of shit, and he couldn't believe that Stuart and Fat Toney were actually buying it.

"Ah, the million dollar question. I, my friend, only do strategic fucking, which is quite different from revenge fucking and appears to be the type Mrs. Barrett has employed with you."

"Stuart, Spanky is full of shit!" Rick slapped the back of the seat.

"What's a strategic fuck, Spanky?" Fat Toney asked, ignoring Rick's outburst.

"A strategic fuck is the preferred tool of most women. It involves a specific person. Women know why they are going to sleep with a specific someone and what will happen after they have slept with that person. They do what I like to call a S.W.O.T. analysis. And it's very effective, I might add."

"Guys, I'm telling you, Spanky is full of shit! No woman I know does any of this bullshit!"

"You're young and stupid, Rick. What do you think this is? Huh! Before that woman screwed you, believe me, she did a S.W.O.T. analysis on your ass. And let me be clear what I mean by that. Erin Barrett is not one of those chickenhead around-the-way-girls you're used to dealing with. She's a politician's wife, which means she's probably seen a lot more than you ever will. She plays an entirely different style of ball than you're accustomed to.

"Before she fucked you, Mrs. Erin Barrett knew: your Strengths, your Weaknesses, the Opportunities you provided, and the Threats you presented. She had done a S.W.O.T. analysis on you, son. She picked you because you are Rick Casner, the nephew of Judge Stacy Hastings and Sheila Casner-Hastings -- her husband's albatross."

"Okay, smart ass, if that's the case, why didn't she just go after Stuart? He's their son for Christ's sake!"

"Another good question, and I would venture to say because you were an easier target. You're younger, wilder, more daring and less scrutinizing. In other words, you're young and dumb, which was precisely the point."

"Okay, Spank. But that still doesn't answer the question about how we got here."

"We got here, Stuart, because Mrs. Barrett knew that by fucking Rick, she could accomplish several things. First, she probably just wanted her husband to know that she could screw around too. Maybe the senator didn't respond the way she would have liked. Let's say he didn't get upset in the least bit; obviously, that option didn't elicit the desired response. So, on to the next option -- put the senator in a compromising position."

"And this was accomplished through supplying Rick with the information about my parents' murders?"

"Correct. Stu, I would bet my last dollar that Mrs. Barrett knew that Rick would tell you and that you would question Barrett about it. She knew Barrett would react the way he did, leaving you feeling betrayed."

"And angry enough to do something about it."

"Precisely. Mrs. Barrett's ultimate goal was probably to have the senator spin his own web of deceit and entrapment. She would come out smelling like a rose -- hands, squeaky-clean." Spanky turned toward Rick and Fat Toney. "That, is what is called strategic fucking."

"This is bullshit, Stuart. First of all..."

"Shut up, Rick! She played our ass. Point fucking blank! She played us. Pimped us. Used us. Outsmarted us. However you want to classify it, she did it. But it will not happen again! You can betcha' life on that!"

"What you mean by that, Stu?" Rick asked.

"Just what I said, cuz, just what I said!"

The more he sat and thought about what Spanky had just said, the more sense it made. Maybe they were being used. Barrett's wife could have been using them.

Hell hath no fury like a woman scorned.

Spanky was right; Erin Barrett had probably been hoping just to embarrass the senator. A little indecent exposure, if nothing else. Never in her wildest dreams could she have guessed what was about to happen. But alas, revenge resides in many hearts. And his was no exception.

He watched the big, white cat scurry back across Third Street. At the same time, an image of his parents' ravaged bodies flashed before his eyes. Their murders had happened on his father's fifty-third birthday, during an intimate dinner. A very special dinner that his mother had been planning for over a week.

He closed his eyes and saw his mother's beautiful smile, red hair, and freckles. She had been small in stature, but a firecracker in action. Feisty and fashionable was how his father often described her.

On the night they were killed, his parents had dropped Tish off at his place so that they could have privacy. He remembered them being happy that evening; in fact, they had been downright giddy. But his mother's smile. Only one word could even come close to describing it -- electric. It was the same smile most kids exuded on Christmas and birthdays. And yet that evening, in spite of it being his father's birthday, his mother had worn it.

Sheila Casner-Hastings had always been the rock in the family and a pillar in the community. A loving wife and a devoted mother. And just as suddenly, she'd become a tragic victim. An innocent bystander. Someone in the wrong place, at the wrong time. Much like the young lady with Barrett at the present moment.

But unlike his mother, he believed that this young lady

was intimately aware of Barrett's wrong doings. Her being here proved that. It was just too bad for her that she'd decided to keep Barrett company on this night. He had no other choice. Being used or not; it was time to finish this thing, once and for all.

He motioned for Spanky to circle the block, then stop across the street. Fat Toney would activate the bomb from there. In his heart, he had known that Barrett would never divulge the identity of the person who had hired his parents' killer. As much as he now hated to admit it, deep down he had always known it.

If anything, he should have been mad for ignoring the writing on the wall. Had he been so eager to believe in the goodness of man that he had ignored common sense?

He knew Barrett was used to playing politics. Playing one side against the other. Screwing people over and not having to answer for it. But Barrett had to know that he didn't play by society's rules. He lived by a different code of conduct. Barrett had forced his hand. And in the process had committed a tragic error. Senator Paul Barrett had fucked over the wrong man. And for that, he would die.

———◦———

Fat Toney got out of the Suburban, walked toward the clinic. With every other step, he licked his crusty lips and pinched his big nose. Smiling, he inhaled the danger involved in this act. For a split second, he hesitated, not out of fear, but because he wanted to savor the moment. He had heard that there was nothing like the adrenaline rush before a kill. Now he understood what the statement meant. The butterflies that one would expect had long since dissipated. He was ready to read the headlines.

Stripes would be earned with this murder. Stuart had

wanted to do it himself, but he had begged and pleaded. Of the four, Stuart had the most to lose. Stuart had a sister who depended on him, and she had lost too much already. Stuart had acquiesced.

Fat Toney stood facing the clinic. The bomb had been programmed to detonate approximately three minutes after he entered the last number. He had played this scene over and over in his head. Whoever had joined Senator Paul Barrett was going to die with him. There could be no turning back. The stakes were too high. His future too bright.

He caressed the detonation device in his clammy hands. He could feel the power of his tiny friend. After this was over, he'd keep her as a souvenir -- a special momento. Something to be looked at and cherished for the rest of his life. He stroked her surface as he would a new lover. Her warmth was orgasmic.

Carefully, he began to trace her pleasure points. The One felt good, but the Two felt better. He skipped over the Three, opting to tease it instead. The Four, Five and Six, he fingered slowly, gently. The Seven and Eight were almost faded away from overuse, so he skipped them as well. They could use the rest, he figured. The Nine was all shiny and new, a recent replacement. He just grazed its surface. Then finally, the Queen Bee. The source of his imminent pleasure -- The Zero. Fat Toney looked at it standing so regal like. Calling attention to itself. Screaming. TOUCH ME, TOUCH ME.

He looked at it like a man getting ready for sex. They were two entities destined for each other. Both possessing the thing that the other longed for. Both unable to go any longer without experiencing the other's touch.
TOUCH ME, TOUCH ME.

He could hear it calling him. Calling his name loud and clear. Wanting no other man but him.

"Yes, baby," he answered, as he traced the outside of its

body, stroking it with his nails.

Fat Toney held his new lover up to his eyes. He wanted to see her by the moonlight. She was beautiful -- a little seasoned. Not like he typically preferred his lovers, but that was okay. She was special.

He pulled her to his mouth and traced her with his tongue. He could taste the salt on her skin. Delicious. He could feel the wetness on her surface. Inviting.

Her ready light came on.

He could feel her trembling in his hands. He was going to please her. He was going to give her what she wanted; what she was now begging him for. He held her tightly. So tight that it would have been difficult for anyone to delineate between them. They were a perfect fit -- a destined pair. Soul mates.

Slowly, he reared back and slammed his finger into the Queen Bee. A low hum sprang forth from somewhere deep inside. Fat Toney sighed and gasped, ooohed and ahhhed, twisted and turned, then smiled.

His breathing was short and heavy. Sweat was pouring. He wiped his forehead with the sleeve of his sweater and looked at his new/old lover.

Her satisfaction light came on.

He had pleased her, as she had him.

Gingerly, he kissed her one last time before bidding her goodnight.

ACT ONE

FIVE YEARS LATER

NORMALLY HONEST
PEOPLE ...

CHAPTER 1

A VOICE was the first thing he heard. Was it a woman's voice or was it a man's voice? He was having difficulty making it out. No it was definitely a woman's. She was giving the forecast for the day's weather.

"A cold front approaching. Rain possible." Rick attempted to open his eyes, but the stinging sensation made it impossible. Briefly, a faint memory of earlier events registered in his mind. So far, every attempt to raise himself from the dampness had been unsuccessful. His legs wouldn't cooperate. They felt pinned down, making it difficult to get to the bathroom.

He'd been collecting these video moments for six years. They helped make up his legacy -- videos of the women he'd loved. The videos had already helped to make him some extra money; some a little, some a lot.

But now her jealousy was threatening to destroy it all.

She should have been happy to be part of the ones that came before her. Most women would have been impressed with his sphere of influence, his creativity, his imagination. So much imagination. Yet, her inability to understand the big picture had caused her to act irrationally.

He'd lived in this house for four years, had helped design it. It had eight bedrooms and four bathrooms. An indoor bridge led over an indoor pond, which contained tropical fish. It had all the accoutrements that money could buy. Three years before, it had been featured in *Atlanta* magazine.

Everything had been built to his specifications. Including his private playroom, which was located in the basement directly underneath the master bathroom. Only the truly uninhibited ones knew of its existence. Thousands of women, thousands of tapes, dozens of little toys and gadgets.

It was a wonder to behold.

These trinkets were stored in a special cabinet. Truly magical moments they had helped produce. Moments even he had a hard time believing. Some of the tapes were downright disgusting, but that was what they wanted. And he always aimed to please.

This room existed just for these goodies; these glorious achievements. This modern day shrine was his way of honoring; his way of partaking in life's perverted pleasures. The room was cleverly concealed and could only be accessed in one way -- sensors.

As a child, he and his mother had traveled all over the world. From each place they'd visited, he had secured a souvenir. The souvenirs, he kept in the basement, enclosed inside a glass trophy case that ran the full length of the basement wall.

The private playroom could be accessed by aligning the special sensor from one of the souvenirs with the one located on the basement wall. Unless one knew which souvenir contained the sensor and the location of the sensor on the wall, the room couldn't be accessed. And even then, one had to know where the key to open the cabinet was located. For these reasons, exposure had never been a concern.

But somehow she'd stumbled onto the room; at least that was the lie she used.

The Nosy Bitch.

And now the water threatened to destroy it all by caving in the bathroom floor.

When the house was built, the builder had cut corners by using substandard materials in the bathrooms. By the time he had found out, it was too late. He had already moved in and since then, he had repeatedly put off having any of the bathrooms redone.

Three months ago, he had started to notice water damage in the ceiling of the private playroom. A plumber had warned that it would only get worse as more water accumulated. Immediate replacement of materials had been recommended. Procrastination had always been his bad habit. Now it threatened to destroy a large portion of his happiness.

Was everything now being destroyed because of one bad habit?

His babies.

His toys.

His conquests.

His plans.

His legacy.

Damn her.

Rick tried to slow his breathing. The last thing he needed was to have a panic attack or worse, an asthma attack. "Calm down, Rick," he told himself. He could still save his temple, but first he needed to get control of himself.

He could still get to the bathroom.

From what he could remember from the argument, Rick believed that he was lying next to the fireplace. The smell of burning wood permeated his nostrils. If his guess was correct, the bathroom was approximately thirty feet from him.

With his arms extended, Rick felt around for familiarity. Any piece of furniture would give him a better indication of his location. His outstretched arms came back empty.

This wasn't good.

In the distance, he could hear the voices of a man and a woman. Then he heard nothing.

CHAPTER 2

MASCARA RAN down her face as she rushed from the house to the car. Looking at her watch, she saw she didn't have much time. Her top lip was numb from the blow and her eyes were puffy from crying.

Teri tossed her toiletries on the passenger seat of the SUV and rushed back into the house. Blood from her mouth had stained her nightshirt. She took it off, threw it on the wet carpet.

Searching the room for something else to put on, Teri ran to the closet, headed to Rick's armoire. She flung it open, grabbed one of his old sweatshirts. Even though her head hurt from when he'd yanked her hair, she easily slid into it. It would also cover the bruise on her left arm where Rick had assaulted her.

Rick had physically harmed her. That fact couldn't be denied.

Teri threw the suitcase in the SUV, wiped the tears from her eyes. She ran back into the house for the last of her belongings. When she entered the bedroom, she saw Rick squirming like a captured animal. Although his feet were bound, Rick's hands were close to the fire poker. Could he be trying to attack her again?

She didn't plan on finding out.

Teri kicked Rick in the head with her boots, rendering him unconscious. She then dragged him to the center of the room where it would be more difficult for him to get free.

Teri looked at her watch again. She had to hurry up. There was no telling how long Rick would be out. She thought about turning off the television. "Fuck it," she mumbled. It wasn't her concern anymore.

She looked at the water overflowing from the bathtub onto the floor. A planned bubble bath cut short by his accusations. She shuddered remembering the look in Rick's eyes when he had attacked her. Pure rage. All she had done was ask him a question. A question that she believed she had a right to know the answer to.

Why did he have that den of perversion in the basement? And more importantly, why did he have videotapes of them having sex?

Instead of answering her, Rick had become belligerent. Yelled and cursed at her. Called her an unappreciative bitch and pulled her out of the bathroom by her hair. Rick had slapped her and swung at her like she was a man. But because he had been drinking and doing God knows what else, she had avoided the full contact of his blow.

And in self-defense, she had retaliated.

During the struggle, she had noticed that Rick smelled of

fresh soap, like he'd just taken a shower. Did he think she was that stupid? Obviously. How long had she been so stupid? Even a day would have been too long, she concluded.

She wasn't mad, just relieved. At least she had destroyed the tapes of him and her. No more physical evidence that their lives had ever been intertwined existed. She was almost certain of that, or at least as certain as one could be under the circumstances.

Still, she never would have thought that Rick would have stooped so low to begin with. How could he have done that to her? How could he have violated their innocent and special moments? The things that they had done with each other. Special things, he had called them.

Again, Teri shuddered at the memories.

But why would she have been perceived differently from the other women? She'd seen the hundreds of tapes. My God, she thought. Did those other women have any idea? Of course some did; some had even been down in the basement, happy to star in his pornographic productions. And there had been so many of them. Most seeming to be of a certain stock: well-bred, well-known, oozing money.

However, she would not be on that list. What she did and who she did it with was between her and that person, no one else.

After she'd viewed the first videotape, certain things had become crystal-clear. The most obvious, that she had gotten in over her head. The next ten videotapes had only served to reiterate that fact. Therefore, she had decided to walk away. Chalk it up as another one of life's lessons and move on.

And that's what she had told him.

But he had become verbally abusive and attacked her. Accused her of snooping through his things. His things, his house. Twenty-four hours earlier, it had been their things. Their things, their house.

How quickly things had changed.

—◦—

Grabbing another bag from the closet, Teri hastily packed the last of her belongings. It was time for her to move on. She had clearly overstayed her welcome, but first she needed to change cars. She knew Rick would probably report the SUV as stolen, because that's what she would do. The police would track her down. They would tell him. He would come after her.

Good thing she'd always believed in emergency planning. Unbeknownst to Rick, she had purchased a car -- just in case. He would not expect her to be so savvy, but that had always been his attitude toward her. He had never respected her mind. And now she had proof that he had never respected women period.

The Toyota Camry she'd purchased had been left in long-term parking at Hartsfield International Airport, ready at a moment's notice. She would leave Rick's SUV in short-term parking where it could be found by Tish later.

After she had viewed the third videotape, she had purchased three airline tickets: a one-way ticket to Los Angeles scheduled to leave later that morning; a one-way ticket to Vancouver, British Columbia scheduled to leave one hour after the Los Angeles flight landed; and a one-way ticket to Rio de Janeiro scheduled to leave one hour after the Vancouver flight landed.

She charged it all to the charge card Rick had bestowed upon her. She had always had her own money, but Rick had preferred her to use his. At first she'd had a problem with it; now she was glad that she had gotten over it. It would not take Rick long to figure out what she had done, but that was okay because he would be wrong.

—◦—

Teri looked at her watch again. She then double-checked the bedroom. It was now 6:32 a.m. Rush hour traffic would begin in less than an hour. She had a long trip ahead of her and an even longer time to think about her future. However, she needed to hurry because they were predicting a severe storm for the East Coast. If the weather got too bad, she'd have to get a hotel room.

Rushing from the bedroom closet, Teri made a mental check of her list: clothes, books, laptop, pictures, jewelry, cash, and a few of the videotapes for a friend.

She looked down at Rick lying on the wet carpet covered and surrounded by his disgusting perversions. She then glanced at the empty bottle of nail polish remover and the baseball bat. They had saved her life. Had she not thrown the nail polish remover in his eyes, she would be the one lying on the floor instead of him.

Once again, she shuddered at the thought.

Teri ran out the door, jumped in the SUV and spun out of the driveway. Without looking back, she headed south toward the airport.

CHAPTER 3

ALPHARETTA, GA
COUNTRY CLUB OF THE SOUTH
6:38 A.M.

THE MAN watched as the silver Land Cruiser sped out of the driveway of the million-dollar estate. He had waited hours for some activity inside the residence, even though he knew exactly where the home's occupants were at all times.

He knew Rick had been at the Ritz-Carlton in Buckhead for seven of the last eight hours. He knew Teri had come home around 11 p.m. to find a light on in the hallway leading to the basement. Feeling scared, Teri had tried to call Rick, but obviously Rick was unavailable. She then called him, Raymond Sexton, or as she would know him, Security Officer Harold Sprint.

After doing a search of the periphery and the inside of the

property, he had informed Teri that there was no sign of forced entry. But before leaving, he had casually mentioned how he and his wife were also swingers. He had mentioned that it was a splendid idea for them to have a private playroom for those activities.

Sexton knew Teri would have no idea about the room he was referring to. As expected, she had been confused, so he had apologized. Teri had threatened to report him to his supervisor if he didn't come clean. That's when he had showed her Rick's private playroom with the toys, gadgets, and tapes. For six hours, Sexton listened while Teri watched tapes of Rick's perversions. Weeks prior, he had removed the ones that were of importance to his employer. Others he had taken for his own viewing pleasure. He couldn't resist. Rick Casner was a man after his own heart.

Hours earlier, his team had removed the majority of the surveillance equipment from the residence. He would finish the rest, before the Feds moved in. His team had already been dispatched for phase two.

After she had tired of watching the tapes, Sexton heard Teri run what sounded like a bath. He heard her hum a Tracy Chapman song. At the same time, he watched Rick pull into the driveway.

Then he heard all hell break loose. But that was the way he had planned it.

The disturbance had been loud. So loud in fact that he had thought about intervening, but that would have been too risky -- raised too much suspicion. So Sexton sat and listened. And waited.

―◄○►―

Sexton waited approximately five minutes after the Land Cruiser left. He entered the estate, turned off the running water. He dragged Rick over to the bed, lifted his head, and placed it against the railing. He hadn't been instructed to kill him.

So that Rick would not unexpectedly regain consciousness, Sexton injected a muscle relaxant into his system. This ensured that Rick would be out a few more hours. Teri had bound Rick's feet, rendering movement difficult if he regained consciousness.

With Rick taken care of, Sexton went to work. First, he checked the residence to see if Teri had left any clues, she hadn't. She had been thorough in her packing. "Good girl," he mumbled.

Sexton noticed the cut on Rick's arm. He saw the baseball bat, the bloody nail file, the empty bottle of nail polish remover. From their position, he could tell they had been the defense weapons. The nail file in particular had produced a pretty nasty cut, but Rick would heal. And that was more than could be said for some of Rick's victims.

Sexton's eyes followed the trail of blood drops leading to the doorway. Doubting that the drops could be Rick's, he knew they were Teri's. Angry, he planted a powerful kick from his size twelve boot in Rick's ribs. "That was for Teri," he mumbled.

Rick grunted.

Sexton removed the remaining surveillance equipment from the residence. He didn't want any surprises awaiting the Feds when they arrived. Next, he went to the basement, destroyed any videotapes featuring Teri that had been missed, and removed any incriminating documents connected to his employer. Once he was satisfied there, Sexton walked back to the kitchen.

Two minutes later, Sexton walked into Rick's heated four-car garage. From the kitchen, he had taken a canister of sugar. He poured the sugar in the gas tanks of Rick's brand new 600 Mercedes-Benz SLK and 911 Porsche Boxster. Finished, he tossed the empty canister in the wastebasket.

After thoroughly rechecking the residence, Sexton walked back to the patrol car, drove to the office, and signed off duty -- for good. Raymond Sexton picked up his cell phone and dialed his employer. Phase one had been a complete success.

CHAPTER 4

SENATOR JOHN Knight placed the phone back in its cradle. With a smile on his face, he walked to the door, picked up his morning paper, and headed toward the kitchen. He glided over to the counter where the coffee had just finished brewing and poured himself a cup. There was nothing like good news and a fresh cup of coffee to start the day.

From the kitchen cabinets, Knight removed the cookware he would need for that morning's masterpiece. John Knight considered himself a gourmet chef. Those who dealt with the senator in the political arena might have a less favorable description, but he didn't care. Knight knew that he was good at his job and that was one of the only things that mattered to him.

Dubbed by the *Congressional Quarterly* as a future leader of the Senate, Senator John Knight was a rising star. However, just like his predecessor, he had an Achilles heal. Senator John Knight was a nymphomaniac.

He loved sex of almost every variety. It consumed his thoughts, which at times proved to be detrimental to him as a legislator. Although his primary job required him to do work on behalf of the good people of Georgia, this often collided with his penchant for frequenting the most exclusive sex clubs in the country. This happened to be his secondary job and one that he took just as seriously.

Besides his seats on the Senate Finance, Intelligence and Judiciary Committees, unofficially, one of his duties was also to serve as pointman for any sexcapades or sexual disasters. This was a duty that he had inherited from his predecessor, the late Senator Paul Barrett.

For two decades, he had served as the chief of staff in Senator Barrett's administration. And on occasion, Senator Barrett had been a fuckup of royal proportions. Yet despite his faults, Paul Barrett had become untaintable. And everyone knew why -- John Knight and others.

Although Senator Barrett had been the elected official, Knight and a small group of trusted advisors ran the show. They had been the brains behind the operation. And were at times, ruthless.

They had been known to bribe, threaten, and steal. Nothing or no one had been off limits. And since Knight had been the most visible of the bunch, he was now hated by a good percentage of the other elected officials in Washington, D.C.

Throughout the halls of Congress, Barrett had often been referred to as "Teflon Paul" because no scandal could stick.

His exploits in the Senate had become legendary and the reputation of his chief of staff had grown. According to his own calculations, Knight had saved Barrett's ass no less than two dozen times. But all that had changed five years ago.

—◄○►—

Five years earlier, Knight had assumed the Senate seat vacated by the untimely death of Senator Paul Barrett. As far as the public knew, Barrett had been killed in a boating accident, while fly-fishing. In actuality, Barrett had been killed in a bombing in Miami.

Congressional leadership had decided that it would be too detrimental to public morale if the truth ever came out. Not to mention, some of the leadership had been visibly uncomfortable with exposing the dirty laundry of a beloved colleague, especially since they, too, had utilized the services of this Miami facility. Nothing would be done that could forever stain the United States Congress and the honest men and women who served in it.

A special joint sub-committee of the House and Senate had been instructed to come up with a viable solution. All for the good of the country. Their solution had been that the great senator from the state of Georgia would go out with the honor and respect due him after serving his country for so long. The president had agreed and a plan had been put into action. The FBI had been told to solve the case, but to keep the findings internal. In the meantime, Knight had been appointed by the Governor of Georgia to finish Barrett's term.

John Knight was born in Portland, Oregon. His father was a lumberjack and his mom, a social worker. The youngest of five, John was the only boy among four girls, which caused him to relate to women better than he did men and caused his father to often refer to him as a momma's boy.

When he was thirteen, his father died on a job site. The company was suspected to be at fault and the family sued. A settlement was reached and the Knight family walked away with twenty million dollars. Claire Knight gave each of her children three million dollars and some advice. "Don't blow it."

Intrigued by the hoopla surrounding his father's death, Knight admired the men in suits -- the men who controlled the lawyers. The men who could pay millions of dollars to settle the family's lawsuit and make disasters go away. John Knight wanted to be one of those men. So at seventeen, he moved cross-country to attend George Washington University in Washington, D.C.

Fearing that John would blow his money chasing women and getting into other kinds of trouble, Claire Knight placed the majority of his three million in a trust fund, which couldn't be accessed until he reached the age of twenty-five. Because his financial future was secure, Knight was able to take outrageous risks and pursue his dreams. He became a master at spotting deals and backslapping. And since he was outspoken and brash, Knight naturally gravitated toward the political arena. It provided everything he needed in abundance.

———◆———

Senator Knight stared at the dish and congratulated himself. The omelet looked delectable. He reached into the overhead cabinet and retrieved a set of china. He was in the mood for some self-pampering.

After he had meticulously laid out the china, the silverware and his vitamins, Knight served himself a healthy portion. Embarrassingly, he looked down at his plate and frowned at the amount of food on it. He was obviously hungrier than normal. Last night had been physically draining. If he was going to continue running around with these younger women, then he would need to take better care of himself.

Patting his ample stomach, Knight vowed to start on a diet, possibly as early as next week. Maybe he would even go down to Seaside and spend a week running the beach. He'd have to go alone though; otherwise, he'd get distracted. Women, especially younger ones, tended to have that effect on him. He made a mental note to tell Fred to call and reserve the beach house.

With that matter resolved, Senator Knight picked up the first section of *The Atlanta Journal-Constitution*. When nothing of interest caught his attention, he pulled out the sports section. He was interested to see what moves the Braves were contemplating during the offseason. Although his heart was still hurting from the team's downward spiral in October's championship series, a good year for the Braves translated into an excellent year for him. He'd learned long ago that someone could always be influenced with quality Brave's tickets.

He was halfway through Terrance Moore's column on Gary Sheffield when the phone rang. Looking at the caller ID, Knight saw that it was his chief of staff, Jeff Cirrillo.

"Hello, Jeff," Knight answered in his best cheerful morning voice.

"Good morning, Senator. I hope I didn't call at a bad time?"

"Well actually, I was…"

"Good. Everything's a go for today's ceremony. It looks like the weather has forced us to have the event at City Hall, but that should work just fine. Right now, our only concern will be getting back into D.C. for your meeting with Director Rogers tomorrow morning. We also received confirmation that Sharon Walsh will be making the dedication. Apparently, Mr. Chandler has some other obligations so he will be unable to attend."

Knight shook his head in disgust. The arrogance of his

friend was appalling. He couldn't fathom forking over twenty million dollars for a new inner-city YMCA and not being present for the groundbreaking. The media would be out in droves. But then again, his friend was different.

"Well that's fine. She's a lot prettier to look at anyway. Plus, it'll make for a good photo-op. But I'll give him a call later to bust his balls."

"Good. The car will be there to pick you up in two hours for the meeting with Bill Simmons at Futurus Bank."

"Jeff, about this meeting, is there anything we need to know beforehand? There aren't any last minute developments I need to know about?"

"No, Senator. He's on board and I anticipate that he will have a few of the other business leaders with him. I'm certain they'll be formally endorsing the new proposal by this afternoon."

Knight was in the middle of securing funding for a new public library to be named in honor of the late Senator Paul Barrett. And although he didn't need it, it had been decided that it would look better to have the support of the city's business leaders.

"Do we know who, Jeff? You know I hate going into these meetings not knowing what or who is awaiting me."

"I don't know right now, Senator. But I will by the time I see you."

"All right. Is there anything else?"

"Well, there is the little matter of Fred and that problem he's working on. I don't think he is telling us everything about..."

Knight interrupted him, "I don't want to talk about that now, Jeff. We'll discuss that later in person, in private."

"Yes, sir. Then that would be all, Senator."

Senator Knight hung up the phone, finished eating his breakfast. Today was going to be a good day. He could feel it.

CHAPTER 5

ATLANTA, GA
SENATOR KNIGHT'S RESIDENCE
8:50 A.M.

FRED KING sat in the back of the Lincoln Town Car, thought about the many perks that came with his job. King considered himself to be a man of exceptional luck. As a matter of fact, he would be the first to argue that his luck and family lineage had been the main determinants for his success thus far. Fred knew he possessed few employable skills. More importantly, he knew his limitations. Fred was a political thug; a clean-up specialist, a trusted advisor.

Above all else, Fred was a keeper of secrets.

At least that was what his brother-in-law and sister called him. But Fred knew that the titles had different meanings for both. Coming from his brother-in-law, it meant he was a high-priced gopher. And coming from his sister, it meant he was a loyal confidante.

However, Fred had no problem with that at all. He abhorred the idea of chasing clients and kissing ass. And as long as his asshole brother-in-law was in office and married to his sister, Carmellia, he had a guaranteed job -- though at the moment that marriage was on very shaky ground.

For years, he had tried to make sense of the relationship that existed between his sister and her husband. But he soon learned that if it worked for them, so be it. He would just shut up and enjoy the ride. That was the least they owed him for his troubles.

Fred King was many things; a fool was not one of them.

Fred knew he had a great gig. His friends envied him. Women wanted him. He had an office in Washington and Atlanta with one secretary and one assistant in both. He had the use of a government vehicle and an ungodly expense account.

He also had instant access to every private sex club in the U.S., with the exception of Alaska. And that was only because he refused to go there. But at the moment, he also had a major problem to deal with and less than ten hours to deal with it.

———◁○▷———

The rear doors of the Town Car opened. The two men walked toward the private entrance of the senator's estate. As usual, Jeff Cirrillo was in front. They were hoping the senator would be dressed and ready to go. Neither expected it, but they were still hoping. If they were lucky, the wait would be only ten minutes.

Before they could ring the doorbell, the lady of the house walked out. Carmellia had her poodles with her and appeared to be going on her morning walk. Both men noticed the cell phone in her hand.

"In case of an emergency," Carmellia had said defensively when she noticed them eyeing it.

Neither man believed her.

Carmellia was Fred's younger sister. Ten years younger to be exact. She was thirty-five, adventurous, and easily bored. Carmellia was a former Miss Georgia, who had married John Knight for strategic reasons. They had grown to accommodate each other over time.

John was older and established. Carmellia was the consummate funtime girl. They had been married eleven years and were the proud parents of no children. Two years into the marriage, all pretensions had worn off. Now, they no longer slept in the same bed, and were rarely in the same house.

The senator spent more time in D.C. than he did in Georgia. Doing the work of the people, he often bragged. Carmellia knew every hot spot in both cities, was a blossoming national socialite, a future member of all the right clubs, and a serious fund-raiser for several major charities.

The senator did his thing, Carmellia did hers. Those were the unwritten rules. The senator benefited from Carmellia's high visibility, social graces, and staggering beauty. She was everything he was not and vice-versa. In a strange way, they were perfect for each other. She was the yin to his yang.

Both went to great lengths not to embarrass one another. It was not stated but understood that they could sleep with whomever they wanted, as long as it was discreet. If problems arose, those problems were dealt with, quickly and quietly. Hence, one of Fred's primary responsibilities. And right now, his major problem.

CHAPTER 6

MINUTE SIXTY-FIVE had just elapsed and Senator Knight was finally getting out of the shower. He was running late even by his own standards. Both men understood the situation, so neither was surprised. The senator was a notorious groomer. With the extra media attention surrounding the day's events, ten-thirty would be a blessing.

"So, she called you while she was on her way to Hartsfield?" Jeff asked.

"Yep," Fred answered for the fourth time, clearly bothered.

"And you're sure she hasn't talked to anyone about her involvement with the senator?"

"Hell no, I'm not sure. Right now I'm not sure of a damn

thing. I'm not even sure whether they are involved as you say. Shit, Jeff, I'm still trying to figure out what the hell is going on myself."

"Well let's talk about what you do know," Jeff said suspiciously.

Fred wanted to smack the little prick, but figured he would probably do irreparable damage. Instead, he brought his hands up, smoothed back his ponytail. A habit he knew Jeff despised.

"Jeff, with all due respect, we've been over this ten times already. I don't see what good going over it again will do right now."

"I'll tell you what good it will do. It will help me understand how this shit happened in the first place. And better still, maybe it will help me understand why I haven't already fired your ass. But please excuse me for taking up so much of your precious time."

"Jeff, I don't know what happened! What I know, you know!"

"I don't believe that shit. Not for one minute do I believe that shit. And you better stop lying to me." Jeff was turning a deep shade of red and pointing his finger. "Must I remind you that a lot of people could get fucked because of this? Things like this have a way of taking on a life of their own."

"Jeff, I understand all of that. I've been around this type of stuff longer than you and know a lot more about this, so back off!"

Fred turned his back to walk toward the bar. Forget the hour, he needed a strong drink. The nerve of this little prick talking to him in such a manner. He had been doing this kind of thing for well over a decade now. Longer than this little shit had been out of his prep high school.

And how dare Jeff Cirrillo threaten to fire him. Jeff didn't have the power and he damn sure didn't have the balls. What the hell did he expect? Did Jeff expect him to betray his own family? If so, then Jeff Cirrillo was terribly mistaken.

Jeff followed Fred over to the bar. He jerked Fred's arm. He was beyond pissed.

"I will not fucking back off you arrogant, insubordinate asshole. And don't you ever turn your back on me again. My fucking career is at stake here and unlike you, I have worked very hard to get to where I am. I don't intend to let you or anyone else tarnish my reputation.

"So please excuse me if I ask you to use your limited intelligence to explain to me why we have some opportunistic fucker threatening to blackmail our boss over some sex shit. Something that is indefensible!

"And second, how some low-life stripper, who just happens to be a girlfriend of one of the largest East Coast strip club owners and suspected drug dealers in the state, has our boss walking around like some lovesick puppy. And while you're at it..." The sound of the front door opening caused both men to turn in its direction. Carmellia was returning from her morning walk.

Carmellia walked into the family room, released the poodles from their leashes. The poodles stopped, looked, seemed unimpressed with the visitors, and headed to other parts of the estate.

"Boys, I could hear the yelling as I was walking up the driveway. My God, what would the neighbors think? If you two can't get along, I..."

Fred interrupted, "We're sorry, Carm. We just got a little carried away."

"Mrs. Knight, please excuse us. We were having a little misunderstanding over a policy issue," added Jeff.

"I can see that, but can't we at least try to be quieter in our disagreements."

"We'll try," they both said in unison.

The tension in the room was thick. Carmellia knew that neither man particularly cared for the other. And rightfully so.

Their loyalties were to different people.

"Wonderful. Now, Jeff, what time would you like for me to meet you guys for the press conference?"

"One-thirty will be fine. You can say a few words on behalf of the YMCA, etc., etc., etc."

Carmellia was on the Board of Directors for the YMCA. It had been her idea to build it in the inner-city. She had wanted something to rival the ones located in the nicer and predominantly white suburbs.

It had been John's idea to enlist the financial help of Chase Chandler -- a prominent businessman. In retrospect, that idea had been a stroke of genius because once Chandler was on board, many other doors had started opening.

Thus, one simple proposal of hers had become a fifty million-dollar community project. A project that would now consist of restaurants, a roller rink, and a baseball park with a bike and run trail. She had even made a new friend in Sharon Walsh, Chase Chandler's fiancée. That friendship looked to be extremely beneficial.

"Wonderful. Then I guess I will see you at the ceremony." Carmellia turned to face her brother. "Freddie, can I have a moment with you in private? I need your help with something." Looking back at Jeff, she said, "Please excuse us, Jeff, but I need to borrow my brother for a minute. That is, unless you have something else to add to the conversation you two were having before I walked in?"

"No, ma'am. I think we were finished."

"Wonderful. Then, Freddie, can I see you in the study?" Carmellia did not wait for Fred to respond. Instead, she grabbed his arm, led him toward the family library.

As Fred walked past Jeff, a cold stare was exchanged. Fred hadn't told Jeff that Carmellia was the one being blackmailed.

And he wouldn't. As long as Jeff thought that the senator was the target of the blackmail, Carmellia would be safe. Besides, everyone was used to the senator's philandering. On many occasions, he had dealt with disgruntled former lovers of the senator threatening to tell all. But this situation was a little different. First of all, this was his sister and second, he didn't know the identity of the threat. Those two things, made all the difference in the world to him.

CHAPTER 7

ALPHARETTA, GA
FUTURUS BANK BUILDING
11:02 A.M.

SENATOR KNIGHT glanced at the list of names that Jeff had given him. There was an impressive group of Atlanta's distinguished business leaders upstairs awaiting his arrival. He decided to make them wait a little longer. This was his moment to shine. Thanks to his ability to align himself with the right people. People like C. Preston Barrett and Chase Chandler. Because of C. Preston Barrett and Chase Chandler, he had pulled off a come-from-behind victory in his re-election bid a month before. Now, he had six more years to work on his legacy.

The meeting upstairs was simply a formality. Nothing more than individuals who wanted to get some face time with him. Individuals who now wanted to be a part of his core group of supporters. The damn spineless ones, he had labeled them.

They should have been supporting him from day one, but they had no allegiance. Not even after all he had done for them over the years. All the legislation he had helped pass. And now they wanted to throw money at him. Fuck 'em. He'd make them wait longer than usual. That would teach 'em to think twice the next time they decided to hedge on their support.

The senator knew that what he lacked in charisma, he made up for in mental acumen. He knew what his strengths were and he played to them. He played to the Barretts and the Chandlers. Those were the only people he cared to please.

———◄○►———

Knight picked up the car phone as he sat in the back seat of the Town Car. Five minutes earlier, he'd dispatched Mutt & Jeff to do the dog and pony show for the distinguished gentleman awaiting his arrival. He punched in the number for the only person he wished to talk to at the present moment. On the fifth ring, the voice mail clicked on. The senator wasn't at all happy with this. He ended the call without leaving a message.

"Maybe she's in the shower," Knight whispered. He desperately wanted to speak to her. He waited two minutes and began entering the numbers again.

The ringing cell phone caught the senator by surprise. The call was registering out of area. For a brief moment, he thought about ignoring it, but figured it could be an important call. Knight answered the phone.

"Hi, John, I just wanted to wish you good luck today at your press conference."

"Thank you. I just tried to call you on your cell phone." He could tell by the static that she was in her car. The reception wasn't that great.

"Well, as you can see, I'm no longer answering that line. But that's one of the other reasons I'm calling you."

"Yes, I see. Is something wrong?"

"No, not anymore. Not after hearing your voice." He liked it when she flirted with him.

"Ah, you do know how to flatter a guy. You sure you're okay? You sound like something is bothering you."

"I guess you could say that. We had a little altercation this morning."

"Who?"

Knight sat up in his seat. She had said the words altercation and we. The bastard had done something to her. He could tell by her tone. If the bastard had hurt her.

"Where are you? I'll send Fred to get you right now."

"No, John, that will not be necessary. I'm fine, but I did leave him."

"What? When? Why didn't you call me? Where are you now?" His heart was racing with the excitement of the news.

"It happened this morning. And I did call Fred to let him know. He said he was going to give you the message. Anyway, I'm driving to New York as we speak, but I wanted to make sure I spoke to you before you called the other cell number and got a surprise."

"Well, I'm glad you called me. I just called the other number, but I hung up without leaving a message. Where are you now?"

"I'm not sure. I think I'm somewhere in South Carolina. But I don't want to go through all this over the phone. Can I see you? I need to give you something."

The words coming out of her mouth were music to his ears. He wanted to see her too. And he would do it tonight.

Damn the consequences. No risk, no reward.

"Okay, I think I can arrange that."

Knight pondered his options.

"Tell you what, why don't you stop in D.C. instead of driving directly to New York. The weather is expected to get kind of nasty anyway. I'll fly in later, after I'm finished here. How does that sound?" Senator Knight was hoping that she was finally ready to give herself to him.

"It sounds like a plan. I've never been to D.C. Maybe you can show me around. That is, if you have the time."

He was a little confused by her comments. He could have sworn that she had told him that she'd been to D.C. But he could have gotten her confused with someone else. There were so many others. Besides, there was no reason for her to lie to him about something so mundane as a trip to Washington, D.C. "Yeah, of course I can show you around. Red carpet treatment and all. You just decide where you would like to go and what you would like to do."

"Thanks, John. You're so sweet. So where would you like to meet?"

"Let me think." Knight rubbed his chin. "Well, it's sort of difficult to explain. And we can't have you get lost, now can we? So, let's do this. Why don't you go to Georgetown and wait for me at Houston's. Take Wisconsin Avenue to M; it'll lead you there. If you have any questions or you get lost, call me back immediately."

"I will. Okay, Houston's in Georgetown seems fairly easy to remember. What time should I be expecting you?"

"Let's say around seven-thirty."

"All right. Houston's. Georgetown. Seven-thirty. Got it."

"Good."

"John." There was a pause in her voice. He didn't know if it was the reception or her. "Thank you for everything that you've done for me. You are truly special. And I promise you,

I won't forget this."

"I think you're kind of special yourself, Teri. I'll see you later this evening." Senator Knight's mind was already brimming with the possibilities. He was so close to having her, he could taste it. He just had to make sure nothing went wrong. "Oh, Teri," he said before ending the call. "What's the new cell number, in case something comes up and we have to alter our plans?"

"Geez, John. I'm sorry, I don't know where my mind was. You have something to write with?"

Knight pulled a business card and a pen from his pocket. "Go ahead," he said.

Teri quickly rattled off the number and said goodbye.

Knight ended the call and placed the business card in his jacket pocket. He took a deep sigh, smiled, and headed toward the expansive lobby of the Futurus Bank building. This was a good situation. He was sure of it.

Indeed, the day had been pretty good. And the night promised to be even better.

CHAPTER **8**

TERI TOSSED the cell phone on the passenger seat as she drove into the Waffle House parking lot. She pulled the Braves baseball cap down over her head and reached for her sunglasses. After stealing a glance at her appearance in the rearview mirror, she frowned. Looking at herself, she knew one thing for certain. She wasn't going to be doing any lipstick commercials for a while, at least not today. And she wasn't about to go into a restaurant looking like she had just gotten into a boxing match.

The Waffle House?

Yes.

Houston's?

NO!

She would wait in front of the restaurant until he arrived. Then they would go some place less touristy. She knew the perfect place. She had lied to John, but he would soon understand why. And then maybe he would agree to help her.

Sitting and thinking about D.C. brought back memories; although at the moment, very unpleasant ones. Tears began to develop in her eyes, but she fought them back. She was through crying.

Teri touched her slightly swollen lip. It had decreased in size, but it was still noticeable. On the way to the airport, she had stopped at a service station and gotten a cup of ice. She'd braved the discomfort because the alternative was worse. She didn't want people staring at her like she was involved with some woman beater, not anymore anyway.

Teri reached back and grabbed her purse from off the back floor. In her rush to transfer things from the SUV to the Camry, she had placed stuff everywhere she could. Although right now, her main concern was locating her wallet. She was starving.

It took her a second, but she found the familiar leather object. She removed the red rubber band that held it together, spilling some of its contents on the back floorboard. "Shit," she yelled, reaching to retrieve the items from the floor. The same thing had happened earlier at the airport.

Frustrated, she shook it with two hands as if she was attempting to strangle and rip it apart. The wallet had been a special gift -- the last thing her mother had given her, which was why she still kept it.

Teri removed a twenty-dollar bill, stuffed the contents back inside, and kissed its tattered surface. She placed the wallet back in her purse, stuffed the money in her jeans, and again checked her appearance. Satisfied, she pulled the baseball cap down a little lower over her face and stepped out of the car.

She had made it halfway to the entrance, when she heard her mother's words. Her mother believed that it was never a good idea to leave a purse or anything else of value in plain site in a vehicle. One of her mother's favorite sayings had been, "Normally honest people sometimes do abnormally dishonest things."

Teri retraced her steps.

After she had placed her purse and valuables out of sight, she realized that she'd become all too familiar with what her mother meant. Her mother had been dead nine years and lately she had been having difficulty remembering the sound of her voice. "Momma I miss you," she whispered, as the tears came down.

◀◉▶

Teri finished her raisin toast and eggs, drank the last of her apple juice, and placed her tip on the counter. If she was going to do everything she'd planned to do before meeting John at Houston's, she needed to get moving. She still had a lot of road to cover and a short time to do it in. It was almost noon and she still had about six hours before she got to D.C.

Teri reached into her purse and pulled out her Palm organizer. She couldn't remember whether or not the person she was now thinking about was still stored. It had been almost a year since she had last thought about him. Did he still live in D.C.? What if he had gotten married? Whatever the case, she'd have to wait to find out.

She scrolled the list of names and thought about how nice it would be to see Seth again. However, as she suspected, his name was nowhere to be found. No big deal, she told herself. Maybe he still lived in the same place. It was a long shot, but she would take it.

Teri placed the Palm back in her purse and thought about her old boyfriend. Seth had helped her get through one of the most difficult times of her life. Yet she had not done right by him. Instead she had left him without a good-bye. No explanation. No letter. Nothing.

But at the time, she felt it was the best thing for everyone involved. However, now she was ready to talk to him. She just hoped that Seth would give her the opportunity to explain.

CHAPTER 9

RICK'S HEAD was pounding. There was a sharp pain in his leg. It felt like one of his ribs was broken. The smell of wet carpet was infiltrating his nostrils. And to top it off, he was having difficulty remembering what had happened. The headache could have come from too much drinking. He remembered drinking. Could he have gotten that wasted? Did he combine his drinking with anything else? He would know shortly because his hangovers usually affected his vision.

Rick opened his eyes.

There was a stinging sensation and his vision was a little blurred, but it wasn't the familiar blur that followed too much drinking. Rick felt the wet carpet under his hands as he pushed himself off the floor and against the bedpost. At least now he knew where the smell came from.

Resting against the bedpost, he looked around the room. The house was a mess. Videotapes were scattered everywhere. Some salvageable, others, completely damaged. Slowly, the events from earlier were beginning to come back.

Pulling himself off the floor and onto the bed, Rick noticed the rope around his ankles. Teri had tied his feet together. He removed the rope and tossed it aside. That's when he saw the cut on his forearm. It wasn't a bad cut, but it would require some medical attention.

Rick took a deep breath and looked to his left. The electronic alarm clock on the nightstand displayed 11:26 a.m. He had been out at least five hours, of that he was certain. He reached for the cell phone lying on the bed. The sudden movement caused a sharp pain to shoot up his side. He touched the bruised area and winced in pain. He had taken a good shot to the ribs, but he knew they weren't broken. He'd experienced that pain before.

———◄○►———

Four messages and one hang up showed on the digital readout. Rick pressed seven to retrieve the messages. The first call had come from Fat Toney. They would be leaving the airport at 7 p.m. for the flight to Miami. Fat Toney would be stopping by to pick him up at 6 p.m. The call had come at 8:45 a.m.

The second call had come from Carmellia. Carmellia was reminiscing about last night's festivities. She wanted more as soon as could be arranged. Her legs were still trembling, she moaned. She had called at 9:34 a.m.

The third call had come from his cousin, Stuart. Stuart wanted to make sure that Fat Toney had given him the message concerning the night's schedule. He also wanted to make sure that everything was finished with the business plan. Stuart had called at 10:22 a.m.

The final call had come from security at the central office. Security was doing a follow-up about the burglary call from the previous night. They had tried to call the main line, but were getting a busy signal. They would be sending a man out in thirty minutes for a follow-up investigation. That call had come at 11:20 a.m.

Rick looked across the room and saw what resembled the telephone scattered into pieces across the floor. He now remembered busting the telephone with the baseball bat. That's when Teri had thrown the nail polish remover in his face.

His stupidity had cost him dearly this time.

Placing the cell phone in his wet jeans and relying on the massive muscle in his upper body, Rick forced himself to stand on his feet. It took him three tries with his bruised ribs, but he managed it. Teri had also whacked him good on the leg with the baseball bat. At that moment, he remembered her telling him that she'd been a pretty good softball player once upon a time. If the pain in his knee was any indication, she hadn't lied.

Pushing the pain aside and using the bed as a rail, Rick hobbled over to the phone jack behind the nightstand. He slid the nightstand over and unplugged the phone cord. He then reached back into his jeans and retrieved the cell phone.

Scrolling through the main menu feature until he found what he was looking for, Rick pressed the callback function for the last number received. He took several more deep breaths while he waited for the call to connect. With each breath, more intense pains shot through his side.

"Central security office," the voice said.

"Yes, this is Rick Casner at 1892 Addison Court."

"Yes, Mr. Casner. We got a call about a possible burglary

last night and we wanted to make sure that everything was all right. We got a busy signal this morning when we tried to do a follow-up."

"Yes, I'm sorry about that. Everything is fine; false alarm. My fiancée was a little spooked that's all, but your officer checked everything out and we're fine. However, thank you for calling to follow-up. We feel much safer knowing that you guys care so much." He took another deep breath and grimaced.

"It's our job, Mr. Casner. We like to make sure that our residents feel safe and secure. And you're sure that we don't need to come back over there?"

"No, no. You have done more than enough, but once again, thank you for checking back with us."

"No problem, sir. You have a nice day and I'm sorry for taking up so much of your time."

"No, it's not a bother at all. Thanks again."

Rick ended the call, placed the phone on the nightstand. Using the wall to balance his weight, he began to strip naked. Removing his clothing would help in two ways. First, not having to lug around the wet clothing would increase his mobility. Second, the wet clothing would not be rubbing against his wounds.

In the mirrors on the walls, he could see the large burgunday bruise. He could also see the cut from the nail file. This little expisode had cost him dearly, in more ways than he was ready or willing to admit.

Rick grabbed the cell phone from the nightstand. He looked across the room to his closet. He needed to make it to the closet; more importantly, his armoire. But with his leg battered up, that task would be difficult. Leaning against the mirrowed wall seemed to offer the best solution.

Rick placed the cell in his jeans, slung them toward the closet. They landed with a thud at the base of the armoire.

Rick beban to slide toward the closet. Once he reached it, he removed the cell from his jeans, placed it on the armoire.

From a bottom drawer, Rick retrieved an old Georgia Tech T-shirt. He caught another glimpse of himself in the mirror. The area around his knee was swollen, but he didn't think the knee was busted. A few pills would help reduce the swelling and if he stayed off his feet, he would be all right. The cut on his forearm wasn't as bad as he first thought, but he was certain that it would require a few stitches.

Rick tore the Georgia Tech T-shirt in half, tied it around the wound. He slipped on the Adidas sweat pants, T-shirt, and sweatshirt. With that done, his attention turned to the most important matter -- his private playroom. Worse case scenario, Teri had only damaged the tapes now orphaned on the wet carpet in front of him. Hopefully, she hadn't done too much damage, if any downstairs.

Rick closed his eyes, took a deep breath, If he was lucky, this would be the worst it would get. His gut was telling him otherwise.

ACT TWO

...CUT FROM DIFFERENT
CLOTH

CHAPTER 10

MIAMI, FL
NAILS AND THINGS
12:01 P.M.

KYUN LEI stared into the face of the woman sitting across from her. The woman had attractive features: long flowing hair, rosy cheeks, sparkling eyes, and beautiful teeth. She seemed to be of South American descent. The type of person Kyun couldn't imagine being the wife of a major drug trafficker, but that's who she was.

After spending the better part of forty-five minutes giving the lady a pretty good pedicure, Kyun had started on her nails. Her instructions were simple: "Take your time," David had told her. And that's what she was doing.

Kyun smiled as she thought about her new love interest, David, the FBI agent. She'd met David two months before at the Playhouse, which was a private sex club.

He had befriended Kyun on her first visit there. She possessed an innocence that attracted him, he had said. He wanted to look out for her, make sure nothing happened to her.

Kyun had been flattered. No one had ever done anything like that for her before. She had been surprised that David had taken an interest in her. She knew she wasn't pretty, at least not in a conventional sense. For years, she had been told that her beauty was more internal. Unfortunately, that internal beauty hadn't attracted many suitors. In fact, she had only had two boyfriends -- Matthew McGinnis and Kevin Kwan. Matthew had been homely-looking and boring. Kevin had been exciting, but married with three children.

On the night she met David, she had been trying to make Kevin a part of her past. That was the only reason she had been at the Playhouse that night. She had figured a good place to start was the private sex club that one of her new clients kept telling her about. And since she had been in the mood to do something wild, the Playhouse sounded like it offered just the thing. She could go there and let go of her inhibitions. No worrying about anyone knowing her family, no worrying about being "noticed."

Kyun continued to massage the hand of the drug trafficker's wife. She wondered if this lady had ever been to the Playhouse. Probably not, she concluded. Rich people usually had private sex parties at their mansions or on their yachts. She'd heard about some of the parties. Scandalous.

Kyun smiled at the lady and continued to think about her recent ride on the wild side. She remembered the night vividly.

Kyun looked at her watch. She had been standing in the same spot for the last ten minutes, debating whether or not to go in. She had been so sure thirty minutes earlier, but now being here, so close, made it difficult.

She watched the couples get out of their cars. Some in mini-vans, others in sports cars -- all ready to pursue some form of sexual pleasure. From the looks on their faces, all seemed unafraid. It was time for her to act or go home. She took a deep breath, smoothed down her dress, and walked toward the door.

She entered the club and was surprised by the reception area. It was more tasteful than she would have imagined. A large chandelier hung in the entranceway, and helped provide a warm, stately feel. Plants were situated in the corner. A lamp rested on a long end table right in front of a full-length gold-trimmed wall mirror, giving the room the appearance of someone's foyer. Music filtered in from another room on the other side of swinging double doors. A couple sat on a couch to her left and filled out paperwork.

Kyun smiled at them and pressed forward. She rounded a corner and was greeted by an attractive female standing in what could only be classified as a greeting/coat-check room.

"Hi. Welcome to the Playhouse," the perky attendant chimed.

"Thank you," Kyun replied.

The attendant could see Kyun nervousness so she knew the approach to take. She asked Kyun a couple of background questions, just to get a general overview of who she was and what her likes were. She supplied Kyun with some information on the Playhouse and asked her to sign some confidentiality and release forms. Once Kyun did that, the attendant picked up a house phone and spoke to someone on the other end. Not a minute later, a very attractive blond guy stood at Kyun's side.

Kyun tilted her head to the side and looked quizzically at the man. Maybe they had the wrong impression of who she was. Things had been difficult in the romance department lately, but surely they hadn't thought she wanted a male escort. Kyun opened her mouth to convey this message, but the blonde smiled. Kyun blinked, her knees buckled, her mind went blank.

"Hello, Kyun," he said. "My name is David and I will be your tour guide for the evening. If that's all right with you?"

"Yes, yes, of course." Kyun smiled, suddenly becoming very conscious about her choice of wardrobe.

David smiled, took her by the hand. His hands were soft, but strong. Gentle, yet forceful.

"You made a good choice by coming to the Playhouse tonight," David offered. "Tuesdays are good nights. A younger crowd, more hip. Normally we discourage members from coming to the club alone." David stopped, turned, and faced Kyun. "Although for some women, we have been known to make exceptions."

The way David had looked at her when he said this, Kyun could feel her face becoming flushed. A lump caught in her throat.

She was an exception.

David held Kyun's hand and escorted her behind a curtain. On the other side, was a glass-enclosed room, with a king-sized bed.

"This is the voyeur room. And these chairs," David gestured to the chairs, forming a circle around the room, "are for people who like to watch."

Again, Kyun felt flustered. She was suddenly thirsty. David squeezed her hand and winked.

"Those people over there," David pointed to the two women and one guy standing in the corner getting undressed, "are getting ready to give a show."

Kyun looked at the three people -- all attractive. The women were in very good shape and teasing each other. She had to do a double take when she looked at the man. Either her eyes were lying to her or he had the biggest instrument she'd ever laid eyes on. David saw her staring, and nodded his head as if he was reading her thoughts.

Others joined them in the room and took seats around the room. Kyun and David watched twenty minutes of the freaky performance, then exited the room.

"That was the biggest penis I've ever seen," David said as they walked down the hallway. Kyun was too awestruck to say anything.

"Can I get you something to drink?" David asked. "Anything non-alcoholic that is. The club doesn't serve alcohol. However, if a customer wants to bring his/her own," David pointed to members walking around, carrying personal drinking cups, "they are more than welcome to go outside and mix it up. We just don't provide it here at the club."

"That's fine. I'm not much of a drinker anyway. But yeah, any type of fruit juice will do," Kyun replied.

David excused himself to get the drinks.

Kyun followed the pull of the music. Although the Playhouse was a sex club, she liked the dance club aspect. She liked to dance.

Kyun was swaying to the rhythm of the music when she felt David's breath on her ear. Again, shivers ran down her spine.

"I see you like to dance," David said and smiled seductively.

"Yes, I do."

"Then maybe you should enter the amateur strip contest later. First prize is two hundred dollars. And I'm sure you would win. Hands down." David looked Kyun's body up and down.

Kyun cleared her throat and brushed her hair back. David was making her feel very sexy. "And how can you be so sure of that?" she asked, turning her body so it stood squarely in front of David's.

"Because I noticed you dancing. You move very sensually, you feel the music. People respect that; I respect that. Besides, you have a nice ass."

David's last comments almost caused Kyun to choke on her juice. Did he just say that she had a nice ass? Of course he had. She hadn't heard wrong. This David guy was laying it on thick. No way was she going to enter a strip contest -- no way.

"I'll think about it," she replied.

———◁○▷———

Kyun excused herself. The drug-trafficker's wife didn't seem to mind. All the thoughts about the Playhouse had caused her to get aroused. She wanted David right now. They hadn't made love in two days and right now she longed to feel him inside her.

She splashed the cool water on her face. It helped, but not much. She looked at her watch. There was not enough time to please herself. Besides, she preferred to feel the warmth of David. Again, she splashed water on her face, took several deep breaths, and rejoined the drug-trafficker's wife. Five minutes later, she was thinking about that first night at the Playhouse again.

———◁○▷———

After the strip contest comment, David had led her to the S & M room. He didn't need to explain the room's purpose to her. Before they had even entered the room, she had seen the televisions suspended from the ceiling showing porn movies. And if that hadn't alerted her, the wall of dildos, vibrators, whips, chains, and paddles had.

In an adjoining room, David had shown her other hanging swings that three couples had been in the process of utilizing for various forms of pleasure. They'd even stood and watched a spanking. Later on, she had admitted that it had been one of the most erotic things she had ever witnessed.

After the spanking, David had shown her the massage room, followed by the six private rooms with various themes, where members could go for privacy. She had observed that several of the doors of the private rooms had been closed and locked. David had explained that those couples didn't want to be disturbed. Pointing to rooms with doors ajar, David had explained that those occupants didn't mind a little company; an invitation for a menage-a-trois.

As David had led her back to the main floor, she remembered passing members giving each other oral sex in the hallways. Other members had also stopped and started watching. To get around the oral action, she remembered having to slide against the walls so that she wouldn't disturb the participants. Even now as she massaged the woman's hands, Kyun could see the image quite vividly. It had been both invigorating and inviting.

From the main floor, she remembered being led to the second floor. David had explained that the second floor provided the most action and led to his favorite room. She remembered thinking and asking how anything could top what she'd already seen. David had replied by simply taking her by the hand.

While leading her up the stairs, David had explained that only couples were allowed on the second floor, no unaccompanied males. Once again, for some females the club made exceptions. He told her that members could lean over the balcony and watch the action on the dance floor or the action in the S & M room, or if they preferred, members could lounge in the sofas that were lined against the wall.

Then David had allowed her a few minutes to gaze over the crowds below. While she had been doing that, David had whispered in her ear that he'd saved the best for last. And without saying another word, he'd escorted her down a hall.

At the end of the hall had been a large, thick blue curtain. But before he'd pulled back the curtain, David had asked her to close her eyes. She had done as had been asked. Immediately, a silk blindfold had been placed over her eyes. Then David had led her through the curtain and down another hallway.

Walking down the hall, she remembered hearing voices, followed by the alternating sounds of sensual moans and involuntary cursing. Next came the passionate exchange of kisses. The sound of skin to skin. She remembered how the smell of sex had lingered in the air. How she'd inhaled the aroma. Not able to see, she had allowed her ears to be her eyes. She hadn't wanted David to take off the blindfold, so he had left it on.

Excitedly, she had listened and took in the sounds and the smells. Minutes had passed and it had become too much for her to bear. She'd begged and pleaded for David to take off the blindfold. He had replied, no. She had survived a few more minutes and had asked again. Be patient and enjoy, she had heard. Then she'd felt softness on her neck.

A sudden warmth had enveloped her body.

Hands of different textures and sizes had begun to touch her. She remembered feeling her dress fall to the floor. She had felt lips on her soft places. Tongues had started to explore her many oceans. She remembered her moistness overflowing. The pleasure had become almost unbearable. The moans around her had begun to increase in volume and intensity. Her moans had begun to echo the others. Her body had shuddered.

And then it had shuddered again and again.

Finally, after she lay spent on the floor, she had felt one set of hands. Nervously, she had grabbed the hands and placed them on the blindfold. She'd wanted to see, to know the source of her pleasure. And slowly, the hands had removed the blindfold.

As her eyes adjusted, her mouth had fallen open. She couldn't believe the picture. She had been standing on a throne, naked. And in front of her had been twelve beds, six on each side of the room. In each bed had been at least two people, in some beds more. All naked and involved in some form of sex. She had been standing in the Orgy Room and David had been standing behind her holding the blindfold.

<hr />

After their brief, but intense encounter in the Orgy Room, David and she had started a conversation and one thing had led to another. They had been on several dates since and David had shared his story with her. He'd told her he wanted to trust her. She had told him he could.

Since then, David had reluctantly asked for her assistance on a case. She was thrilled that he trusted her enough to ask. It was a major turn-on for her. David had informed her that the FBI had been investigating a major drug trafficker who just happened to not only frequent the Playhouse, but also her salon. The drug trafficker had been eluding the Bureau for some time and was considered a danger to society. David had told her that the Bureau desperately needed to apprehend this guy, but they didn't want to draw attention to themselves or the Playhouse. There was a quieter way; a way that all parties would appreciate. Several lives depended on it.

David had shown her pictures of the man and his wife.

She had immediately recognized them. She'd always suspected something was fishy about them. Yes, she would help. It would be an honor for her to help her country.

Because the case was top secret, David had asked her not to tell anyone and risk jeopardizing two years of undercover surveillance. Her country was depending on her. She had told him she'd keep it to herself.

Kyun had let the undercover agent into the salon at approximately 6:55 a.m. To ensure that David's operation ran smoothly, she had cleared space in the tanning room closet. Very thick and expensive drapery had been hung to help provide a place for the agent to hide. Ironically, the drapery looked similar to the ones leading to the Orgy Room. She had also placed cookies and drinks in the closet. Her little contribution.

---◦---

The front door of the salon opened and a new client walked in, Kyun smiled at her and looked at her watch. It was 12:28 p.m. Although she didn't know for certain whether David's plan had worked, she was happy. She had done a wonderful service for her country and she was to meet David later that night at the Playhouse. Somehow he had managed to get the place for the two of them.

Kyun heard the new client ask about the services of the tanning room. It was currently in use, she was told. She smiled at the new client again and continued buffing the nails of the drug trafficker's wife. Now all she had to do was wait for David to call.

When she heard the familiar ring of her cell phone, a smile etched across her face. David had entered his code. Indeed, everything had worked exactly as he had said.

---◦---

Deuce Daley placed the cell phone in his garment bag and tossed the bag in his suitcase. For the most part, his work in Miami was complete and his role as David, the FBI agent, was finished. He would never see Kyun Lei again. And in a few hours, neither would anyone else. His partner, Raymond Sexton, would see to that.

Deuce loved the drama of it all. It was part of the job in which he excelled. The acting, the pretending. Deuce specialized in seducing the weak and vulnerable. For a brief moment in time, he gave them a sense of hope. A sense of purpose. A reason to live. A desire to believe in love, in romance.

Deuce opened the door to the warehouse. His co-workers were already hard at work. They had the man tied up, blindfolded, and naked. They appeared ready to get very creative with their form of torture. Now, it was just a matter of when.

Deuce looked at the torture devices assembled and squirmed. The thought of what was about to happen to the man would not soon be forgotten. It would be one of the sickest acts his coworkers had ever performed.

Phase two was now complete.

CHAPTER 11

ATLANTA, GA
GLADYS KNIGHT & RON
WINANS' CHICKEN AND
WAFFLES
12:35 P.M.

STUART LOOKED across the table at Tish. She looked more and more like their mother with each passing day. He noticed that Tish even wore the same style of glasses their mother had worn. She had turned into a beautiful young lady. One that he was proud of.

He couldn't believe that it had almost been ten years since their parents' deaths. A lot had happened in that time. His life, their lives, had changed in so many ways. Back then, he had been very wild, very angry, very violent. But time and responsibility mellows a man. The beautiful young lady sitting across from him had saved his life. She would never know that, but she had. If it had not been for Tish, he hated to imagine what or who he would have become.

Stuart stared at the items on the menu. His thoughts, someplace else, in some other time. His thoughts were back in Miami. He would be going back there today for the first time since that night five years ago. He had been thinking about the days leading up to that event a lot lately. They had gotten away with murder. And as crazy as it sounded, that bothered him.

In the five years since that night, he had had a lot of time to reflect. When one human murders another, the image of that person never leaves the mind. When one murders several people, those images are multiplied. They become affixed to the psyche, feeding on themselves. Almost like an extension, so to speak. And if one is really lucky, an extension that can peacefully co-exist with the rest.

He had come to terms with his involvement in the murders. Those actions had been a reflection of who he was then. But every so often, a part of him wondered whether he had done the right thing.

Ironically, as he had gotten older, he had begun to understand why Barrett might have acted as he had. Divulging the identity of the person responsible for his parents' murders would probably have ensured an untimely death for Barrett himself. Yet, had Barrett been an honorable man and told him that, he would have respected Barrett's position. He would have hated it, but he would have respected it. For him, it had always been about principles.

At the time, Barrett had been the chairman of the Senate Select Committee on Intelligence, and privy to all kinds of classified information. Information that Stuart didn't give a damn about, other than the information pertaining to his parents' murders.

Through their correspondence, Barrett had led him to believe that he would help. Barrett had promised him that information and had even accepted money for it, only to later renege on that promise and then feign complete ignorance when confronted about it. And now five years later, that simple gesture is what bothered him the most.

The look on Barrett's face had been the look of complete and utter ignorance. Not to mention, every detail surrounding the Miami event had been swept under the rug. It was as if the truth behind Barrett's death threatened something greater. That something greater was the thing that interested him, and the sole purpose for him going to Miami tonight. It was still very much about principles.

——◄◦►——

Stuart smacked Tish on the head with his menu. "So, what are you in the mood for?"

"Umh, I don't know. Everything looks so inviting."

"Well, I think I'm gonna have the Midnight Train," Stuart sang.

Tish scrunched up her face. "Stuart, please don't clear the restaurant with your horrible singing."

"Girl, please, you know big brother can sing. Watch this."

"Stuart don't," Tish pleaded, but she knew it was too late. Her only option would be to hide under the table and pray that no one noticed.

Stuart stepped out of the booth, cleared his throat, and proceeded to sing -- loud and off key. Gladys Knight's *Midnight Train to Georgia* was the featured selection. For added measure, he asked a couple of guys sitting at the next table to act as The Pips. Tish was thoroughly embarrassed, but she laughed with everyone else in the restaurant. Stuart and his makeshift Pips were truly a spectacle.

After his third bow, Stuart sat back down in the booth.

"Are you happy now?" Tish asked, shook her head, and smiled.

"I got you to smile didn't I, so yes I am."

"Are you guys ready to order yet? I know you should be after that mini-concert." The waitress looked at Stuart and laughed.

"No autographs today, thank you."

"Don't pay him any mind. He hasn't taken his medication today," Tish said. The waitress winked that she understood.

"So, what can I get you two?"

"I'm having, what else, the Midnight Train," Stuart sang.

"I guess I should have known that." The waitress smiled, writing Stuart's order down.

"And I'm having the Uncle Ron's," Tish answered.

"Damn, someone is hungry," Stuart blurted out.

Tish's expression changed. Stuart wondered whether it was something he'd said. "What's wrong, baby girl?" he asked, grabbing his sister by the hands.

Tish shook her head, but Stuart could tell that she wasn't being completely honest. Tish could never hide her feelings about anything.

"You sure?"

"I'm fine, Stuart," Tish said quickly.

Stuart let it pass. He knew not to push. Tish shared her feelings only after she had processed them. Whatever it was, he knew she was still working through. He changed the subject.

"So, how are finals going?"

"Good. I have one more."

Tish began tapping her fingers on the table.

"Yeah, and how are the internship prospects looking?"

"Excellent. I should know something by the end of the week."

Stuart noticed that Tish seemed nervous, almost uncomfortable. Her table tapping was getting faster. He chose not to comment on it. Smiling, he said, "I'm very proud of you for finishing your undergraduate degree early. I'm sure Mom and Dad are smiling as well."

"Thank you, Stuart."

Tish took Stuart's hand, more to stop the table tapping than anything. She was surprised he hadn't mentioned it. Not too much escaped him.

Tish playfully bit her brother's hands. He had their father's hands. Big and strong. In a way, that's who Stuart had become to her -- a brother/father. Just like a father, he had sacrificed a lot for her. And just like a daughter, she wanted him to be proud of her, as she was of him.

Over the past five years, Stuart had turned his life around. He'd become a successful and respectable businessman. Not too long ago, she had worried about him. He had a good heart, but sometimes his heart caused him to make bad decisions. Decisions like going into the strip club business with their cousin, Rick. She was never happier than the day Stuart had told her that he was selling out. She had prayed every day to hear him say those words. She loved Rick, but he was, as her mother often said, "cut from different cloth."

Rick's actions over the last twenty-four hours only help reiterate that fact.

"Tish, are you gonna tell me what's wrong? Or do I have to come over there and tickle it out of you?" Stuart's words brought her back to the present.

"No, no, no." Tish scooted away from Stuart's reach. "I'll tell you, but you have to promise not to say anything."

"Come on, Tish. You know me better than that."

"I'm serious, Stuart. Give me the promise."

By her demeanor, Stuart knew Tish wasn't kidding. He placed one hand in the air and the other on his heart.

"Okay, I promise not to betray what my sister tells me in confidence." He felt silly making their secret promise, but it had always been their thing. And some things one always cherishes. Always. "Satisfied? Now tell me what's bothering you."

Tish took a deep breath.

"Teri called me this morning as she was heading to the airport."

"And, what's so…"

Tish snapped, "Stuart, please, just let me finish."

Stuart frowned, sat back in his booth. Tish never, ever raised her voice, especially at him. Something was bothering his sister. Something she was having trouble dealing with.

"Something happened between her and Rick this morning. Something very bad, Stuart." Tish stopped and allowed her words to sink in. "Teri left him," she said a few seconds later.

"Did she tell you what happened?"

"Yes. She wanted me to know that she had left Rick's SUV at the airport."

"Did you call Rick and tell him this?"

Tish's look turned cold, and Stuart knew that this time it had been something he'd said.

"I'm gonna pretend that my brother didn't ask me that," Tish said through clenched teeth. Before, she could continue, another waitress came back with their food and placed it on the table.

"Can I get you guys anything else?" The new waitress asked, looking more at Stuart.

"No, thank you," Tish responded, not too pleasantly. The new waitress turned, smiled half-heartedly, and walked away.

Stuart waited for the waitress to be far enough away, before resuming conversation. "Is there a reason you're not planning to tell Rick about any of this, LaTisha?"

"Yes, there is. And if you knew the whole story, you, Stuart Parker Hastings, would feel the same way." Tish stood from the booth and headed to the restroom.

Stuart knew that it would be pointless for him to ask Tish

any more about her conversation with Teri. Tish was loyal, just like he was. And because he had promised her his silence, there was no way for him to tell Rick. But something else was wrong with his sister. He could see it in her eyes.

Stuart leaned back in his seat and tugged on his soul patch. The new waitress walked by, smiled, and stopped one booth over. Although she was supposed to be taking an order, Stuart could feel her staring at him. He decided to ignore her. At the moment, his life had too much drama. He also decided to let the situations with Tish and Rick play themselves out. For now, that was all he could do.

————◄○►————

Tish floored the black BMW down Interstate 85. She had to get to Rick's SUV before it was discovered. She didn't know why; it was just a feeling she had. Teri had been a very dear friend to her and she wanted to make sure nothing had been left behind. Teri deserved a clean getaway.

Although Rick was her cousin, he was an asshole. And now apparently, a woman beater. Tish pushed the anger back down. Violence never solved anything, she reminded herself. She couldn't believe what Rick had done to Teri.

Tish steered the car into the short-term parking lot. She knew exactly where the Land Cruiser was because Teri had told her. She pulled her car into the parking space beside it. It would only take her a minute to check the vehicle. Teri had left the keys underneath the passenger side front tire.

Tish squatted down, scooped up the keys, deactivated the alarm, and climbed inside. The inside of the SUV was clean. Teri hadn't left anything; at least nothing that looked important. With her fear put to rest, Tish opened the door and stepped out. She had barely extricated herself from the vehicle, when her lunch made a reappearance.

Suddenly light-headed, she allowed her body to fall back against the SUV. At the same time, she wiped the beads of sweat that had appeared on her forehead. She didn't feel so good. Possibly a virus, she thought. Lately she hadn't been feeling well. But she had chalked it up to stress and sleep deprivation. A quick visit to the Emory Clinic would do the trick.

Tish looked at her watch. There was just enough time to stop by. If she was lucky, Gina would still be in. She slowly crouched down to place the keys back under the tire. Now would not be the time for sudden movements.

The envelope rested about three feet under the vehicle. From its appearance, some type of legal documentation had to be inside. Tish used her foot to retrieve it. She looked at it, opened it, and smiled. It was definitely important.

In her hands, she held the contract for Teri's new house in New York. That woman's intuition of hers had been correct.

Tish opened her car door and tossed it on the passenger seat. She then picked up her cell phone and dialed the Emory Clinic. She still had her biggest final to take and there was no way the flu or any other bug would affect that.

CHAPTER 12

LANE "TURK" Reynolds loved being an FBI agent. He loved that he was authorized to carry weapons and could shoot to kill. He loved that he possessed the power to deprive suspects of their freedom and had the ability to send them to jail for life. He loved that he could eavesdrop on private phone conversations and videotape bedroom theatrics. But more than anything, Turk Reynolds loved the feeling of catching his prey.

He found it amazing how much information could be obtained about an individual by monitoring their mailbox or sifting through their trash. As a rookie agent, he'd realized that people threw away all kinds of incriminating information.

And after twenty years in the Bureau, he was still surprised to learn that most damaging evidence usually resulted from telephone records or income tax returns. Surprisingly, people tended to be very carefree with this type of personal information. Grandma Bell and Uncle Sam had provided him with very lucrative leads.

Smart and intellectually curious, Turk possessed a dry wit and a lean physique. He sported a shiny bald head, bushy eyebrows, a thick goatee, and steely eyes that seemed never to flinch. When he was angered, his northern accent became more pronounced. When he walked, it was with an air of confidence developed through living a rich and adventurous life. Throughout the Bureau, he was considered one of the best field agents ever.

Unknown to most, he was also part owner of a private intelligence firm. This firm specialized in gathering and disseminating top-secret personal information. The firm was known for doing excellent work and was therefore in constant demand.

From its inception, the firm was discreet about the assignments it accepted, meaning all clients had to be referred from a reputable source. The assignment would then be accepted only after a thorough background check of the party requesting the investigation had been completed. Once an assignment had been accepted, a non-refundable fee of fifty thousand dollars had to be wired to an offshore account. Upon the completion of the assignment, another fifty thousand dollars had to be wired.

All information gathered by the firm was labeled and cataloged, ensuring that regular updates could be done every couple of months or so. However, under no circumstances was all the information gathered on a person relinquished. For obvious reasons, this information was kept in a high security storage facility housed in Arlington, Virginia.

Turk was staring at some notes when one of his pagers started ringing. Of the two pagers that remained attached to him at all times, this time the two-way was the culprit. It was to the voice mail for Langham & Associates, the firm in which he was a partner. In total, there were six partners in the firm - three were general, two were silent, and Turk was a combination of both.

Langham & Associates had been structured so that the three general partners and Turk performed all the work. Turk's duties entailed intelligence dissemination, which meant that any information requested by a client couldn't be released without his approval. And that approval was only given when he had reviewed the intelligence packet himself. This was done to ensure that no highly classified information slipped through the cracks.

Turk picked up the two-way and read the message. As he'd figured, it was from a man who called himself "The Conduit."

Message: "Hello, this is The Conduit. My client appreciates your completion of the assignment. I don't have to remind you that all information that was obtained in your investigation be kept strictly confidential. As always, fifty thousand dollars has been wired to your account at the designated location. If we have the need for any additional services, we will not hesitate to get in contact with you."

This was not the first assignment the firm had completed for "The Conduit," whose real name was Fred King. He knew who King was. He knew who they all were. He knew King served as a front for someone else. That someone else he knew as well.

What had surprised him about this request was the subject's sex. Usually King wanted information pertaining to a female. Rick Casner did not fit that profile. This had been an interesting request. One that he planned to investigate further. Turk wrote a note to investigate the matter when he returned from vacation. He placed the note in a new file folder and placed the folder in his briefcase. He then deleted the message.

———◦———

Turk stood from his chair, stretched, and walked over to the coffee maker where the last of the morning's coffee rested. He had already exceeded his allotted cups for the day, but what the hell? He was in the mood for some adventure. Besides, no one was around to see him. No harm, no foul.

After he had taken his third sip, Turk reached into his briefcase and pulled out a gray envelope. The envelope contained the information on Casner that had been sent to King. Because of the recent scrutiny surrounding Casner, the information hadn't been updated in months, not that King would be able to tell the difference. The information was still very detailed.

Enclosed in this particular packet was information on Casner's background and business associations, as well as any past criminal activity. In short, King would be receiving enough information to do any number of things.

Turk opened the envelope and reviewed its contents.

He had just finished reviewing the packet when Special Agent Stan Belinda knocked on his door. Belinda was heading up the D.C. portion of a major undercover investigation code named CASTEL.

For five years, Belinda had headed up the drug squad in the New York field office, which was how they'd met. Six months prior, Belinda had accepted a special position in the Washington Metro office. High profile cases would be his domain.

A tad over six feet tall and possessing a biting sense of humor, Belinda was a favorite inside the Bureau. He'd been nicknamed "Mr. Tenacity" because of his relentlessness. Not only was he known for taking a no-nonsense approach to crime solving, but he also possessed an exceptional memory.

In fact, Turk had thought so highly of Belinda that before he accepted the promotion to head Washington Metro, he insisted that Belinda be transferred from New York to work with him. At the time, Belinda was in the middle of another major undercover drug operation, but now he belonged to WFO.

"Hey, Boss." Belinda smiled, walking in the door.

"Hey, Stan. Sorry I haven't had the opportunity to spend a lot of time with you lately." Turk rose from his chair and extended a hand.

Belinda shook it, then took a seat. "Don't sweat that. I can find my way around any city. Not to mention, it looks like you have other things occupying your mind these days."

Belinda pointed to the vacation balloons swirling around in the air. Turk looked at them as well and smiled. The four women in his life had sent them. Not that he needed to be reminded.

"And it couldn't have come at a better time," Turk replied.

"Now you're sure you want to go on some God-forsaken cruise and leave us common folk here to deal with society's darlings? I know how gut-wrenching this decision must be for you," Belinda teased.

"I struggle with it every minute of every hour."

"You should. You mind?" Belinda pointed to the jar on Turk's desk. "Haven't had lunch yet."

"Go ahead."

Belinda grabbed a handful of the colored Jelly-Bellys that sat atop Turk's desk. He tossed half in his mouth and plopped back down on the well-worn leather sofa next to the door.

"So, what do you think about my e-mail?" Turk asked.

"You want our guy to approach Stuart Hastings?"

"Yeah, what do you think about it?"

"Our source said it looks doable. He thinks that after Hastings sees what we have and what we want him to do, he could be willing to help us. But he says that if Hastings senses that we are trying to nail his cousin, forget about it. I'm told that their family dynamics are very unique to say the least."

Turk pulled the hairs in his goatee, but still said nothing.

Belinda continued, "I get the impression that Hastings is loyal to family and friends. From what I'm told, it would have to be something very serious for him to turn his back on family, Turk."

"And you don't think the Miami thing is serious?" Turk asked, still pulling the hairs in his goatee.

"I don't know. It could be the straw that breaks the camel's back. Hastings' and Casner's relationship hasn't been the same since Hastings cashed out of the adult entertainment business five years ago." Belinda grabbed another handful of the Jelly-Bellys. "I was told that Hastings struggled a long time about whether or not to get involved in the Miami deal."

"Well, I have to believe that when Hastings finds out that Casner used him as a bargaining chip to get involved with other illegal dealings, he'll think differently."

"We'll see. You could be right. From what our source tells me, Casner seems to be involved in a lot of other shit these days. Stuff that I'm certain Hastings wouldn't approve of. Especially since he has been legitimate for so long."

"I'll tell you what I find interesting," Turk leaned back in his seat, "that Casner would use the Hastings' murders as enticement into the deal in the first place."

"Well, to tell you the truth, that move surprised me at first too, so I asked our source about it. And the way it was explained it to me made perfect sense."

"So what did this source tell you?"

Belinda had not told Turk the identity of the source and Turk hadn't pursued the issue. As long as this source continued to produce tangible results, Turk planned to let him run his own investigation. Things worked better that way. Plus, Belinda was experienced enough to know when to ask for assistance.

"In short, Casner found out about Benito Escada by accident. From what I'm told, Casner videotapes what goes on in the private rooms of his clubs. And apparently, one of the dancers and Escada had become quite friendly. Evidently, Escada was totally wasted one night and started talking. He started blabbing about what he did for a living and other things. One of which, pertained to his last visit to Atlanta and the guy he spent the night in jail with. This guy just happened to be the guy who killed Hastings' parents. Casner has it all on videotape, according to our source."

"You shittin me?" Turk asked, dumbfounded by what he was hearing. "Where are these videotapes?"

"Casner has some type of secret room in his house where he keeps them. I'm told that Casner has a who's who on some of these tapes."

Turk pulled out a yellow steno pad from his drawer and jotted down the information that had just relayed. "Has this source seen this room and these videotapes?"

Belinda nodded. "Apparently on this one particular tape, Escada boasts about actually meeting the man who contracted the murders."

Belinda's last comment got Turk's full attention. If this information was correct, Escada was more important than anyone knew. But why was Escada sitting on this? Who could have had Benito Escada that scared? Turk wrote the questions on the steno pad and circled them.

"I'm told that on another tape, Escada brags about being a top lieutenant with the Cortez cartel. Obviously, that's when Casner's interest in Escada changed. Escada became a business opportunity at that point."

"So much for family loyalty." Turk shook his head.

"Well according to our source, this is where Casner ran into his problem. On one hand, he had vital information that could repair the relationship with his cousin. And on the other hand, he had the profit potential involved in doing business with the Cortez cartel. Trouble was, he couldn't act on either without causing suspicion."

"So what did he do?"

Belinda grabbed another hand of Jelly-Bellys. He was beyond hungry. Between chews, he said, "Casner got one of his dancers to get Escada to talk about his work and what he would do to improve productivity. And lo and behold, what do you think comes out of Escada's mouth?"

"I can't begin to imagine," Turk responded.

"Are you familiar with the new way that drug cartels operate?"

"Educate me."

"It will be a monumental task, but I'll try my best," said Belinda. "From my work on the drug squad, I've learned that these cartels function like Fortune 500 companies. They have the same type infrastructure that a GE, Coke or any other major corporation would have. In fact, it is not uncommon for these organizations to send family members to law school or graduate school.

"In that sense, like any other major corporation, employees are given bonuses for submitting quality proposals. People that directly impact the cartel's bottomline are highly compensated. In some cases, promotions or demotions are handed out contingent upon job performance.

"Anyway, I bet you didn't know that our boy, Benito

Escada was pissed for being bumped down a level. That's how we got him as an informant in the first place."

Belinda waited for Turk's reaction before he continued. He had told Turk something that he didn't know. Turk's facial expression said it all.

"And here's the kicker. Apparently, even now after he has agreed to become an informant for us, Escada is still trying to win some brownie points within the cartel."

Turk wrote another note on his pad.

"Our source says that in the videotape, Escada is telling the dancer that they need reliable cell phones. Preferably high security, state of the art high-tech phones. Escada is complaining about the current cell phone service. Everything from poor quality to high cost. I'm told he essentially lays out Casner's sales pitch and marketing strategy."

"Son-of-a-bitch."

"Right. Escada handed everything to Casner on a silver platter. Hastings Communications, is one of the largest providers of telecommunications services along the East Coast. Casner would have to be stupid not to capitalize on that opportunity."

Turk was loving this. Videotapes, cell phones, sex, drugs. This was good. "So then what happened?"

"What do you think?"

"Well, if I'm Casner, I let Hastings know who Escada is and what information he can provide."

"Right. But, you don't tell him about the other shit that you're planning to do. Let him know enough so that his curiosity is peaked."

"In other words, do a soft sell."

"Correct. Tell him that you'll do all the leg work, he will only have to provide the technical support. Hell, better yet, start another cell phone company, with you two as partners of course. He can even be silent if he prefers because you really want to protect him, in case anything goes sour. Then, after the relationship has been established with Escada, hit him up for the information about the Hastings' murders."

Turk stood from his chair and walked over to the window. He was mulling over the scenario Stan had just painted. He had to admit, it made perfect sense. Stan's ability to summarize a complex situation was one of the things that made him so damn good.

"And this is what the source said happened?"

"Pretty much. Turk, if you're Rick Casner, you find a way to get this deal done because it will provide you with the best of both worlds."

With his case made, Belinda grabbed another hand of the Jelly-Bellys.

"So, the only flaw in Casner's plan is that he doesn't know that Escada is an informant of ours?"

"Correct."

Turk heard the uneasiness in Stan's reply. He had an idea what it was.

"Uncomfortable with Escada, I take it?"

"Do you really want me to answer that?"

Turk smiled. He had the same reservations, especially now after hearing what Stan had just relayed to him.

"I take it you've come up with another option?"

Belinda nodded.

Turk looked at his watch and walked back over to his desk.

"Then you can tell me all about it over lunch. And you owe me a box of Jelly-Bellys."

CHAPTER 13

THE PAINKILLERS had begun to take effect. Now he would be able to function with a clear head and move around with minimal difficulty. He'd fucked up, big time. That part was evident to him. The part that wasn't clear was exactly what Teri planned to do with the stuff she'd taken.

Teri had not only taken a few of the most recent tapes and that night's plans, but also the preliminary plans from Senator Barrett's murder years before, which he had kept in a file on the laptop. He had always been a pack rat and now he deeply regretted it. In her possession, Teri held enough incriminating information to destroy him and a few others ten times over. He had to act fast.

The ringing doorbell broke Rick's train of thought. It had to be Fat Toney. He had called Fat Toney thirty minutes earlier and told him to drop whatever he was doing and get over there.

"What's going on, Rick?"

"I got a problem that I need your help with."

"Shit, I can see that." Fat Toney stepped into the foyer. "What the hell happened to you?" He noticed that the house was trashed.

"Teri took off this morning." Rick walked toward the kitchen and sat at the bar. Fat Toney followed.

"What do you mean she took off? As in left?"

Rick shot Fat Toney a glance, then stood, and walked toward the refrigerator. What he wanted was a drink, but it was too early. Plus, he needed to have all his faculties in order to function effectively the rest of the day. A bottle of orange juice would have to do.

After tossing a few Excedrin in his mouth and chasing them down with the Tropicana, Rick answered. "Teri claimed a burglar was in here when she came home last night and that she had to call security. She claimed that the door to the private playroom was open when security checked out the house." Rick finished off the Tropicana and threw the bottle in the trash.

"And you think she's lying?"

Rick chose to ignore the question. "Anyway, as you can see," he pointed to the damaged tapes on the counter top. "Teri destroyed a few videotapes and took several more with her when she left. From what I can tell, it looks like she only destroyed the ones pertaining to the last six months. And mostly the ones pertaining to her. Fuck!" Rick yelled and banged the counter with his fist. "Fucking bitch! Fucking inconsiderate bitch!" He yelled and banged the counter again, knocking some of the damaged tapes on the floor.

"Damn, that's messed up. I bet you had some good shit on these too." Fat Toney bent down to pick up a few of the tapes. Damn, he thought, as he read their contents, some of them were his favorites.

Rick shot Fat Toney another look from hell.

"What?" Fat Toney asked in defense.

Visibly disgusted with his friend's inability to see the bigger picture, Rick excused himself to use the bathroom.

———◦———

While Rick busied himself in the bathroom, Fat Toney made his way through the damaged area and into the master bedroom. Rick was right. Teri had done some extensive damage.

She had gotten Rick good, real good.

However, another matter concerned Fat Toney more. One of the videotapes. The one featuring him. The one Rick didn't know about.

Although now Teri did provide him with the perfect cover for the other tapes he'd taken, he still needed to know the whereabouts of this one particular tape. Had it been destroyed or did Teri have it? He was almost certain that Rick hadn't seen it; otherwise their conversation would be quite different.

Rick wouldn't have been as calm.

Fat Toney looked around the bedroom. He had to find the whereabouts of that tape. A lot depended on it. If Rick was correct about the tapes and Teri had taken that particular one, then right now he was in the clear. And as long as Rick didn't trust Teri and she stayed gone, everything would be fine. He just had to make sure that Teri stayed gone.

———◦———

"What's that smell?" Fat Toney asked as Rick walked into the bedroom.

Rick was about to respond with a smart comment when he realized that Fat Toney wasn't referring to his recent bathroom trip.

"The wet carpet. Teri was getting ready to take a bubble bath when I got in at dawn. We had some words, things got physical, water overflowed from the bathtub, shit went haywire."

Rick didn't plan on giving any more detail. There were some things that no one else needed to know. Some things that needed to be kept private between a man and a woman. Right now, he just needed Fat Toney to help him pull things together again.

"Man, that ass must've been pretty good for you to be laying up all night with it. You a bad muthafucker, Casner." Fat Toney smiled and nodded his head in approval.

Rick just stared at him again.

"Anyway. Teri hit me with one of them damn stun guns I keep in the nightstand. Got me real good, too." Rick rubbed his side where Teri had zapped him. "You figure I was already fucked up from partying all night, so it just knocked me right out. When I came to, the carpet was soaked. But, that's not the problem."

"Then what is?" Fat Toney was a little afraid of Rick's response.

"Teri took the plans for our little side arrangement when she bolted with the laptop. You know, the shit we wanted to set up with our friends in Miami."

Fat Toney's eyes widened. "You mean the distributorship? Oh shit, Rick! What we gonna do? What if Teri takes what she has to the police? Fuck, Rick! We could all end up in the Federal Pen."

"Man, calm down! I don't think Teri understands how to

access the files and even if she did, I don't think she would take them to the police. If I know her, she'll hold on to the information in case she needs it for something. But I'm figuring she has no idea what's in her possession."

"For everyone's sake, I hope you're right."

Me, too, Rick thought.

"So how you gonna find her? I mean, if she went through all the trouble that she did to leave, I doubt she still hanging around here. Do you have any idea where she might be?"

"That's what you're gonna help me with. We need to get some of this taken care of before I leave for Miami tonight."

"Wait a minute, Rick. I thought all four of us were going to Miami?"

"Teri, is more important at the moment don't you think?" Rick held up one of the damaged tapes and tossed it in the trash. "Plus, I think that I can handle the situation down there. The situation right here is the one that's bothering me. We might even get lucky and Teri might call or stop by."

"Fine. Whatever you think is best," Fat Toney said with a disappointed look on his face. He had been looking forward to hitting the clubs and the girlie bars, not to mention the Playhouse. He hadn't spent much time there since they'd opened it six months ago. He had been hearing some very good things about it. "Damn," he mumbled. But Rick was the boss and there was a slim possibility that Teri would return to the scene of the crime.

"I think that would be best. Besides, Teri didn't have any money of her own. Everything she had, I gave to her." Rick stopped as if he was remembering something very valuable. A broad smile spread across his face.

"What?" Fat Toney asked.

"Charge card."

"What?"

"Let me have your company charge card." Unsure of why

Rick wanted his charge card, Fat Toney reluctantly surrendered it.

Rick walked to the kitchen. Fat Toney followed. Grabbing the phone on the counter, Rick dialed the number on the back. Fat Toney still looked confused.

"Teri used a charge card for everything," Rick whispered, covering the phone with his hand. "I bet she's used it today already. If she has, we can find her that way."

Fat Toney marveled at Rick's ability to function and focus under pressure. He would have never thought of that.

"Yes, hello. Can I get my most recent transactions from you? I can. Good! How about the last twenty-four hours?"

Rick gave Fat Toney a thumbs up.

"Sure, Rick Casner. Account number 2606-7368-0429-5421." Rick wrote down the information and hung up the phone. He then called the travel agency, whose information had been given to him. Five minutes later, he'd gotten what he needed. "Teri bought three airline tickets." He scanned the departure and arrival times for all three, his eyes zeroing in on the last one. He smiled, said, "Teri's headed to Brazil."

"Brazil?"

"It's a long story, but I still want to make sure that's where she is. And, I want to know where she's going when she gets there. But that obviously means the Land Cruiser was left somewhere at Hartsfield. At some point during the day you have to go get it. Teri may have left a clue to her whereabouts in it. She wasn't the smartest person in the world you know."

Fat Toney wasn't too sure about that. Teri was a lot smarter than Rick was giving her credit for. He wasn't about to underestimate her. Rick had made that mistake and look where it had gotten him.

"What's with Brazil and the other flights?" Fat Toney asked.

Rick rummaged through the damaged tapes. He smiled

when he found one that he thought could be saved.

"Teri likes to travel. She always talked about the different places she's been, but I usually just tuned her out. Damn, now I wish I would have paid more attention to her rambling ass. The good thing is, as long as she's out of the country, we're okay, for now. And as long as she continues to use the charge card, we'll be even better because then she'll be leaving us a trail.

"But just in case that trail runs cold, I figure she talked to Tish or someone. Someone will remember something Teri told them about her travels. I want you to go talk to some of the girls at the club. But first, get one of the guys to ride to the airport with you. No, on second thought, take a taxi. And go alone. We don't need anyone else knowing about this, you understand?" Rick gave Fat Toney a serious look to reiterate his point.

"In the meantime, I have to come up with some alternative plans for tonight. I think I may have saved an earlier version of the plan on a disk somewhere. Shit, we just can't let Stu's ass know about any of this. There would be no way for me to explain any of this to him. No way he would understand..." Rick's voice trailed off as he said this.

"Hell, I get the feeling that Stuart's already looking for a reason to back out of the deal anyway. And I'm sure that I don't have to remind you that we need him to get this deal done."

"So what about Teri and Brazil?"

"I have a few connections over there. They can make sure that if she lands in the country, she'll be detained." He gave Teri credit; she had been smart. Unfortunately, she had underestimated his resources.

"Do you need me to do anything else?"

"Yeah, call your doctor friend and tell her to get her ass over here."

"What for?"

Rick pulled up the sleeve of his sweatshirt to show Fat Toney his bandaged cut.

"This is what for."

CHAPTER 14

```
ATLANTA, GA
CITY HALL
2:05 P.M.
```

MAYOR   BILL Durbin sauntered to the mic.
Durbin was the happiest of any of the people on the dais. He
was a hometown hero, who had graduated from Morehouse
College and Emory Law School -- an individual destined to be
a two-term mayor and possibly more. He had grown up on the
south side of the city, earned his stripes by working hard on
the city council, and was regarded as one of the finest people
in local politics. He was also the catalyst who planted the seed
in the head of Carmellia Knight about the community project.

Mayor Durbin cleared his throat to get everyone's attention. The event was being broadcast live.

"Good afternoon to all who are here to witness this momentous occasion. It is with great pleasure that I stand before you today to announce the plans for a major development in our efforts to help revitalize the inner-city. But before I do that, I want to ask Carmellia Knight to stand."

Carmellia stood and was greeted with a standing ovation from the people on the dais and in the audience. Senator John Knight leaned and kissed Carmellia on the cheek. Today, he was playing the role of supportive husband.

"About one year ago, I had the pleasure of spending some time with Mrs. Knight at one of our monthly meet and greets. As many of you who have followed my administration know, we generally use that as a time to eat and socialize; some would argue that this is all we do. However, on occasion we have been known to get something productive done."

Most of the room laughed. They all knew about Mayor Durbin's sense of humor regarding his girth. It had helped make him very popular in all pockets of the city.

"Seriously though, folks, at that meeting Carmellia and I struck up a conversation about revitalizing our inner-city. Now those of you who know me, know how passionate I am about this issue. It was one of the issues I campaigned on. In fact, I'm sure I have bored many of you about it. Isn't that right, Chairman Pennington?" Laughter again filled the room as the mayor looked at the head of the city council.

"Anyway, I left that conversation very impressed by Mrs. Knight's commitment to the community. I walked away thinking that one day we would love to enlist her help in doing something. I didn't know what, but I wanted her energy in helping us to get something done. Obviously, I wasn't alone in my thoughts.

"Less than one week later, Carmellia Knight came down to my office. Uninvited, mind you." There was another round of laughter. Mayor Durbin turned to his press secretary. "You see,

Reggie, I told you that open door policy thing would work."
More laughter. "In all seriousness, folks, she came to my office
with the idea of building a state of the art YMCA in the inner-
city. I was floored. I thought that it was a good idea and one
that I would love to help make happen." Mayor Durbin
turned to face Carmellia.

"Well, Carmellia, you made it happen and then some. On
behalf of the city of Atlanta, I salute you." The Mayor led the
room in another round of standing ovations.

"Now after we give you a sneak peak at this project, we'll
take your questions. So without further delay, I present to you,
the Chandler Sports & Recreation Complex."

Mayor Durbin pointed to his press secretary, who turned
down the house lights and started the elaborate video presen-
tation. Ooohs and ahhs filled the room for the entire five-
minute clip. When it was over, Mayor Durbin stepped back
up to the mic.

"Ladies and gentleman, Mrs. Carmellia Knight."

———◦———

Carmellia finished her speech and answered questions about
her motivation for the project. The moment was more exciting than she'd imagined it would be. She liked the spotlight
and adored the accolades that it brought.

Out the corner of her eye, she noticed him. It was a subtle gesture, but she noticed it. He would be something new,
something totally different from the rest.

Although Rick was great in bed, he was a little too dangerous for her tastes right now. Freddie was right about that.
She'd fuck him a couple of more times to get him out of her
system. Her approval rating in the state was high now and she
needed to capitalize on it. Plus, now that she was seriously
thinking about divorce, being involved with Rick Casner on

any level would not help her cause. But this new piece of eye-candy could prove to be very beneficial.

Carmellia excused herself, walked back to the dais. He was still watching her. Even though her back was turned, she could feel his eyes pouring over her body. She added a little extra "umph" to her walk, turned in time to see him staring. He was definitely interested. That he couldn't deny. Nor, did she want him to.

Carmellia pulled out a pen and her business card. What she was planning to do could backfire, but what the hell, she thought. Nothing good in life came without risk. And worse case scenario, she could always deny it. She'd throw out the carrot to see if he would bite.

Carmellia wrote a simple note on the back of her business card. She did it in a way that he would notice. A sudden rush of energy came over her. She looked over her shoulder, saw John talking to him. He wasn't paying much attention to John. In a sleazy kind of way, it turned her on to know that her husband was now jollying it up with a man she planned to fuck very soon.

Carmellia eased up to them, slipped her arm under John's. Very subtly, she slipped her card into Mr. Eye-Candy's hand. He took it as if he had been anticipating it. John didn't notice a thing.

Carmellia smiled.

Mr. Eye-Candy smiled.

Now, it was just a matter of scheduling.

CHAPTER 15

THE SMELL of chicken prepared in several delicious flavors was in abundance. And as usual, Pork Chop was manning the stove. He was dancing to a melody that only he could hear.

Stuart opened the door and walked in. "Chop!" he yelled, but got no response. Stuart waved his arms, in an attempt to get his grandfather's attention. At the same time, Pork Chop started singing. Pork Chop had a habit of singing songs completely different from what was playing over the restaurant's sound system.

"Hey, Chop!" Stuart yelled again, stopping Pork Chop in mid-belt. Pork Chop looked over his shoulder with a grimace, signifying that he didn't take to kindly to being interrupted. Pork Chop was known for cursing anyone out, for any thing. Rumor had it, he had even cursed President George Bush out when he was still Governor Bush. No one questioned the validity of the story.

One never knew which side of the bed Pork Chop would wake up on. If it was the right side, meaning he was in a good mood, then the restaurant would be packed because he would allow his employees to come to work. If he woke up on the wrong side, take-out was the order of the day. Many an employee had threatened to quit the Wing Leader, but no one ever did. Working for Pork Chop guaranteed a certain measure of celebrity status. In Hotlanta, Pork Chop was the Soup Nazi.

"Stu-Stu, my punk-ass grandson. What cha know?" Pork Chop smiled, exposing perfect white teeth.

"Same shit I knew yesterday only more of it."

"Right-right," Pork Chop responded, still smiling.

Stuart figured he must be in one of his good moods.

"You scaring the people away with that singing."

Pork Chop was a worse singer than he was, which meant that Pork Chop was a terrible singer. But, since Pork Chop was, as he liked to call himself, the best damn chef in Hotlanta, everyone tolerated it. People traveled miles just to sample his wings. His recipe's rivaled the Colonel's. However, Pork Chop only cooked a certain number of wings each day. And when that day's blessing was done, it was done. Pork Chop was a temperamental soul, stubborn as the day was long.

"You should be the one to talk. Remember, I've heard your singing too," Pork Chop said, tossing an apron in Stuart's direction. When one entered Pork Chop's kitchen, one worked.

Stuart tied the apron around his waist, and waited for his grandfather's obligatory gesture. Pork Chop spoke in gestures. He could convey anything he needed to say with a snap, nod, or point. Stuart got the "wash those chicken wings" point.

For the next five minutes, the only sounds heard came from the faucet and the fryer. Stuart looked at his grandfather. There was a peacefulness about him. He was a man comfortable in his skin. Stuart wondered if he would ever experience that feeling.

"Boy, is there a reason you keep staring at me?" Pork Chop asked, with his back to Stuart.

"How you know I'm staring at you when you got your back turned?"

"Cause I just know."

"Then how you know I wasn't looking at that press conference?" Stuart motioned toward the small television above his grandfather's head.

Pork Chop looked up at the television, shook his head. "You got my new phone?" He asked a minute later, pointing at his current one beeping on the kitchen table.

Stuart turned off the faucet, removed his apron, and picked up the phone he'd given his grandfather the previous month. It looked as if it hadn't been answered in as much time.

"Chop, damn. When's the last time you checked your messages?"

"Don't need to. Those who need to contact me, know the best way," Pork Chop said, holding a small container and shaking it. He sniffed it, apparently, didn't like the smell, and tossed it in the waste basket.

"So, tell me again, why I'm bringing you a new phone?" Stuart removed the box from his briefcase, placed it on the steel table.

"Cause, I said for you to," replied Pork Chop.

Stuart hated when his grandfather answered questions with his parental stock answer. Maybe, he had read his mood incorrectly.

"How you know that no one important hasn't tried to get in contact with you? Shit, Chop, how you know that you ain't win the lottery or that Auntie Dee and Auntie Livvy didn't get in an accident. Either one of them could be laying up in a hospital needing a blood transfusion or something?"

Pork Chop stopped what he was doing and looked at Stuart. "Have your numbers changed, Boy?"

"No, sir."

"Have Peaches' numbers changed?" Pork Chop called Tish, Peaches. If you were lucky enough to be given a nickname by Pork Chop, it meant he liked you.

"No, sir."

"Then, like I said, those who need to reach me, know how. And your aunts been taking care of themselves for a long time. As for the lottery, I ain't played it in three years. Not since that asshole took office. I wouldn't give Roy Barnes a pot to piss in, much less a dollar." Pork Chop glared at the television.

Stuart laughed at his grandfather's hatred of Governor Roy Barnes. He didn't know the full story, but rumor had it the current governor had made a disparaging remark about Pork Chop's wings. Political suicide.

"Chop, you shouldn't talk about your elected officials like that," Stuart said and continued to laugh.

"Boy, you trying to get me riled up. You know I can't stand that..." Pork Chop stopped his statement and went back to seasoning his wings. He continued to mumble to himself. Stuart turned to make his way to the restroom.

"Look at that S.O.B, standing right smack dab in the middle of the press conference? Like he had something to do with the YMCA project. I didn't see him at any of those preliminary planning meetings. Not a one of the executive board meetings. But there he is. Look at him, standing up there grinning like a cheetah."

It had been a long time since Stuart had seen his grandfather this worked up.

"He is an opportunist. And an ungrateful one at that," Pork Chop concluded.

"Chop, why aren't you at the press conference?" Stuart asked, laughing.

"Cause ain't no way in hell I was going to be on the same stage with Barnes. They'd had to pull me off him, or shoot me dead, which I'm sure he would have instructed them to do. And I be damned if I was going to play nice in front of the cameras. Been there, done that."

Stuart knew how much his grandfather loved the YMCA project. He had been specifically recruited by the mayor to help with it. It took Carmellia Knight's coming down to Auburn Avenue and having lunch at the Wing Leader to get his grandfather to agree. And although the building would be called the Chandler Sports & Recreation Complex, in certain parts of the community, it was being called The Robert Casner Sports Complex. One day soon, Stuart planned to sit down and pick his grandfather's brain. The man was a living legend.

"Chop, you ever gonna tell me what happened between you and the governor."

Pork Chop stopped seasoning his meat, looked at his grandson. "You ever gonna tell me what happened between you and RJ?"

"Chop, damn. You never gonna let that go, are you?"

"Nope. Not as long as I got breathe in my body."

"I'm trying, Chop. I swear to God..."

"Watch your mouth, boy. Ain't no need to disrespect the Lord."

"Sorry, Chop. Rick and I are working on our relationship."

"Good."

"As a matter of fact, I'll be seeing him later today."

"Is that right?" Pork Chop smiled.

"Don't act like you don't know? I know Rick told you already."

Pork Chop nodded.

"Then, how you gonna stand there and play me like that, old man?"

"Cause I like to make sure I have my facts straight. And if you call me old again, you gonna be removing my size thirteen from your ass."

"Can't kick what you can't catch," Stuart said, smiling.

"No, but I can shoot it."

"You wouldn't do that because then that would leave you with only one grandson," Stuart said as he made his way toward the restroom.

"I said I'd shoot you, not kill you," he heard his grandfather reply from the kitchen.

———◦———

Stuart looked at the wall of fame adorning his grandfather's restaurant. During the Civil Rights Movement, his family had been on the front line. Looking at the pictures, Stuart felt his family's power. He couldn't help but feel proud. He turned in time to see his grandfather walking out of the kitchen, carrying two beers. He handed one to Stuart.

"How you doing, son? And don't bullshit me. Something must be bothering you to get you to come to Auburn Avenue," Pork Chop said, as he took a deep swallow of his beer, and motioned for Stuart to take a seat.

"Damn, Chop, that hurt."

"Truth sometimes does," his grandfather said, before getting up to get another beer.

"So what are you getting at, Chop?"

"Stuart, don't think I don't realize what the day is, or how long it's been. That was five years ago, time to let it go. You did what you had to do. You did the right thing."

"I'm not to sure about that," Stuart said, rubbing the bottle with his thumb.

"Son, come on out and say what you thinking." Pork Chop hated people to beat around the bush. He gave, and respected, bluntness. Stuart had always been too much of a thinker. RJ and him were different in that way.

"It's nothing," Stuart said, rising from his stool. "I'm just a little geared up for this Miami trip. Tonight will be my first time back since that night."

Pork Chop nodded his head, stared at his grandson. Stuart was lying, but in due time, he would come clean. Both of Sheila's kids were like that. Independent thinkers, she called them. He had another name for it. "All right. I'll leave it be."

Neither man said a word for about thirty seconds, then Pork Chop broke the silence.

"How's Peaches doing?"

"Don't rightly know," Stuart said, causing his grandfather to spit out his beer laughing.

"Boy, what the hell did you just say. 'Don't rightly know'. Well ain't you educated. Just goes to show you that all the schooling in the world can't remove country," he said still laughing. Stuart laughed with him.

"Okay, Mr. 'Don't rightly know,' remember to look after your sister. She's the only one you got."

"I'm trying, Chop. I'm really trying. She just going through something right now, I suppose. And you know how Tish is, you know, when she wants you to know."

"Shit, both of ya'll just like yo mama. Sheila was the queen of keeping stuff bottled up," Pork Chop said, then excused himself to use the restroom. Damn imported beers kept him pissing, but he loved them too much to give them up.

———◄○►———

"Whatever happened to that girl you had chasing behind you? Thought you had her looking after Tish?" Pork Chop asked, returning from the restroom.

"You mean, Gina?" Stuart frowned. "Too much drama, that's what."

Pork Chop looked at his grandson and laughed.

"The Casner Curse," he said, smiling.

"Naw, Chop, Gina just crazy."

Pork Chop grunted, took anther swig of his beer. "It's been a minute since I've seen Peaches. Maybe I can talk to her. Find out what's bothering her."

"I'd appreciate that," Stuart said, and looked at his watch. He had to get going.

Pork Chop beat him to the punch by rising from his stool. "Son, I'm just doing what's right," he said and tossed his unfinished beer in the trash.

Stuart understood what his grandfather was implying.

The two men exchanged hugs and knowing glances. Stuart picked up his briefcase and headed for the door, Pork Chop picked up his apron and headed for the kitchen.

"Stuart," the sound of his given name, stopped Stuart at the door. He turned to face his mother's father. "I know that one day you'll tell me what happened between you and Rick. A man can't do nothing until he's ready to, you get what I'm saying."

"Yes, sir."

"And, son, I don't expect you to understand Rick, just know he means well. You and Peaches were raised different from him. Dee-Dee did the best she could, but she will never win mother of the year, you get what I'm saying."

"Yes, sir."

"And besides, ya'll, the last of the Casner men. You two

need to look out for one another. Family is all you got, you hear me. At the end of the day, family is all you got."

Stuart nodded that he understood.

DUNWOODY, GA
128 SPAULDING DRIVE
3:08 P.M.

TISH HELD the home pregnancy test in her hand. Why? She had no earthly idea. There was no way she could be pregnant. No way.

Because of an accident on Interstate 85, she hadn't been able to make it to the Emory Clinic in time to catch Gina. She had tried to reach her on the cell, but it just kept rolling over to voice mail. After the fourth try, she realized it was Tuesday; Gina's spa day. She reluctantly left a message.

It was just her luck that the clinic had started its winter break hours, which according to Gina meant that everyone treated work like one big break. She had gotten there a few minutes after two, and it was just like Gina to have left early. Of all the days, Tish thought.

The incompetent fools working the reception desk had been of little help. No one seemed to have a clue. They all seemed too busy watching *As the World Turns* and gossiping, to help the few students who needed it.

It was only after she had barfed in the waiting area did they pay her any attention. And even then she had to fill out all the stupid paperwork and give them every piece of documentation she had on her person, did they inform her that an emergency had come up and the doctor had left the building. Apparently, Gina hadn't been the only staff member to leave early.

To make matters worse, no one seemed to have any idea when the good doctor would be returning. That's when she lost it. She had always made it a habit not to act "ignorant," but sometimes.

Tish laid back on the bed, looked at the other items that had been in the bag. Before they had kicked her out of the clinic, or politely asked her to leave, depending on who was telling the story, one of the nicer girls had given her a "care package."

Because so many college students got pregnant during the winter, the clinic was providing materials informing students about making educated decisions. Included in the "care package" were condoms, ibuprofen, a coupon for a free pack of birth control pills, a video on STDs, and a home pregnancy test. Late night study sessions obviously led to other things, it was concluded. Tish looked at the use of her school tuition and shook her head. She got up and went to the bathroom.

———◄◦►———

Tish rushed to her purse to get her cell phone. She had dozed off. It was almost 4 p.m. Gina's name was displayed on the caller ID.

"Girl, damn, where you been?" Gina began. "I've been trying to get in touch with you for like thirty minutes. Don't tell me you've been studying on this beautiful day."

Tish stretched her arms, waited for a pause in Gina's ranting. Gina talked a lot and one had to get a word in whenever the opportunity presented itself. Ready. Set. Go.

"Hmm, I was taking a nap," Tish said, continuing to stretch.

"What? You, a nap! Girl, please! You know you're a vampire!" Both laughed at the joke. "I'm coming over to your place right now. As a matter of fact, I'm pulling into your subdivision as we speak. Get up and comb that nappy head of yours. My daddy just gave me an early Christmas gift. You'll never guess what is was, so I'll go ahead and tell you. Can you say Black Card!" Gina shrieked.

Gina was a rich, spoiled brat, but that's what Tish loved about her. They had become best friends because Gina had the hots for Stuart. And Tish suspected that Stuart would deny it, but she saw the way her brother's eyes lit up when he talked about Gina.

For all of Gina's quirks, she was the perfect person for her brother. Although, Gina was materialistic, one knew that up front. Gina did not conceal her desire to spoil herself or have others in her life spoil her. With Gina, one got what one saw.

"Gina, you know I need to be studying for my physics exam." Tish protested, even though she had already studied an entire week for it and was certain she would ace it.

"Girl, damn, where have you been?" Gina said. "What's your gate code?"

"Press #, then 0793," Tish replied, heading to the bathroom.

Gina entered the gate code, continued talking. "Uncle Phil had to leave to go out of town, family emergency. All exams have been canceled. Whatever you had on yesterday, will be your final grade."

"Girl, you should have seen some of those sad faces outside his office. Just plain Jerry Springer sad. Crying and all. And you know it was the ones who hadn't cracked a book all semester. Talking about they're gonna sue."

As much as she tried not to, Tish couldn't help but laugh. Gina's uncle, Phil Bershon, was Dean of the School of Medicine. He also taught Quantum Physics. He was notorious for canceling exams at the last minute.

"Well, it's a good thing I had an A," Tish said, while brushing her teeth. "Have you parked yet?" she asked, before rinsing out her mouth.

"Yeah, so come and open the door. Oh, and bring your keys, you're driving. My car is packed to the hilt with bags. No more room."

"First of all, I never said that I was going," Tish said, tossing water on her face, then patting it dry.

"Girl, stop fronting. You don't have nothing else going on, and I need you," Gina whined.

Tish heard the doorbell chime and walked to the door.

"And why do you need me?" she asked a smiling Gina.

Gina closed her cell and walked into the condo.

"Because, other than me, you have the best taste of anyone I know," she said, leaning to kiss Tish on the cheek. "I'm thirsty. Do you have any bottled water?" she asked, heading toward the kitchen.

Tish laughed at her friend and went to change clothes.

CHAPTER 17

ROBERT "PORK CHOP" CAS-
NER was a well-connected man, anyone who knew him,
knew this. He was seventy-five, and looked fifty. Had never
abused any substances and kept what vices he did have to a
minimal. After a lifetime of traveling the world, the Wing
Leader was his refuge.

He had graduated from Howard University with an
undergraduate degree in economics and a Law Degree two
years later. Throughout his lifetime, he had been a lawyer, a
diplomat, a delegate to the United Nations, a commissioner of
the FCC, and had served on the boards of nine major corpo-
rations.

Robert Casner was a powerful man, anyone who crossed him, learned this. At sixty-two, he retired from government work. His beloved wife of thirty-seven years was dying and he chose to be with her during her final months. Because he was a restless soul, Pork Chop needed a hobby, and Grace knew this. Although she appreciated his attentiveness, Grace knew he needed to be kept busy. Pork Chop Casner was the kind of man who needed to have a project. He needed a destination. He had yet to realize that life was about the journey.

One day while they were talking about their travels, Grace noticed how Pork Chop always identified places by food. She jokingly suggested that maybe he should try to duplicate cooking a few of those dishes. Immediately, after saying it, Pork Chop seized the idea. He enrolled in one of the finest culinary institutes in the world. And because of his connections, apprenticed under well-known chefs the world over. On the night before Grace passed, Robert "Pork Chop" Casner prepared her a meal fit for a queen.

———◦———

Pork Chop pulled up to the gate, waited for the security officer to exit the booth. The security officer smiled and handed Pork Chop the clipboard.

"Good afternoon, Mr. Casner. How are you doing today?"

"I'm fine, and yourself?"

"Doing just great, sir," the security officer said, accepting the clipboard back. He looked at it and smiled, "I'll only be a minute," he said before disappearing back inside the booth.

While he waited for the security officer to issue him clearance, Pork Chop turned up the volume of the talk radio program. He understood the need for security, so this inconvenience was tolerated. He also realized that his grandson had things he wanted protected.

Pork Chop turned down the volume of the radio when he saw the security officer returning. There was a look of disappointment on his face.

"I'm sorry, sir. I'm not getting an answer from Mr. Casner's estate."

Pork Chop's facial expression didn't change.

The security officer leaned closer to the vehicle, his eyes roaming nervously. "I could try again if you'd like?"

Again, Pork Chop nodded.

The security officer turned to re-enter the booth, then stopped. "Look, Mr. Casner," he whispered, looking around nervously, "I'm sure you're here about the incident last night. Since I've been on duty, the phone company and a doctor have come through." The security officer raised his head and looked over his shoulder. Satisfied that no one was looking, he said, "I'm gonna let you through. I'm sure Mr. Casner won't mind. Just keep it between us, okay?"

Pork Chop nodded and smiled. He had learned long ago that sometimes it was best to remain silent.

———◄○►———

Rick looked at the tapes along the wall. He had arranged everything for easy access. The contractor would be able to get in, do his work, and leave. He took a deep breath, closed his eyes. Physically, he would be fine. Emotionally, it would take a while. Teri had gotten to him. It was only now that he was coming to that realization.

Rick sat in the recliner, interlocked his hands behind his head and stared up at the ceiling. How was he going to make this right? And in the end, would it be worth it? These were just two of the questions that occupied his mind.

Rick stood from the recliner, stretched his legs. Modern medicine worked wonders for injuries. Other than his bandaged ribs and leg, he was okay. The Vicodin would take care of the pain.

Rick pressed play on the remote. He had been able to salvage one of the tapes of Teri and him. They had been compatible in so many ways. They had had so much fun. Sexually, she was his equal, if not better. It had taken his ego a minute to digest this, but he had never had illusions of being with any virgins. He preferred seasoned women; worldly women. Hell, he had lost his virginity to a hooker in Shanghai, so who was he to judge.

Teri had brought out a softer side in him. Taught him to look at things in a whole new light; with fresh eyes, she liked to say. His actions last night had been an attempt to reclaim his more animalistic desires; to prove that he was still the man and could do as he pleased. He knew that staying out late was pushing the envelope, which is probably why he did it.

Again, Rick closed his eyes and massaged his bald head.

"Son, you wanna tell me what happened here?" Pork Chop asked, pressing the stop button on the remote control.

Rick looked at his grandfather, gave a half-smile. Pork Chop did a quick scan of the room, took a seat on the leather sofa. He had seen the mess upstairs and in the garage. He had figured it out already, he just needed to hear it from his grandson.

"Had a little water damage," Rick replied looking at his grandfather.

"Hell, son, I can see that."

Rick knew that his grandfather was the one person he could come clean with. There was no need in lying to him. "I fucked up, man," he began.

"Go on," Pork Chop said.

"Teri left me. And, she did some serious damage in the process." He gestured to the condition of the house.

Pork Chop nodded.

Rick stood from the chair, started pacing. "She said that a

burglar broke in last night and that's how she stumbled on the room. Said that this room was open. But, man, you know how difficult this room is to access."

Pork Chop nodded again. He had helped design the room, so of course he was aware of the difficulty involved in breaching it.

"So, I'll ask you again, what happened?"

Rick knew what his grandfather was asking and also knew there was no way for him to avoid telling him. He sighed, then told Pork Chop everything.

CHAPTER 18

FAT TONEY cringed as he heard the smooth jazz coming from inside the building. He hated coming to these types of places, but he had no choice. He had something important to do.

It had taken them nearly two hours to clean up the mess at Rick's place. His doctor friend had sewn Rick up with twenty stitches, and had given him a prescription for painkillers.

Fat Toney looked at the bottle of Vicodin in his hand, then tossed it on the passenger seat of his Land Cruiser. Teri had left her mark indeed. She had trashed every one of Rick's cars. Bitches don't appreciate shit, he had said to Rick when they discovered the damage. Now, maybe Rick would start listening to him; maybe he would stop getting so caught up all the damn time. He couldn't remember the number of women Rick had fallen for. Each time, each one, possibly being "the one."

Fat Toney turned off the radio, grabbed a breath mint. Rick had told him to make sure his breath was fresh. No telling whom he would see, Rick had told him.

While he waited for the mint to work its magic, Fat Toney glanced at the sheet of paper on the passenger seat. So far he'd completed two of the items on the to-do list Rick had given him. He'd just left the car dealership where he dropped off payment for Rick's brand new Range Rover. It would be delivered to the house in a couple of hours.

He was still amazed at how people did special things like that for you when you had serious money. Very shortly, he would have money like that. Thanks to Mrs. Carmellia Knight.

Fat Toney smiled, stepped out of the Land Cruiser, and activated the alarm. He doubted anyone would try to steal his ride, but he knew there were haters everywhere.

He approached the entrance to the building. The black BMW he was instructed to look for was parked next to a handicap spot. He looked inside, saw a few items that he recognized as belonging to the owner, shook his head, and laughed.

Rick was right; women were predictable.

Rick had told him that if they got lucky, Teri would have called either Tish or Gina. Women always talk to someone Rick had lectured him. They would find out very shortly, but they would have to be smooth about it.

He had wanted to just call and ask, but Rick told him that that approach wouldn't work. Rick said that women were too slick for that and would smell them coming a mile away. Rick had a better plan; one that would ensure they got what they wanted.

While Rick, Stuart, and Spanky traveled to Miami for the meeting with the Cortez cartel, he would remain in Atlanta and try to learn Teri's whereabouts. Rick also wanted him to hang around the house while the general contractor came by for the damage assessment.

Fat Toney glanced at his watch. He had less than two hours to complete all but one item on the list. The trip to the airport would have to wait until later. Rick, Stuart, and Spanky would be leaving soon, which would provide him with uninterrupted access to Rick's tapes. He had to make sure that he hadn't missed anything.

———◄○►———

Fat Toney opened the tinted glass door and stepped inside the building. Within seconds, his nostrils encountered a sweet smell. It took another second for his eyes to adjust to the soft lighting. When they did, he looked for the reception area. He found it located to his right.

As he approached the counter, he couldn't help but notice how warm and inviting the atmosphere was. A lady was placing freshly cut flowers into a vase. Situated next to the vase, were rows of bottled water and complimentary towels. Fat Toney took a deep breath, tried to remember what Rick had told him to say.

"Hi, how may I help you?" the lady asked.

"Yes, hi. My girlfriend and her best friend are here and I wanted to check in on them. You know, see how their day of pampering was going."

"And you would be?"

"I'm sorry, where are my manners. My name is Toney Pruit. My girlfriend's name is Tish Hastings and her friend is Gina Bershon." So far, so good, he thought.

Rick had instructed him on precisely what to do. He was told not to wait for the lady to find the names on the appointment book. He was to turn on the charm immediately. "Tell you what," he said, leaning forward and touching the lady on the hand -- just like Rick had shown him. "I was trying to surprise them as part of an early Christmas gift and if you could help me do that, I would truly appreciate it." He continued to smile for added measure.

"I see, and how can I assist you with that?"

"Can you tell me what they're having done today? Better yet, don't even bother. Why don't you just go ahead and give them the royal treatment."

The lady's eyes lit up. He had said the magic words. Again, Rick had been right. He handed the lady a card and told her to charge the services to him.

"Of course, of course. I'm sure they will be so surprised," she responded.

"They deserve it," Fat Toney said with as much sincerity as he could.

While the lady was informing whomever about the changes for Ms. Hastings and Ms. Bershon, Fat Toney made small talk. He found out that she was the owner and that this was her newest location. She gave him a brochure that listed the other locations as well as the spa's services. He thanked her and reminded her not to say anything to either of the ladies about who had paid for the services. He promised her more business if she kept her word. She promised. He thanked her again and left.

Everything had happened exactly as Rick had predicted it. Now, all they had to do was wait a few hours before making their move.

———◦———

The silver Mercedes SLK hardtop convertible parked next to the Land Cruiser. The occupant of the vehicle was making no attempt to hide. In fact, the woman was making every attempt to be seen by the man she had been following.

She had pulled into the parking space next to the SUV moments after he had. She had followed him while he ran his errands. She had watched him stop at the black BMW and look inside. He did not know that she was following him. People only noticed her when she wanted them to. And right now, she wanted him to notice her.

Elana Futora wore very tight jeans, three-inch boots, and a plunging v-neck sweater that more than advertised her physical endowments. She did not need to wear a wonder bra or push-up bra or any other fashion trend of the day. Her own breasts served her just fine, thank you.

Her long auburn-tinted hair was pulled into a tight bun and covered by a Bebe baseball cap. In one hour, it would be dyed another color, something that would accentuate her high cheekbones and piercing gray eyes. She stood five feet ten inches and wore a size 5/6. She was simply beautiful.

She had been in Atlanta for ten days and had tracked Toney Pruit's movements. She knew how often he went to the bathroom and what he liked to eat. She knew what his favorite hangouts were and whom he was sleeping with. She had been in his house several times and inventoried everything in it. Things that were of importance had been either duly noted or taken.

She would secure the duly noted items shortly and her mission would be completed. In less than twenty-four hours, she would be on her way out of the country again.

Elana looked at the photo in her folder. The guy was a little heavier, but definitely the same person. She watched the guy walk out of the salon smiling. At the same time, she stepped out of her rental car and walked toward the building.

She wanted to make eye contact with him. This was something that she needed to do -- a little mind-fuck, it was.

As he approached her, Elana purposely dropped the books and her keys. Toney did as expected and acted like a gentleman. He retrieved her items and stood to hand them to her. Their eyes meet long enough for her to be satisfied.

Toney Pruit was definitely the man who had killed her brother. And now it was time for him to suffer the same fate.

ACT THREE

...TOKEN OF MY APPRECIATION

CHAPTER 19

KIP ROGERS looked calmly at the wet sidewalk below his office window. He loosened his tie, unbuttoned his collar. After he took the last sip of his Diet Coke, Kip discarded the can in the wastebasket and headed to his private bathroom.

As the Director of the FBI, his office overlooked the Justice Department and Pennsylvania Avenue. In essence, that meant he occupied the largest office space in the building. And because of his love of nature, a large portion of that space was filled with plants and flowers.

Phyllis, his executive assistant, had handpicked every flower and plant in the office from the neighborhood Lowes Home Store. Each one had been chosen for a specific reason.

And although it was Phyllis' job to water the inner garden on a daily basis, he had decided to do it today.

Kip walked out of the bathroom carrying an antique Chinese water container that had been a gift from a long time business associate. He walked over to the ficus, watered it. He walked over to the roses, watered them. He proceeded to water every plant and flower in his office. He was trying to calm down and watering the inner garden was the third step of a five-step process.

He liked his office, especially since the inner garden gave it a relaxing aroma. However, some days that aroma was appreciated more than others. Today was one of those days.

Kip placed the water container on his desk and continued to take deep breaths. Other than his love for nature, the rest of the office was decorated with minimal but tasteful furnishings. He walked toward the sitting area and rearranged the chairs in front of his desk. It was time to begin the fourth step in the calming process.

Kip looked at the antique coffee table in the lounge area. In the middle of the coffee table was the picture book, *Home Run: My Life in Pictures* by Hank Aaron. Lying atop the coffee table picture book was a glass enclosed gold key. Atlanta Mayor Maynard Jackson had given the key to him when he helped in the capture of the Atlanta Child Murderer. Continuing with step four of the calming process, he took in the vases and the plaques, the volumes of books.

Kip allowed his eyes to travel along the wall, stopping at a corner entrance, which led to the back room. Located in the back room, he kept a secure phone, another couch, and additional momentos of his days at the Bureau, including the Distinguished Intelligence Medal. For celebratory purposes, he also maintained a wet bar, which he typically opened up on Fridays for agents who had successfully completed major cases.

Kip looked at his desk. It was a beautiful desk -- not too large, but functional. He didn't like ostentatious. On the desk rested several color-coded briefing books, as well as a few weekly reports. On the right bottom corner of the desk rested a yellow-covered booklet, which contained undercover review-board-operation minutes. Part of his duties as director of the FBI required him to review all undercover category-one proposals. Category-one proposals pertained to major undercover operations. As of that morning, one hundred category-one cases were scheduled to go through the undercover review-committee procedure. Those procedures had been enacted to address all concerns on third-party liability, legal, tactical, and human resource issues.

For a brief moment, he thought about some of the undercover operations up for review. Some were a complete waste of time and energy, and others would never make it through committee review. Also resting on his desk was a blue-covered booklet that was prepared each week for him. Unlike the yellow booklet, which contained undercover category-one proposals, the blue booklet gave a rundown on current major cases. And it was very detailed.

Material on light green paper in the booklet could be made public. The rest had to be kept confidential. An appendix to the booklet showed how a division utilized agents within seven sections: civil rights and special inquiry, counterterrorism, drugs, investigative support, organized crime, violent crime and major offenders, and white collar crime. Kip walked over to his desk and sat in his chair. He was now ready to start the fifth step in the calming process.

——◄�► ——

Kip stared at the blue booklet in front of him. It contained the sources of his problem. He massaged his temples and closed his eyes. At this very moment, he hated his job and was trying real hard to remember why he had come out of retirement to accept it. Langham & Associates had been doing great. He had enough money and other toys; therefore, he didn't need the political headache associated with it. The president had just called him for an update on the CASTEL case, which he didn't have yet.

Oh, how the day had begun with so much promise.

Kip Rogers had gained national attention when he was special agent in charge of the Atlanta field office. At his direction, the Atlanta office had arrested the bomber who'd killed Judge Stacy Hastings and his wife Sheila Casner-Hastings. Unfortunately for the Bureau, that person had never made it to trial. And worse, had never divulged the identity of the person who had hired him. That person had been poisoned while awaiting arraignment.

Four years later, still the special agent in charge of the Atlanta office, another bombing had taken place, but this time in Miami. Though the bombings had been completely different in nature and execution, he had suggested that they were in some way tied together. This hadn't gone over well with a few powerful men; thus, he had been instructed to busy himself with other things.

Disgusted with the politics surrounding that bombing, he resigned in protest after twenty-one years of FBI service. One year later, following a quiet internal reorganization, he had been brought back as director.

He had accepted the directorship only as a special favor for the president and only under the condition that he be allowed to fully reinvestigate both bombings. Those cases had haunted him for years, and had led to the formation of Langham & Associates. So either as a government employee or a civilian, he would solve them. It had taken the president four years, a re-election, and a threatened letter of resignation to fully understand this.

The Bureau had known all along that the Hastings' bombing was drug-related. Judge Stacy Hastings had been suspected of accepting illegal favors from drug cartels for administering lighter sentences. The thought of a possible federal probe into these allegations had led the cartels to seek a permanent resolution.

The Miami bombing, it was learned, was tied to the Hastings' bombing. Stuart Hastings had been the mastermind behind the bombing, but Toney Pruit had carried out the act. Erin Barrett, Senator Paul Barrett's wife, had confessed to setting the entire event in motion. However, since there was no public record of the incident occurring, no formal charges could be brought against any of the parties involved.

Director Kip Rogers hadn't been satisfied with that, so he had approached the president with an idea. Against great opposition, the president had given his full support and a major investigation code-named CASTEL had been born.

From the start, Kip had known that CASTEL would be no ordinary investigation. It involved sex, drugs, politics, and public figures. It also required multiple joint investigations between several field offices, and a significant investment of financial resources. And now it seemed to be coming apart at the seams.

———◦———

Kip pressed the intercom for Phyllis.

"Yes, Director Rogers."

"Phyllis, is everyone in the conference room?"

"Yes, sir. And Special Agent Buchman is holding on line three."

"Thank you, Phyllis."

With the blue booklet tucked under his arm, Kip entered the conference room. Everyone seated around the table stopped what they were doing. Seated in the room were Deputy Attorney General, Clive Fordham; the Associate Deputy Director over Criminal Investigation Division, Janet Lighty; the Associate Deputy Director over Intelligence Division, Victor Horowitz. Also present were Special Agent Lane Reynolds, SAC of Washington Metro; Special Agent Stan Belinda, and Assistant U.S. Attorney Christian Walsh, head of the U.S. Attorney's office organized crime strike force.

"Good afternoon, Janet, gentlemen. Thank you for coming on such short notice. I'll try to be brief." Kip took a sip of water, cleared his throat. "As of approximately noon today, Benito Escada has disappeared."

Most of the faces around the table took on a frown.

"I don't have to tell any of you what this means to our investigations. But, before I go any further, we have Special Agent Dale Buchman of the Miami field office on the line." Kip pressed the button on the phone to address Special Agent Buchman.

"Dale, I know this has been a terrible day for you, but I need you to brief us on what transpired today. Did Phyllis tell you who was going to be sitting in on this conference?"

"Yes, sir."

"Then you can begin. Please speak up so that everyone will be able to hear you."

"Yes, sir. As everyone present knows, for the last three months the Miami field office has been working in association with the Atlanta and Washington Metro field offices in a joint investigation code-named CASTEL, the purpose of which we're all aware of.

"On the Miami end we wanted to infiltrate and bring down the massive inflow of illegal drugs in the U.S. Over the past few years, we have been able to penetrate two of the four largest illegal narcotics cartels, the Cortez and Medellin. Six days ago, we had everything in place to set up the meeting between Hastings LLP and the Cortez cartel. However, that mission was aborted for reasons beyond our control."

Everyone in the room looked at Deputy Attorney General Fordham, Kip included. He made no attempt to hide his contempt for the man. He wanted him to feel the disdain that the majority of the room held for him.

Because of Fordham, Benito Escada had become a hostile informant. Fordham had been in charge of working out the deal with Escada, and had tried to play hard ball when it wasn't necessary. At the time, Escada was willing to do whatever the Bureau asked; that is, until Fordham tried to curry political favor by making Escada his whipping boy.

In the end, Fordham had pissed Benito Escada off to the point that he had refused to negotiate with anyone at the Bureau or Justice. During the six days it took Kip to win back Escada's trust, massive amounts of drugs had disappeared and several undercover agents had been killed.

"Dale, please continue," Kip said.

"The purpose of that aborted mission was..."

Fordham interrupted, "Agent Buchman, I think we all understand the purpose for the aborted mission. You can skip to what happened today if you don't mind."

"Yes, sir. Agent Carl Stinick and Agent Melissa Martinez were conducting a routine surveillance on our contact Mr. Escada and our undercover agent, Fagan Alvarez. As you know, Benito Escada is not only a high-ranking lieutenant with the Cortez cartel, but more importantly, he had recently become a valuable informant. Agent Alvarez was working in conjunction with Escada to arrange the meeting between Hastings LLP and one of the Cortez brothers.

"The purpose of that meeting was to establish a partnership where Hastings LLP would provide telecommunication services to the entire Cortez organization. From a Miami field office standpoint, the significance of having access to any information conveyed over cell phones goes without saying. I'm sure that Special Agent Belinda can fill us in on the status of Hastings LLP."

Belinda spoke, "A little over three weeks ago, we learned about a second purpose that had developed for that meeting. We found out that Rick Casner and his partner, Toney Pruit, had privately proposed to serve as East Coast distributors for the Cortez cartel's drug operations."

Agent Buchman continued, "That meeting was scheduled to happen shortly after the conclusion of the other meeting. From what we know, sometime between 11a.m. and 12:35 p.m. Benito Escada and Agent Alvarez were getting a mani-cure/pedicure."

"Did you just say a manicure/pedicure?" Deputy Director Lighty asked.

"Yes, that would be correct."

Kip interrupted, "Deputy Director Lighty, every Tuesday at the same time Mr. Escada and Agent Alvarez would go to a place called Nails & Things. It was one of the weekly perks that Justice had to grant Escada for his continued coopera-tion."

Fordham averted eye contact again and suddenly became very interested in something on the floor.

"Continue, Dale," Kip said, shaking his head.

"At around 12:30 p.m., Agent Martinez entered the spa to check on the situation. Upon her entrance, Agent Alvarez dis-cretely signaled that Escada had gone into the tanning room. Two minutes later, Martinez casually inquired about the use of the tanning room and was told that it was occupied.

"After about a five-minute wait, Martinez had one of the employees check on the tanning room's availability again.

When they did, they found the door locked, but received no answer from inside the room. Thinking that something was not right, the spa manager accessed the room. Escada was nowhere to be found and a window in the tanning room had been opened. His clothing was still in the room.

"We found evidence to suggest that someone had been hiding in a closet and right now we are treating it as a kidnapping. Our best estimate would be that by the time Agent Martinez entered the establishment, Escada had been gone at least fifteen minutes, if not more."

Everyone around the table was quiet. No one was ready to admit the obvious; without informant Escada, the likely success of CASTEL had been significantly reduced.

"Agent Buchman, how many men do we have looking for Mr. Escada?" Assistant U.S. Attorney Walsh asked.

"We have over two hundred agents helping with this search. Right now, it is our top priority. We are very quietly asking around and knocking heads."

"Agent Buchman, this is Deputy Director Horowitz, I have two questions. First, will we know if Escada has compromised this mission or any other mission in any way if we find him? And second, assuming he is not found, do we have other informants or agents in place who could commence the mission at a later date?"

"Sir, the answer to that first question is, no. We will not know whether he has compromised our undercover agents or other missions. However, even with all the security measures we had in place, it would still be hard for us to know what Benito Escada knew. He was very connected as you know. In my opinion, I suggest that we treat the situation as if he had compromised the mission. I think that would be the safest course of action.

"As for our ability to commence at a later date, I think that all depends on the first question. But to answer your question.

Yes, we do have other informants in place. Although not at the level of Escada, we still have them. However, I caution that it would take us at least three months, maybe more, to divert suspicion and get this thing rolling again. I also think it would be smart for us to remember that this will be the second aborted meeting in less than a week. Either one of the parties could decide to walk away."

For about twenty seconds, the room remained silent as everyone searched for a solution.

"Dale, how much confidence do you have in Agent Alvarez?" Belinda asked. He had been prepared for something like this.

"I don't understand your question, Stan."

"Stan, are you talking about what you and I discussed earlier?" Turk asked.

Belinda nodded.

"Well, do you two mind filling the rest of us in?" Fordham cut in.

"Yes, sir. Dale, Agent Alvarez has had contact with others within the Cortez cartel has she not?"

"Very limited, but, yes. Her main contact was with Escada but he did introduce her as his girlfriend at several cartel functions. We were very adamant about that."

"Director Rogers, do you mind if I…"

Kip interrupted. "No, no, Stan. Go right ahead. This is your area of expertise."

"Thank you, sir."

"Okay, Dale, let's make several assumptions here. Although I hate to do this, I think our options are limited."

"All right I'm listening."

"Okay. First, let's assume that the mission has not been compromised by Escada. Let's also assume that Agent Alvarez has paid attention at these cartel functions and that the Cortez brother whom they were to meet tonight finds her engaging.

Do you think she can..."

Agent Buchman interrupted, "I see what you're getting at, Stan. I think that Agent Alvarez can pull it off, if we need her to. But I must caution you that this is her first undercover operation."

"Agent Buchman, we have no choice. This meeting is to commence tonight. I'm sure Agent Alvarez knows the danger inherent in this type of mission," Fordham chimed in.

Kip was close to losing it, but he kept his composure. "Dale, how soon can you get in contact with Agent Alvarez and give her the new game plan?"

"With any luck, sometime between now and 7 p.m. She and Escada were scheduled to meet with the Cortez brother at 8 p.m."

"Dale, do your best to get in touch with her and work out a plan for tonight. I want a status update every hour on the hour. We'll work out everything else on this end," Kip said.

"If Escada resurfaces, how do you want us to handle it?" Agent Buchman asked.

"Neutralize him," Fordham answered quickly. Everyone in the room looked his way, then at Kip.

Kip said, "No, Dale. You are to detain him and interrogate him. Find out whatever you can, by whatever means you can." He refused to look in Fordham's direction. If he had, he would have seen that the man was seething. Seething because he had just been made to look like a complete ass.

"Yes, sir."

"That will be all, Dale. Good luck."

Kip sat back in his chair as another possibility entered his mind. His people had invested too much in this thing to let it fall apart. It was time to take the offensive. Time to roll the dice. "I have an idea," he said. "I want to arrest Toney Pruit."

He then laid out his reasons. Once he was finished, every-one agreed with his plan, including Deputy Attorney General

Fordham. They all also agreed that if they were lucky, months of work and thousands of dollars wouldn't be blown.

If they were lucky.

CHAPTER 20

WASHINGTON, DC
RONALD REAGAN NATIONAL
AIRPORT
7:02 P.M.

FRED ENTERED the password to access the Net Bank account. He made the transfer and watched as one million dollars vanished. He thought about putting a trace on the money, but knew that would prove pointless. Whoever was blackmailing Carmellia would undoubtedly have the receiving bank transfer the money into several different accounts seconds after receiving it.

Fred sighed. He had done the right thing. Besides, it wasn't like it was his money. The money had come from a special account that John had set up years before for situations such as this. He closed the Net Bank site, saved the wiring instructions he'd been given. Who knew if that information would come in handy at some point in the future.

The blackmailer had been very creative and careful so far, but he had gambled enough to know that sooner or later one's luck changed. He planned to be around when that change occurred. His only problem then would be his course of action. One thing was for certain though, in less than an hour he would know a lot more about Rick Casner.

Fred held up the gray Langham & Associates envelope he'd received earlier in the day. He still hadn't gotten a chance to look at its contents yet. Jeff had been glued to his hip all day. He'd been lucky that the courier had delivered the package while Jeff had made a trip to the bathroom. Otherwise, the little shit would have been even more of a thorn in his ass.

Fred slid the envelope back into his briefcase. It had been a hunch, but he had played it. He didn't trust Casner. Too many things about him didn't add up, nor could he shake the timing of everything. Carmellia had had many affairs, but the blackmail had occurred shortly after she had started her fling with Casner, which naturally made him a prime suspect.

Carmellia had worked too hard building her image and he had worked too hard protecting it to allow someone like Casner to destroy it or taint it in any way. That was why he had paid the fee of the blackmailer, without hesitation. And why he had contacted Langham & Associates.

He just wished that he were back in Atlanta where he could really dig into the meat and potatoes of the report. It was guaranteed to be good reading and very informative, that he knew for certain. If nothing else, Langham & Associates was very thorough -- almost a little too thorough.

Fred wondered what, if any, information Langham & Associates had on him. A cold chill ran up his spine at the thought of anyone knowing some things about him.

He nervously looked around the waiting area. Thogh he didn't see anyone suspicious looking, but one never knew.

When he had an opportunity, he planned to do more research on Langham & Associates. This company was almost too good to be true. Hell, maybe he could work with them in some capacity. Surely they would be able to use someone with his expertise.

Under the circumstances, that actually wasn't a bad idea, he concluded. With everything happening so fast lately, he hadn't had the time to put together a solid contingency plan. His current situation was now shaky at best, but maybe he could salvage something from it.

Fred looked around the lounge to make sure the assholes were still talking to the Assistant U.S. Attorney. By chance, they had bumped into him in the private lounge. He knew the conversation would last at least fifteen minutes, so after minute five, he'd excused himself under the guise of needing to make a few phone calls. He'd made the calls, now he was checking his new e-mails.

Fred glanced over at the three men sipping drinks and backslapping. Not a one of them had a thing to worry about. All three were rich and respected; all three had bright futures.

It was a forgone conclusion that Assistant U.S. Attorney Christian Walsh was quietly building support to run for governor of Georgia. Damn, that would be major, Fred thought. He could see the good ole boys of the KKK dropping dead from heart attacks. He chuckled at the image.

Then there was his asshole brother-in-law. John would make out just fine if he had to resign under any scrutiny or scandal. He had long ago figured that John would either end up heading some think tank, making some ungodly sum of money or he'd become a well-paid public speaker. John would definitely write a couple of books.

He could see John following in the footsteps of Newt Gingrich and Ollie North.

And lastly, there was Jeff. He knew without a doubt that

Jeff would land on his feet. In fact, he didn't put it past Jeff to be planting notes in one of U.S. Attorney Walsh's pockets right now about his imminent availability. The conniving prick, that was definitely Jeff's style.

Fred looked over at Jeff backslapping and ass kissing. Jeff was in his element. Almost as if he knew Fred was looking at him, Jeff pretended to laugh a little harder. It was as if he was saying, "I will leave your drowning ship in a heart beat and I will always come out smelling like a rose."

And he didn't doubt it for one minute. Jeff would always have granddaddy's money and connections behind him. But then again, it wasn't like Jeff was a slacker. On the contrary, Jeff was very intelligent and hard working. He actually had some semblance of respect for the jerk. Jeff was just so damn smug.

Still, the little shit would land another gig, latch on to some other politician. People with Jeff's skills and connections usually just changed team uniforms. The Jeff Cirrillo's of the world would always land on their feet.

Fred felt his head start to spin. He loosened his tie, reached for the glass of water on the table. He needed to think. He needed to cover his ass. This thing with Carmellia could end up blowing up in his face and then what? And who was to say that the blackmailer wouldn't come back for more?

Fred opened the program on his laptop containing his electric Rolodex. If he had to, he'd contact every name on the list. He would start with the A's. No, he would wait. A move like that would make him seem desperate and probably set off a few alarms. But hell, he was desperate and the alarms would sound eventually anyway.

"Think, Fred," he told himself.

"But don't do anything stupid," he countered.

"Don't show your hand yet," spoke another voice.

"Bullshit, you have resources at your disposal; use them or

lose them," interjected another one.

His head now hurt from the thinking and the stress. He didn't do stress, but today that seemed to be all he was doing. And as if dealing with the blackmailer hadn't been stressful enough for him, now Carmellia was thinking about a divorce. He wondered whether Carmellia would change her mind, if she knew about the blackmail; although right now, he had no intentions of telling her. Carmellia deserved to be happy and he was determined to do everything in his power to ensure that happiness.

Besides, he really couldn't blame her. She'd stayed in the loveless marriage out of necessity. But with the pending success of this YMCA project and the other doors that would be opened because of it, Carmellia didn't think she needed John anymore. She felt that she would be more valuable divorced than married. A hot commodity, she'd called herself; especially now that John was globetrotting after some twenty-four-year-old. The country would embrace her, just like they did Ivana Trump.

Well, Carmellia deserved to be viewed like Ivana and he would make sure of that. Now it was time for Fred to look out for Fred.

———◄◦►———

Using the laptop, Fred accessed the emergency fund that he had set up for his personal retirement. Over the years, he had gradually siphoned off tens of thousands each year from his expense account. Over a ten-year period, that figure had grown tremendously.

He had invested the money wisely, meaning no tech stocks for him. He only bought what he knew. Plus, if his scheme was discovered, he wanted to be in a position to replace the money rather quickly. No need to be greedy. Besides, some of the new high-tech stocks, he couldn't even pronounce. But he believed in the Dow Jones, even though the good old standards had performed terribly when compared with the high-tech darlings.

Fred looked over at the group. They looked to be finishing up their meeting. He quickly entered his code to access the account. He just wanted to sneak-a-peak. The numbers came up and a smile crept over his face. The figure had grown more than he thought.

Cautiously, he had only checked it once a year. He'd actually hoped that he wouldn't have to resort to taking it, which was why he didn't tempt himself too often by looking at it. Or why he never considered it his. But his days of thinking like that were no more.

Fred straightened up a little bit. He felt new life enter his body. He was rich, very rich. Now he just needed to move it somewhere safe -- the Cayman Islands or someplace like that. He would do that later.

Fred saw the men shaking hands, so he knew they were finished meeting. He closed the program and began to pack his laptop. By the time John and Jeff made their way to where he was, Fred was ready to go.

CHAPTER 21

WASHINGTON, DC
HOUSTON'S
7:28 P.M.

SENATOR JOHN Knight stopped the car in front of Houston's. He had insisted that Jeff ride in the Town Car. The senator had taken Fred's car, which Fred had been more than happy to relinquish since he'd been sent back to Atlanta to work on the "special project."

For some reason, Jeff had protested vehemently, but the senator had already made up his mind. Fred didn't need to be in D.C. right now anyway. His services were needed back in Atlanta taking care of the latest problem. Jeff needed to take a cue from him and stop wanting to know the who, what, when, and why. Blanket denial worked wonders.

While back in Atlanta, Fred could dig up information on

Teri's former boyfriend. He didn't even know the prick's name, but that was something for Fred to worry about. Jeff would just have to get over this little thing he had for micro-managing. They had bigger issues on which to focus.

Knight made a mental note to speak with Jeff. Although Jeff was talented and liked, he needed to remember who worked for whom.

Knight looked in the rearview mirror to check his appearance. He had brushed his teeth at the airport and had gargled with mouthwash on the drive to Georgetown. Over preparation was a good thing.

Knight reached into his briefcase, pulled out a bottle of Bvlgari Black cologne. It had been a gift from one of his younger, hipper, female friends. He sprayed a tad behind his ears, massaged it into his skin. He smoothed his eyebrows and straightened his necktie. When he was happy with his appearance, he stepped out into the cold air.

A car's horn beeped behind him, but he didn't look. However, when he heard his name, he turned toward the direction of the sound. It took only a second for his eyes to recognize the person.

She was sitting in a white Toyota Camry wearing a baseball cap and sunglasses. He wanted to ask her how she could see with the sunglasses on, but figured that wouldn't be an appropriate greeting.

"Hi, sexy. You going my way?" Teri asked.

Knight made his way over to the car.

"Get in."

He did as instructed.

"Aren't we eating at Houston's?"

"Nah, I found a more private place for us to talk," Teri said and pulled out into traffic.

Knight didn't object. It was clear who was in charge.

"So, are you okay? You mentioned you had some trouble?" he asked, adjustomg the seat to fit his frame.

"I'm fine. I just discovered some disturbing things, that's all. Things that I need your help with." Teri said this without looking in his direction.

"Sure, if I can. But why don't you give me a hint as to where we're going? Maybe I can offer a short cut." Knight nervously reached for his seat belt.

Teri knew she was driving rather fast; she always did. She also noticed John's uneasiness; she smiled. "Nah, I think I pretty much got this part covered. Don't tell me you're scared of a little excitement, Senator?"

"Well, no. I like excitement." Knight shifted uneasily in his seat. "It's just that I prefer it in other areas. Areas that don't compromise my physical well being."

Teri took a quick right down a residential street, which caused Knight to grab the dashboard. He noticed she was heading north toward Maryland. She'd obviously been studying a city map, he figured.

"You might want to get comfortable, we have a long night ahead."

Knight was tongue-tied. Something told him that Teri had different things in mind from what he had.

CHAPTER 22

TERI PULLED the car into the garage of the Tudor style house. Knight sat with a look of confusion on his face. Teri hadn't said much on the thirty-minute trip into the suburbs, but he now knew that she'd lied to him about having been to D.C. What else had she lied to him about?

When the garage door closed behind them, Teri got out of the car. Knight hesitated.

Maybe he was making too much out of the situation. Teri probably had friends and this was one of their homes. She was probably trying to protect him. Couldn't it be that? Couldn't it be that she just wanted to have him some place safe? Some place special. Yeah, that's what it was. She was just trying to make him more comfortable. But she didn't have to lie to him about it. Oh well, to each his own, he concluded.

His fears put to rest, Knight stepped out of the car, walked into the house. Before the door closed, his theory was permanently destroyed.

———◦———

John Knight walked around the living room and took in the photos. The pictures were of Teri growing up. He assumed the woman in the picture was her mother. The woman looked vaguely familiar, but he couldn't place her.

He continued to walk through the family room. More pictures of Teri and her mother. Going to the zoo. Playing in the park. Teri riding a bicycle. Teri ice-skating. Teri and her mother horseback riding. Teri celebrating her birthday. Teri and her mother playing in snow.

"She was so beautiful," Teri said from behind him.

"Your mother?"

"Yep."

John could see the sadness in Teri's eyes. There was a deep sadness there, a sadness that he would never understand.

"She died from breast cancer nine years ago this month," Teri said, teary-eyed.

"I'm so sorry to hear that, Teri."

John traced his finger over the picture of Teri and her mother horseback riding.

"I take it you guys were close?" He remembered his relationship with his mother.

"Very. We spent every day together. We even had the same birthday, July 26th." Teri said this, then excused herself. Minutes later she came back carrying two mugs. "Apple cider?"

John accepted a mug.

For the next ten minutes he looked at Teri's family photo

albums, while she busied herself in the kitchen.

"Can I get you another cup of cider?" Teri asked, walking back in the room and wiping a tear from her eye.

"No, I'll do it. I need to get up and stretch my legs anyway. Why don't you have a seat? You look exhausted."

"Thank you. I would appreciate that." Teri handed John her mug and leaned her back against the couch, just like she had done all her life.

"So, I take it you grew up in this house?"

"Half and half. We lived abroad half the year and stayed hear during the holidays mostly. My mom moved here two weeks before she had me."

John returned from the kitchen with two steaming mugs of cider. He handed Teri one, sat next to her on the carpet. "What about your father? I don't see any pictures of him around."

"I don't keep them out in the open. It wasn't something that I was allowed to talk about growing up."

"Why is that?"

"Why don't you see for yourself?"

Teri placed her mug on the coffee table; she removed a necklace from around her neck. Attached to the necklace was a small skeleton key that John hadn't noticed until that moment.

Teri held the skeleton key in her palm, smiled down at it as if it unlocked the door to one of life's greatest treasures. She placed it on the coffee table. From an end table, she removed an antique jewelry box. The outer surface of the box appeared to be some type of map. John squinted, his eyes trying to make out the locations. Teri saw him, smiled.

"These are the places my mom and I traveled," she said. "My father was only able to make a few of these trips. When my mom died, I had a replica of the travel map we used to plan our destinations, transferred on her old jewelry box. The jewelry box had been a gift from my grandmother to her, and will one day by my gift to..." Teri's voiced cracked and she couldn't finish the sentence. But there was no need to; John understood.

John noticed the box had three letters carved on top. He wondered what the letters stood for. He could barely make out the letter K. One of the other letters appeared to be an S. Someone's initials possibly? They looked to be the creation of a child.

Teri grabbed the skeleton key off the coffee table, inserted it into the jewelry box, turned it three times, and removed an item wrapped in crepe paper. She removed the crepe paper, exposing a small videocassette. She held the cassette in her hands, hugged it, kissed it, and handed it to John. "I have to go wee-wee," she said, embarrassed. "And something tells me, you need to see this for yourself. The entertainment system is in the wall unit," she said, pointing to its location.

John pressed "play" on the VCR. The red, white, and blue Barrett for Congress banner was the first image he saw. Paul looked a lot younger; as did most of the people with him. The film had been shot at least twenty-five years before. He recognized most of the people. Some still worked in politics. The most noticeable were C. Preston Barrett, his mentor; Al Cirrillo, his chief moneyman; and a woman he now knew to be Teri's mother.

John turned up the volume and listened to Paul's victory speech. Paul had always been charismatic. He'd always been the golden boy. Paul thanked everyone for his or her hard work and dedication, but singled out one person he identified as the key to his victory -- Helen French, Teri's mother.

Teri French. He had never asked Teri her full name.

John continued to watch the home movie. There was footage of Paul and Helen embracing. Footage of Paul and Helen in the delivery room. Footage of Paul holding a baby and looking extremely happy. Dance recitals, birthday parties, family outings. In all the years he had known Paul Barrett, he could not remember seeing him smile as much as he did in this footage.

John grabbed the photo album he'd been looking at earlier, shook his head in astonishment. Most of the pictures that he'd looked at of Teri and her mother had been taken from this film. Paul had been there for what appeared to be most of the significant events in Teri's life.

John sat in amazement and wondered how Paul could have accomplished something like this without his knowledge. How could he have missed so much? Who had been helping Paul hide this enormous secret? The answer hit him like a ton of bricks. The who was staring him right in the face.

CHAPTER 23

TERI RETURNED from another room and took a seat on the floor next to John. The truth was out. She'd let him know her true identity. Now she prepared for the potential onslaught of questions.

"So, Paul was your father?" John asked with the hint of a smile.

"Yep. He met my mom at a political rally. Love at first sight type of thing. But, coming from where he came and being who he was, their relationship was a definite, no-no. Plus, that whole marriage thing for him was a bit of a problem.

"So he kept her hidden away or should I say us hidden

away, bought this house for us, paid all the bills. Private school, etc. He provided almost everything we needed." John noticed the distance in Teri's voice when she said this.

"So what happened?"

"Well, good ole Grandpa Barrett forbid Daddy from seeing Momma. Threatened to cut him off financially if he didn't stop. Promised to banish him from the family if he continued. Said it would destroy the family politically and socially. From what I understand, that was initially why Uncle Al hung around -- to make sure the family image stayed intact."

Teri lowered her voice and poked her chest out as she said this. But underneath her bravado, John could hear the hurt in her voice.

"Uncle Al controls the family purse strings as you well know. But then I guess over time, he developed a soft spot for the relationship between my parents."

"So, Al Cirrillo knows about your existence?"

"Of course. He was the one who would help Daddy sneak away to spend what little family time we did have together. He allowed Daddy to use him as a cover. As a matter of fact, most of the footage with all three of us together, Uncle Al shot. After my mom died, he even helped me convert some of it to these pictures."

"Well at least that explains why your father couldn't catch a fish to save his life, despite all the fishing trips he and Al went on." John laughed at the memories.

Teri nodded her head in agreement, laughed with him. "Daddy didn't do fish."

They laughed for a few more minutes, each one remembering the fond memories of the man they loved. Teri noticed John's expression change. She could tell that his feelings were hurt. She touched him on the arm.

"Teri, why didn't you tell me this when we first met, or at least after we started to spend time together? I would like to think that we developed some type of trust. As for your father, I can't believe he didn't trust me enough to tell me this."

"I didn't know if you would believe me if I told you. And what was I supposed to say? Hey, Senator Knight, congratulations on the re-election. By the way, I'm the African-American daughter that one of your dear friends forgot to tell you about. You would have thought that I was some fruitcake."

"Yeah, you're probably right."

"Furthermore, it's not like Uncle Al and Grandpa have been very forthcoming with information about my father's death. They didn't want to talk about it. As a matter of fact, the last time I brought it up, they told me to let it go. Hearing that from them," Teri sighed and looked away, "hurt."

"Honestly, John, I didn't know whether you would say the same thing. I mean, why would you want to continue rehashing that tragic event?" Teri pressed "rewind" on the VCR, looked at her father's smiling face, then pressed "pause." "Why would anyone want to keep rehashing that tragic event?" Her voice trailed and John knew she was reliving her losses.

John touched Teri on the shoulder. She smiled, took his hand in hers.

"John, you have to remember that what I'm telling you goes against a lot of what you thought you knew. It brings into question your faith in a lot of people. Most notably, Uncle Al and Grandpa. Plus, I didn't know until tonight whether or not I could trust you. I didn't know if you would help me."

He understood. He probably would have done the same thing.

"As for my father, I believe he loved you like a son. I know he didn't want to disappoint you because he constantly said so. He liked you, John, that I do know. As a matter of fact, I never heard him say one bad thing about you, which coming from him, was the ultimate compliment."

John smiled when he thought of Paul Barrett thinking of him as a son. At times, he wished he had been the man's son. Paul had been a good man in his eyes. Not a perfect man, but still a damn good one.

"I think he wanted to tell you, but I also believe that Uncle Al and Grandpa talked him out of it."

"Why would they do that?"

Teri shrugged. "That's something you'll have to ask Uncle Al and Grandpa. I'm sure those two old coons have lots of secrets," she said. Teri grabbed both mugs, headed for the kitchen.

John sat wondering why two people he cared for like family had been keeping him in the dark. Damn right, he planned to ask Al Cirrillo about this situation. And Al had better pray that he had a damn good excuse. He wasn't going to ask C. Preston Barrett a thing. The man didn't have to justify his actions. C. Preston had practically treated him like a son. Had made him an honorary Barrett. But Al would get an ear full.

While he sat and pondered Al's possible responses, another thought entered his mind.

"Teri, did Al know where you were?"

"Why do you ask?" Teri responded with a perplexed look on her face.

"It's probably nothing. I guess I was just wondering if he knew that you were in Atlanta, and about us?" John felt silly making the last statement in light of her current revelation.

"No, he didn't know about us." Teri smiled, walked out of the kitchen, and again sat next to John on the floor. "I speak to Uncle Al a couple of times a year just to touch base, but he never knows where I may be contacting him from. He says I have a Gypsy soul. Imagine that." Teri shrugged and laughed. She excused herself again to go to the bathroom. Hot liquids tended to have that effect on her.

John continued to think about what Teri had just told him. And he wasn't liking one bit what his gut was saying.

CHAPTER 24

TERI HAD removed her baseball cap when she exited the bathroom. Her hair draped her shoulders. It was the first time John had seen her without some type of head covering. She was definitely more beautiful, he thought. Watching Teri shake the tangles from her hair, John noticed the resemblance to Paul. She had Paul's eyes and his smile. Why hadn't he noticed this before?

Teri tossed the cap on the chair behind John and again took up residence on the floor. She resumed the conversation as if it had never ended -- another trait of Paul's.

"I think the last time I spoke to Uncle Al, I was in Puerto Rico. That was around my birthday." Teri looked at the fire, stood up, and walked toward it.

"So, Al had no idea you were in Atlanta?"

Teri picked up the fire poker and stoked the logs.

"Nope. When I visited Atlanta six months ago, I had no intentions on staying. I didn't think I could be that close to Daddy's childhood home and not be tempted to drop by."

"Were you able to resist?"

"No, I wasn't," Teri responded with a look so innocent it touched John in a way that not too many other things had. "At the time, I was living in Miami. I was there hoping that I would stumble onto some answers about Daddy's murder."

When Teri said this, she looked to see what John's response would be.

"You were in Miami inquiring about Paul?"

Before she answered, Teri took a seat in front of the fire. Yet again, another one of Paul's habits.

"Not really, I was there inquiring about the bombing." Teri watched John's mouth open wide with the shock of another one of her revelations. She continued, "I knew about the abortion clinic because I'd asked Daddy to help a friend who was in trouble. And remember I told you that Daddy didn't do fish. That was our little code for spending family time.

"John, I just want to know the truth. I don't care about the other lies that were told. I understand politics enough to know that sometimes we, the family, are better left not knowing. I just want to know who killed my father. I think I deserve to know that."

John could see the tears welling up in Teri's eyes again.

"I was supposed to be with them that night in Miami, John," Teri said, wiping the tears off her cheeks.

"What do you mean you were supposed to be there?"

"The young lady my father took to get the abortion was my best friend and roommate." Teri removed a handkerchief from her pocket and wiped her nose. John wondered how many days she had cried herself to sleep.

"John, you should have seen her. She was so scared, so

afraid."

Teri closed her eyes as if she was reliving the moment. John had no doubts that she had lived that night a thousand times over. Probably sitting in the same spot.

"I mean, when I first met her, she was this courageous and spirited person. She was a cheerleader. Very active socially, but disciplined academically. That girl really knew how to burn the candle at both ends." Teri chuckled.

"I called her, Fireball -- Carol 'Fireball' Dorsey. And then she changed. I mean, it wasn't an overnight change," Teri wiped her nose again. "It was more subtle than that. She just became different -- distant. That lasted about a month or so and then she was right back to the same old Carol, at least for a little while anyway."

Again John could tell that Teri's thoughts trailed off to some other time, some other place.

"Do you think it was drugs? Teri, it sounds like it could have been from what you're describing." John offered this analysis while he tried to make sense of the situation. It wasn't like rich college kids didn't do drugs. He knew better than anyone did.

"No, I'm fairly certain that it wasn't drugs. At least not like speed or LSD, nothing like that. Carol was too health conscious for that. She always got on me for drinking an occasional beer."

Teri thought about John's suggestion a little longer. Shaking her head, she dismissed the notion. "No, I'm positive that it wasn't drugs."

"Then if it wasn't drugs, what could it have been?"

John thought he might already know the answer to that question. A lot of things were beginning to fall into place for him now.

"Truthfully, John, I think it was a man. I kid you not. I remember Carol coming in some days on cloud nine. Then other days, she would be curled up on that couch like a baby." Teri pointed at the couch John was leaning against. "For a period of time, I had no idea which roommate I would be coming home to."

"You ever meet the guy she was involved with?"

John's mind was already brimming with possible answers.

"No, Carol didn't want me to. She said she was trying to protect me from her mess. Whatever that meant. And then a couple of days later she told me she was pregnant. John, I just remember her being so scared. I really believe she thought the guy would try to hurt her if she tried to have the baby.

"I also got the impression the creep was a public figure, someone very powerful. Carol never said it, but that's the impression I got. Something told me that he could possibly even have been married, but who knows. Fireball had her secrets, as we all do. Anyway, I begged her to talk to my father. John, I didn't know what else to do. I figured Daddy would be able to help her."

Teri started laughing, startling John.

"What's so funny?"

"I remember the look on Daddy's face when I asked him if he knew of any good abortion doctors. Oh, John, you should have seen him. He tried to play it calm and cool, but I could see it in his eyes. He thought I was asking for myself."

"I would have loved to have seen the look."

"Oh, John, it was priceless." Teri laughed, clapping her hands together.

"I bet. So who else knew about the trip to Miami?" John couldn't shake the feeling he had. Something wasn't adding up.

"I don't know. I was hoping you could answer that for me. I figured Uncle Al or Grandpa talked to you about it. Weren't you running the office?"

"Obviously not that well," John mumbled. He took a few seconds to reflect on what Teri had just told him.

"John, are you all right?"

"Yeah, I'm sorry. I was thinking about something. I wasn't involved in the Miami thing. And out of respect, I don't bring it up. As a matter of fact, I didn't find out about Miami until after your father had been killed. Teri, I'm ashamed to say that I don't even know the particulars of the incident. I was in Portland visiting my mother at the time. Your father threatened to fire me if I didn't go."

John smiled as he remembered the debate between him and Paul about the trip. They had argued for days about it. And had Paul not threatened to fire him, he wouldn't have spent any time with his mother before she passed. It was funny how some things worked out.

"Anyway, your Grandfather, Al, and others had already decided upon a course of action by the time I found out. And they had other plans for me. I guess they were trying to keep me focused on making the transition from chief of staff to senator."

"I see," Teri said sadly before she excused herself again.

———◦———

While Teri was gone, John thought about the events of that night. Initially, it had bothered him that a lot of decisions concerning his future had been made without his input, but he understood why. He was on the other side of the country spending some precious time with his mother, and time was of the essence. Or was it?

Ironically, his mother died one month after Paul did. One of his greatest joys had been that she had the chance to see him sworn in as Senator John Philip Knight III. Most importantly, he had been given a chance to say good-bye. Teri hadn't been given that chance with Paul.

In the five years since, he had never investigated the accident surrounding Paul death. Why was that? he wondered. Then he remembered, because C. Preston had asked him to leave it alone. And he had.

Here he was talking about being Paul's friend and he hadn't really gone out of his way to inquire about the incident in Miami. Had he been that power hungry back then? And why hadn't he looked into it since?

It was very easy for him to find out that information; he had assumed all of Paul's committee seats for Christ's sake. But unlike Paul, he didn't have good relations with his comrades in the Senate. A couple of them had long memories and they would rather walk through fire than help him. But still, there had to be someone who would be willing to help him.

John pinched the bridge of his nose, stroked his chin. He had friends at Justice whom he could ask, but how would that go over? Would they become overly suspicious? What the hell, he would have to find out. Teri deserved to know the truth, and so did he.

He noticed Teri's Palm sitting on the counter. It was the same model he owned. He wondered if she used it a lot. He never used his, which was why Jeff kept it. But he knew it had saved his ass on many occasions. Jeff kept all of the appointments on it; otherwise, he would never get anything accomplished. Maybe one day he would sit down and read the manual. Better still, maybe he would get Jeff to show him the basic functions, at least have a general overview of how everything worked. In no time, he too would know how to beam people.

John leaned his head back on the couch, then just as quickly jerked it up. He knew whom he could ask. And this person would definitely help.

CHAPTER 25

CHEVY CHASE, MD
1917 BROHMWELL COURT
10:18 P.M.

JOHN FOLLOWED Teri back to the den. She
had given him a tour of the house. But even with her self-pro-
claimed abbreviated version, it had taken a while. The house
had five bedrooms, three baths, and a finished basement,
which was rented out as an apartment. A sign above the door
leading to the basement read Kevin's World.

The house was a little over twenty-years-old, but had
recently been remodeled. The kitchen had been upgraded and
the carpet looked to be less than a year old. It was cozy, also in
a very upper-middle class neighborhood. A great investment
with a prime location. The kind of quiet residential neighborhood where kids played football in the street during the fall
and sold lemonade on the corners in the summer -- a family

neighborhood.

Every week a housekeeper came by. Every so often, a family friend would use the main residence for a peaceful respite. But more often than not, the upstairs remained unoccupied. Rarely did Kevin venture upstairs, Teri told John. The basement was his domain. John was tempted to ask more about this Kevin, but held his tongue.

Teri said that she kept the place because it had been and would always be, her home. One day she planned to come back for good, but not right now. It was still too much for her to deal with on a day to day basis. Too many memories.

The neighbors were friendly and kept an eye on the property for her when she wasn't in town, which amounted to a month or so every year. Plus, she knew that Al usually had a security team check on it at least once a day.

Teri would be leaving for New York before noon the following day. John made sure he had the correct address. They made preliminary plans to visit some museums and see a few Broadway shows. Teri told him that she looked forward to the visit. John asked her why she had chosen to live in New York. Teri replied that it offered plenty of distractions, something that she desperately needed right now. John agreed.

They made pizza and salads and Teri talked about the different places she'd been. She told John about how after her father had been killed, Al and her Grandfather had insisted that she go see the world. How for five years, she'd traveled the globe. Looking, searching, learning, but never forgetting.

She'd visited every continent and mastered four languages. She told him about teaching English to a tiny village in Capetown. How she lived amongst the Aborigines in Australia, about her love of authentic Spanish artifacts, her obsession with Asian culture.

Teri mentioned the places that she would love to visit again and the places that she would never visit again. John listened attentively and asked questions when he wanted more detail. He now understood that she had been through a lot in ten years. She had lost two parents during that time. But, she didn't seem jaded by it all. In fact, she still seemed sort of naïve to him, which he found very attractive.

In the midst of all their talking and laughing, John promised to help Teri get the truth about the events surrounding the deaths of Paul and her best friend. He suspected that he already knew some of the truth, but he wanted to know everything before he shared it with her. He would get part of the story tonight and any missing pieces tomorrow morning at his meeting with FBI Director, Kip Rogers.

<hr />

Before Teri knew it, it was almost 11 p.m. and the snow had started to accumulate. She noticed John check his watch.

"I guess I kept you a little longer than I should have, huh?"

"I can think of no other place that I would have preferred being."

"Thanks for everything, John."

Teri walked over and gave John a big hug and a kiss on the cheek. She held him tight, almost as if she was afraid to let go. Finally, after such a long time, she had shared some of her pain with another being who understood, someone who was willing to help her. She'd found a friend in John Knight. Teri kissed him on the cheek again.

"And to what, pray tell, do I owe the honor of the second kiss?"

"Oh, just a token of my appreciation."

"Your father used to say that."

"Yeah, it was a saying of my mother's he adopted." Smiling, Teri walked to the kitchen to retrieve her keys.

"You sure you feel safe driving back to the city? The snow appears to be coming down pretty hard," John said, staring out over the front lawn through the plantation blinds.

"What, you don't think I can handle a little snow? Didn't I just finish telling you about traipsing over the globe in search of deadly adventures?" Teri said this as she slipped on her hiking boots.

"Like I said, are you sure you want to drive in this snow?" John joked, putting on his jacket.

"Well, since you don't trust my driving, you can walk back into the city." Teri looked at her watch. "It should only take you about…eh…three hours to get there. That is, if you don't freeze to death first."

"Okay, I guess I can stand one more roller coaster ride tonight. Just promise me you will at least drive the speed limit, preferably fifteen miles below it."

"Ah, come now what fun would that be?" Teri stood from the couch, grabbed John by the arm, and walked toward the door. He stopped before she grabbed the doorknob.

"Teri, you had something for me when I talked to you earlier?"

"Yeah, I almost forgot. You're not gonna like it." Teri shook her head, then rushed up the stairs. Seconds later, she returned carrying a small travel bag, which contained a few of the videotapes. "Here, I think you need to see these."

A look of confusion enveloped John's face. "What are these?" he asked, pulling out one of the tapes.

"When I called you this morning, I told you that Rick and I had an altercation."

"I remember." John frowned and touched her lip. "I never knew his name was Rick."

"Yeah, well anyway, Rick owns the club where I was bartending and apparently, he has a penchant for videotaping certain adult activities. He's obviously been doing it for quite a while." Teri raised her eyebrows to signify her meaning.

"What does any of that have to do with me, Teri?"

"John, read the strip on the side of the tape."

John's mouth dropped after reading the title. He couldn't believe what he was reading. "Are you sure that's what's on these tapes?" He was not believing what he was reading.

"Pretty sure. I skimmed through a couple of them last night, which is another story. But it's pretty kinky stuff," Teri replied frowning.

"How did you get them? And what was he doing with them?"

"You mean, besides starring in a few of them? I have no idea. But, John, he had hundreds of them. I only grabbed a few after our little altercation. Anyway, after watching a few of them, I figured it would be best if Rick and I parted company. A scandal involving any of these people would destroy a family. And my involvement in it would surely disappoint Grandpa and Uncle Al," Teri said sarcastically. "I can fill you in on how I came upon them on the drive back into the city."

"Okay, start talking." John opened the door and started walking toward the Camry.

"Nope, wrong one," Teri shouted. "We taking Big Shirley." She pointed to the big, red monster truck.

John hadn't noticed it when they pulled into the garage or maybe he had. He couldn't remember. At the moment, other thoughts were occupying his mind.

"So, tell me about this Rick guy."

John looked at the other titles of the tapes and the dates. This couldn't be happening, he thought. This was bad, very bad.

"You mean the former love of my life? Let's just say that Rick and I both had a very interesting childhood. And I learned it's a very small world," Teri replied.

"I'm all ears. I want to know everything," John said.

CHAPTER 26

FAT TONEY hit the light switch and entered the basement. He pulled the small skeleton key out of his pocket and approached the bookshelf -- the key had been removed from the jewelry box that Rick kept in his armoire. He had just gotten off the phone with Rick and learned that the meeting in Miami hadn't taken place yet. Benito Escada was apparently not one who believed in punctuality. Rick had said that Stuart was getting a little antsy, which made Fat Toney grateful that he wasn't there. Stuart had little patience and could be very anal when things weren't happening according to plan.

Fat Toney opened the bookshelf and bypassed all the souvenirs except one, the autographed baseball from Chase

Chandler -- an item more valuable than its appearance. It had been reconfigured with special sensors that allowed it to serve as the master key for entrance into Rick's private adult playroom.

Fat Toney removed the baseball, making sure that he didn't disturb anything else in the process. If he broke anything, Rick would be very unforgiving. He held the side of the baseball with the sensor directly in front of the sensor located against the basement wall. There was a small beep, the walls parted, and he walked inside.

Each time he entered the room, he marveled at its existence. Who, but Rick would have thought of something like this?

Fat Toney pressed the red button on the wall and a large projector screen descended from the ceiling. He picked up the remote, resting in the recliner, and pressed "play." Within seconds, the image of Rick and Teri, engaged in naked wrestling, came on. He wasn't surprised that Rick had been watching a tape of Teri. He would have done the same thing. Teri was one of the finest women he had ever had the pleasure of knowing.

Fat Toney hit "stop" on the remote, flipped the control switch for the room's lights. As much as he would have loved to, he didn't have the time or energy to finish watching Rick and Teri. That would have to wait until another day. Instead, he headed toward the wall where Rick kept most of the videotapes.

As he was about to reach for one of the tapes, Fat Toney heard what sounded like footsteps. He cocked his ear to the right, listening for any other noises. He didn't hear anything, but that didn't mean much. Maybe Teri *had* barely missed an intruder the night before. He didn't plan on taking any chances.

Fat Toney looked around the room for anything that could serve as a weapon. His heart rate quickening, he grabbed a nearby paddle and walked toward the stairs, all the while listening for other signs of trouble. Suddenly, the safety and security of Rick's house didn't exist.

Fat Toney walked to the top of the stairs, scanning the room for anything out of the ordinary. He checked every closet and every bathroom. When he was completely satisfied that it had just been his imagination, he headed back down to the basement, but not before activating the motion detectors for the upstairs and main level.

Once he was back in the confines of the playroom, he resumed checking the tapes. Starting with the very first one on the top left corner, he proceeded to read the titles left to right, top to bottom. While he had been busy running errands earlier in the day, Rick had rearranged the room so that the general contractor could do his assessment.

The fact that Rick was organized made this task very easy, all the tapes were catalogued by date and subject. Most of Atlanta's prominent ladies occupied a space on Rick's wall of fame. How Rick had managed to sleep with these women still amazed him. It was like there was a secret society of these ladies and they took pride in sleeping with the same man -- like it was some type of competition. Or maybe they liked the danger and excitement Rick provided for most of them.

Fat Toney pulled out a tape from six years before that featured Rick and Erin Barrett. The tape had been made months before the incident in Miami. In fact, it had been the catalyst for the playroom.

After Rick had realized that Mrs. Barrett had used him, he had struck back. That same night, Rick sent her copies of the two of them engaged in sexual acts with the dates of the occurrences prominently displayed. There had been dozens of them, with Oscar worthy performances from the lead actress in all of them. That gesture had gotten Mrs. Barrett's attention and cooperation. And from then on, Rick had started videotaping, and in some cases blackmailing, every woman he slept with.

That night in Miami had taught Rick a valuable lesson.

Fat Toney placed the tape back on the shelf and continued scanning the wall, stopping at the more recent ones. The tapes of the last six months were of particular interest to him; those featured Mrs. Carmellia Knight.

Carmellia was freaky. She had done things that most men only dreamed about a woman doing. Rick had dedicated an entire section to her, just as he had Erin Barrett. From the looks of things, the women had comparable sexual appetites. Maybe it had something to do with being a politician's wife.

Fat Toney read the strips along the side of the tapes. Just as with Erin Barrett, there were several dozen. A few of the more politically damaging ones, he had taken for purposes of blackmail. Most involved Carmellia and several men and women. *High Profile Orgies I, II, III, and IV,* going up to *XXX,* Rick had titled them. They were like something straight out of a porno movie. Fat Toney had contemplated replacing them while Rick was in Miami, but Rick had already noticed that they were gone. His only option was to keep them -- not that that was a bad option.

Fat Toney pulled out one of the more recent Carmellia Knight tapes and smiled. Thanks to this tape and others like it, he was a million dollars richer. He had sent the package the day before and had received confirmation that his conditions had been met. The money was now resting comfortably in an offshore account. In fact, it had probably already earned him at least a thousand dollars in interest by now.

"Thank you, for being a horny, stupid bitch, Carmellia," he yelled. "Thank you, thank you, thank you. And my bank account thanks you as well." He laughed loud.

With a look of satisfaction, he placed the tape back on the bookshelf. He wasn't worried about the police or any other law enforcement agency getting involved. Carmellia Knight had too much to lose and didn't want the political black eye, which was why she had been chosen in the first place. And now, with her increased media exposure because of this new project of hers, the timing couldn't be better.

Fat Toney smiled at his good fortune. He had learned the art of blackmail from Rick years before, when Rick still liked to blackmail women after he'd slept with them. It had never failed. Each target had been quick to anti up. People tended to be very cooperative when they had a lot at stake and secrets to protect, Rick had taught him.

What surprised him, was that none of the women had suspected that Rick was the blackmailer because most of them continued to sleep with him afterward. Over a year ago, Rick had stopped the blackmailing practice for reasons unknown. However, when Fat Toney had seen the Carmellia Knight tapes, he couldn't resist. She was easy money -- like taking candy from a baby.

Fat Toney shifted his focus to the tapes for the month of October. The Halloween tape was the one that had him concerned. It had been placed among the other tapes by accident. He was lucky that Rick hadn't viewed it or hadn't perused the wall as he was now doing. The Halloween tape would have stuck out like a sore thumb.

He didn't see it in October or November. He checked twice more -- still nothing. It had to be in Teri's possession. Fat Toney looked around the room, made sure that everything was exactly the way it had been when he entered. Rick was anal about things being just the way he left them. When he was fairly certain that everything was the same, he exited the room, placed the baseball back on the bookshelf.

It was time for him to pay Tish a visit.

———◄◦►———

Fred King waited ten minutes after the main door closed, then rolled from underneath the bed. He hadn't heard any more noise from upstairs, but he had been very lucky. He could have been killed. Beaten dead where he stood. Doing this had been a stupid idea on his part, but he had hit pay dirt. He now knew who had blackmailed his sister, so the risk had been worth it.

Fred smoothed back his ponytail, thought about the information he'd just stumbled upon. There were so many things that he could do with it -- so many options now available. The Big Guy had been looking for something. Something that no doubt was very important to him. Fred wondered what it could be.

The report from Langham & Associates had provided photos of Rick Casner's business associates. He recognized the guy from the report. Toney Pruit was the name. He wondered what it was that had Pruit so shaken. Whatever it was, he was now very interested in.

Fred opened the door leading from the basement, poked his head out, and peered up the stairs. The house appeared empty and spooky. He quickly closed the door behind him and headed for the garage. He had left one of the windows in it partially opened. He hadn't always been an upstanding, law-abiding citizen. And some old habits…well, he'd just say that from time to time, he still liked to use them. Which had been a good thing tonight.

CHAPTER 27

TISH ACCEPTED the glass from Gina. She took a swallow of the water, then handed it back to her. Gina had just returned from the Kroger where she had purchased another home pregnancy test. They had three different brands, and they were all indicating the same thing.

"I don't understand, Gina," Tish said, the tears starting to flow again.

Gina sat next to Tish and hugged her. She was just as confused. Tish was a virgin so there was no way for her to be pregnant. She had suggested that Tish take the test as a fluke. It seemed like a harmless thing after the day they had.

They had gone to Spa Excellence were they had been given

the royal treatment. The spa manager had given them a description of the man who had paid for their services. With the first word out of her mouth, they knew it had been Fat Toney.

Tish had told Gina about everything that had transpired earlier in the day between Rick and Teri. And they both agreed that Teri was better off. Gina told Tish some things about Rick and Fat Toney that she didn't know. Things that she planned to share with Stuart. Gina knew Rick wouldn't believe it if it came from her.

During their "girl's day out," it had become obvious that they both disliked Rick greatly, for different reasons. They also didn't care for the blind loyalty that Stuart seemed to have for him. To show their appreciation to Rick, they had decided that if he wanted to be stupid enough to try and buy their help, they would make him pay dearly. Since he was paying the bill, they added a few additional items. The spa manager had hesitated at first, but because Gina was such a valued customer, she had acquiesced.

Thanks to Rick and the money he had saved them at the spa, they had gone on a serious shopping spree. Lenox Mall and Phipps Plaza, each had gotten a taste of the Black Card, as they affectionately began to refer to it. In less than three hours, they had completed their holiday shopping. Afterward, they had dined at Maggiano's, and had desert at the Marble Cream Slabery. Until an hour ago, it had been a glorious day.

Gina looked at the shopping bags thrown haphazardly on the bed. She looked at the wrapping paper they had purchased from Walgreen. They had planned to cap the night off by watching *The Real World* and decorating the little Charlie Brown Christmas tree that Tish pulled out every year. But now that seemed like years ago.

Gina wiped the tears from her eyes and continued to hold her friend. She would be there for her and together they would figure out what the hell was going on with her body. She kissed

Tish on the forehead and stroked her back. She gently rocked her back and forth and silently asked God for some wisdom. She crossed her fingers that he was listening.

———◄�○►———

Tish was taking a shower, so Gina began to clean up the place. She emptied the bags and started hanging up the items Tish had purchased for herself. Christmas gifts were left in bags and placed in the hall closet. Gina was placing the last of the bags away, when she heard the doorbell. For a minute, she started to pretend that no one was at home, but since every light in the condo was on, and the television was turned pretty loud, she decided to answer it. It could be Stuart for all she knew.

Gina checked her appearance in the hall mirror and walked to the door. Since Tish's front door didn't have a peep hole, she did the unthinkable; she opened the door.

"Girl, have you lost your ever loving mind," Pork Chop said, walking though the door. "I know your parents taught you how to answer a front door." He gave Gina a discerning look.

"Mr. Casner, I'm so sorry. I just figured…"

Pork Chop raised his hand, cutting Gina off in mid-sentence.

"I don't give a rat's ass how sorry you are. With all the crazies in the world, you gonna be stupid enough to open the door without the least bit of concern." Gina could do nothing but stare at the floor.

"What if I was some rapist or a mass murderer? What would you have done then, missy?"

Gina had never seen Mr. Casner upset. She felt like a three-year-old.

"Gina, did I hear someone at the door?" Tish asked, walking out of the bathroom with a Pink cotton robe on.

"Hey, Peaches," Pork Chop said to his granddaughter. "Is

this how you answer the door, too? This one here," Pork Chop pointed at Gina as if he was picking someone out of a line up, "don't ask no questions at tall."

Tish's eyes widened, Gina had committed a cardinal sin in her grandfather's eyes. Never open the door without asking who it was, was something they had been hearing from an early age. It was one of the few things that Tish knew really bothered her grandfather.

"Gina, I'm sorry, I thought it was Stuart. I thought he was the only person with your security code," Gina said in her defense. Pork Chop looked at her and shook his head. Gina wanted to sink into the carpet.

Tish knew she had to intervene before her grandfather made Gina cry. He could do that with a look, and Gina was very close to getting the look.

"Pork Chop, is everything all right?" Tish asked.

"Hell no," Pork Chop answered quickly. "I've been trying to get in contact with you all day. Ya'll kids gonna be the death of me yet. You, RJ, and Stuart," he said, taking a seat on the couch."

"I'm sorry, Chop, I was…"

"Tish was with me, Mr. Casner," Gina butted in and wished she hadn't. The look she received form Tish's grandfather made her want to run and hide. She took a seat on the couch on the opposite side of the room; tears started to form in her eyes.

"Chop, I'm glad you came by. I've been thinking about you a lot lately. I was gonna bring by some can goods this week for the Hosea Williams Feed The Hungry Drive," Tish began, trying to save her best friend from the wrath of her grandfather. Gina started to say something, but got the hint from Tish to be quiet.

Tish walked to where Pork Chop was sitting and sat beside him. She gave Gina the nod to give them some privacy. Gina excused herself to get something to drink. Pork Chop looked at her and shook his head.

"How is the food drive going this year?" Tish knew that Hosea Williams and her grandfather had been very close friends and that the Hosea Williams Feed The Hungry Drive had always been important to him, but especially this year with Hosea's passing a few weeks prior.

"Thank you, Peaches," Pork Chop said showing his first smile since he had arrived. "I think this year will be a wonderful year for the Drive. This year I want you and your brother to come down and help serve some food," he said, as Gina made her way back into the living room.

Gina couldn't help herself. She really wanted Mr. Casner to like her. "Mr. Casner," she said, "do you mind if I help too?"

Tish had to stop herself from laughing. Gina Bershon helping to feed people, on Christmas of all days, her grandfather had no idea how sacrificial this was for Gina. If she hadn't been too shocked at the notion, Tish would have told her grandfather so.

Pork Chop waited for what seemed to be a long five seconds before he responded. He did it with a nod.

ACT FOUR

BLOOD IS ...

CHAPTER 28

ARLINGTON, VA
4552 LORCOM LANE
11:32 P.M.

C.J. BARRETT popped the tape into the VCR. It always provided the perfect beginning to what would be a perfect day. In less than thirty minutes, he would be twenty-one-years-old and a very wealthy man. Not that money mattered that much to him. He'd been around it all his life. He simply viewed it as another tool for his pleasure. And right now his pleasure, as always, was in giving it away.

C.J. heard the laughter coming from upstairs. He smiled when he thought of the perverted things that were undoubtedly taking place right above his head. For a split second, it crossed his mind to join the festivities, but that would be a distraction. He had to stay focused.

C.J. placed the two Diet Cokes and bowl of popcorn on

the coffee table. Leaning back on the sofa and closing his eyes, he thought about the day his world had changed. He remembered how excited he had been to be turning sixteen. Finally, he would be able to get his driver's license. He had been practicing his parallel parking for three weeks. Had been up until two the night before picking out the right color, the right model for his car. He'd spent seven hours deciding every mile along his private parade.

He had even called three of his friends from Georgetown Day and had an impromptu brainstorming session, which had accomplished absolutely nothing, a complete waste of his time and energy. In fact, he'd gotten so frustrated that he had simply hung up the phone. They wanted to talk about girls, parties and drugs. Things that were secondary in importance to him at the moment. He had called them for some group support, needing someone who could identify with what he was about to embark upon.

This decision would be one of his first major ones. Damn near the most important one that a sixteen-year-old would have to make. But they had not been up to the challenge -- the selfish dweebs. Trust-fund slaves, they were. Not a one cared about anything that wasn't materialistic. Not a one wanted to make it on his own.

Not that C.J. didn't like material things; he did. He just didn't pine over them, except maybe his cars. He had a thing for cars. His cars received extra special attention. They were maintained in tip-top condition. He personally supervised every intimate detail that went into a Barrettmobile, as he had affectionately dubbed them. Every birthday, he received a new one. And every birthday, he gave up the previous year's. It was his way of inflicting poverty on himself.

The old vehicles were given away, usually to some unsuspecting person. From year to year, he had no idea who would be receiving the cars. He preferred to randomly select people.

To give away the third Barrettmobile, he had driven into Anacostia, a section of southeast D.C. known for drugs, gangs, and many other social ills. He'd found an area high school and talked the principal into allowing him to give the car to the senior with the highest grade point average. He had wanted to do it right on the spot. The principal had urged him to wait until graduation, but he had told the principal that that suggestion was bullshit.

His argument had been that the real disciplined and determined kids would achieve regardless of whether or not there was a reward at the end. They would perform with the cameras off, he'd told her. The principal had agreed and the student had been given the car at a special news conference that day -- against his objections.

He didn't understand the need to publicize the event. He hadn't given away the car to make the news. He'd given it away because it was his and because he wanted to. He didn't need total strangers telling him how good he was. What a wonderful thing he was doing. It wasn't a wonderful thing he was doing. And he wasn't good, not by a long shot. He had his reasons for doing what he did. No one else needed to understand those reasons.

After the big to do, he had even suggested to the principal that the family sell the car and use the proceeds for other things. Since the family lived in the projects, the general consensus had been that the car wouldn't last twenty-four hours anyway. And to his surprise, the family had done just that. They had sold the vehicle to an anonymous buyer for over one hundred thousand dollars. The car had only been valued at ninety-five thousand.

Even more surprising to him, had been the family's wise decision to use a portion of those proceeds as a down payment on a four-bedroom house in the suburbs. The rest had been set aside to fund savings accounts, to buy two less expensive cars, and to purchase other necessities. And since the young lady had received a full scholarship to any school of her choice, the family had significantly improved its quality of living. This had made him very happy.

And it all had started on the day of his sixteenth birthday. The day when he found out who he really was. The day he found out that Paul Barrett wasn't his father.

———◄○►———

C.J. was thirty minutes into viewing the tape when the doorbell chimed. He didn't bother to get up to answer it. There was no need to. The person would eventually get the message and do what he always did.

C.J. heard the sound of the door close and the horrible singing of the person who had entered his house. He didn't take his eyes off the television.

"How much did I miss?" the visitor asked.

"The same amount you always miss," C.J. responded, refusing to look at his visitor.

"I see you got the SUV. Is it to your liking?"

"It's fine."

"Do you know what you're going to do with the Mercedes yet?"

"Nope."

"So you still plan on giving it away?" The visitor's question was laced with a hint of irritation.

"Don't I always?"

The visitor grunted.

"Son, if you don't want the damn cars why do you continue to spend good money on them? Why don't you just write a fucking check for Christ's sake if you want to give to charity?"

For the first time that evening, C.J. looked at his visitor.

He didn't say a word. He just stared at him, almost as if he was trying to look through him.

"Look, C.J., you're an adult now." The visitor looked at his watch. "As a matter of fact, you're an adult worth several hundred million dollars and then some. That means from now one, you'll be making your own decisions and other people will be scrutinizing your every move." The visitor paused to allow his point to settle in. "My God, son, in the next couple of years the old man might not be around anymore. And who knows where Erin will be. It'll just be you, C.J. You'll be the last one and you'll be responsible for a lot of shit."

C.J. continued to stare at the television. The tape was approaching one of his favorite scenes. He turned up the volume to really experience the moment. The visitor grabbed the remote from his hand, turned the volume back down.

"Come on, C.J., a lot of people will be looking to you to make smart decisions. I just think it's time you started making them. Damn, son, I can only offer you good counsel if you're willing to take it."

The visitor was more animated and standing directly in front of him. "Do you have anything to say?"

"You're in my way," C.J. responded.

The visitor blew out an exasperated sigh and took a seat.

—◦▸—

Al Cirrillo had been an employee of the Barrett family for over fifty years. He was approaching seventy-two and he was tired, most of his exhaustion coming as a result of the last ten years. He had dealt with every one of the Barrett men. Four generations of them. But this youngest one, he had the stubbornness of four generations coursing through his veins.

What the others lacked, this youngest one had in abundance. He had his great-grandfather's shrewdness, his grandfather's charisma, and his father's business sense. The kid had the complete package, plus the looks.

Trouble if ever trouble did exist.

Cirrillo had arrived in town about two hours earlier, but he'd had other business interests to attend to. Plus, the dance that he and C.J. did usually required him to show up at about the thirty-minute mark of the movie, *The Godfather.*

For five years, they had performed the same ritual. The first time by accident. The last four as sort of a ceremonial right of remembering; not that he wanted to remember that night five years earlier when Paul had been killed. But he had been the one to give C.J. the news.

The look in C.J.'s eyes had been indescribable. How do you deal with the fact that when you celebrate your birthday, you also celebrate the date of the murder of a loved one. Sometimes life can be so cruel, those were the first words he'd said to C.J. that night.

C.J. had been waiting for Paul to return home. As usual, Erin had been out doing God knows what and was en route home. They'd all planned to watch a movie of C.J.'s choosing. C.J. had chosen *The Godfather.*

After they had received the news about Paul, Erin had been heavily sedated and unable to effectively do much of anything for days, so all family duties had fallen onto him, Al Cirrillo -- the Barrett family problem solver.

He had sat with C.J. that night and watched most of the movie; that was when he wasn't busy trying to diffuse the potential scandal that would surface if the truth behind Paul's death became known. Between phone conversations and damage control, he had checked on C.J., and C.J. had shown no outward expression whatsoever. He had shed not a single tear, asked not a single question.

Cirrillo grabbed a handful of popcorn, popped open the extra can of Diet Coke resting on the coffee table, and joined

C.J. in watching *The Godfather*. Al Cirrillo was a traditionalist, if nothing else. Plus, the tape was approaching his favorite scene.

CHAPTER 29

CIRRILLO'S CELL phone rang. He exited the room to answer it. Whoever was calling him was in a bad cell location, so the call ended. While he waited for the person to call back, Cirrillo walked to the kitchen and put on a pot of coffee. He had some paperwork to go over with C.J., and that would take at least a half-hour, maybe more. C. Preston had always made it a point to give C.J. his yearly trust withdrawal during the first hour of his birthday. Cirrillo suspected that this was done to ensure that no one upstaged C. Preston's gift.

Cirrillo rubbed the back of his neck and popped his back. He removed a couple of packs of sugar from a drawer, poured them in a coffee mug. He usually preferred his coffee black, but tonight he had no intentions on staying up late, which is the effect that black coffee had on him.

While he listened to gush from the coffee maker, he noticed the empty pizza boxes on the island. Either C.J. had developed a ferocious appetite or he had company. It hadn't crossed his mind that others would be in the house. He didn't hear or see anyone, but it was a big damn house. Plus, he and C.J. had been enjoying a state of the art home entertainment system.

Cirrillo grabbed a slice of pizza, headed to the garage. He wanted to get a better look at the new vehicle. He had to say one thing about C.J., he knew how to pick cars. Each year, C.J. had topped himself, and this year was no exception.

Cirrillo placed the cell phone in his shirt pocket, climbed behind the wheel of the SUV. He'd like to get this puppy on the road right now. Test it out in the snow to see if it was all that it was cracked up to be. But no one drove C.J.'s cars.

Cirrillo flipped through the CD collection. Half the names he couldn't pronounce and most of the artists looked like crazies. Although again he had to hand it to C.J., he had an eclectic taste in music, everything from classical to country. C.J. was just like his father and grandfather in that respect -- C.J. was opened minded.

Cirrillo closed the CD portfolio and turned on the ignition. The engine purred like a kitten. He could tell that the SUV had some power. He pressed the gas pedal again just for the hell of it. He wanted to power up the stereo system to see what kind of bells and whistles it had, but he couldn't tell how to turn it on. C.J. had always splurged on sound systems.

Cirrillo heard his cell phone ring; he cut the engine.

"Al Cirrillo," he answered, stepping out of the SUV.

"Al, we have a problem," John Knight's voice boomed on the other end.

"John, what are you talking about?" Cirrillo closed the door of the SUV, making sure it didn't slam.

"I just received some very disturbing information!"

"John, calm down. What are you talking about?" Cirrillo was trying not to raise his voice.

"Look, Al, I'm mad as hell with you right now for lying to me. To me of all people. How could you not have told me the truth?" A now yelling Knight asked.

"What truth? John, are you drunk? Have you been drinking?"

"Hell no, I haven't been drinking. Don't bullshit me, Al, I know."

"You know what? Goddammit, John. What in the hell are you talking about?"

"I know about Teri, dammit. And I know about the girl in Miami, Carol Dorsey. I know every goddamn thing."

There was silence on the phone.

"Do you hear me, Al? I said I know about that girl getting pregnant and Paul's trip to Miami to take care of the problem. You son-of-a-bitch. You told me Paul was there for other reasons. You told me it had been bad timing on Paul's part that he was even there.

"In fact, if I remember correctly, you said the doctor had been the intended target. You lied to me. To me, goddammit. I was his chief of staff, Al. And you lied to me. In fact, you're still lying to me. Who killed Paul, dammit? I know you know, Al. Tell me right now, you son-of-a-bitch. And while you're at it, tell me who got her pregnant, Al. Who's mess was Paul cleaning up? Tell me, dammit!"

Cirrillo smoothed his hair back, massaged his temples. He really didn't feel like dealing with this shit right now, but that's what he got paid to do.

"John, where are you?" he asked calmly.

"Al, did you hear what I just said? Is it true? Is what Teri told me the truth?"

Still there was silence.

"John, are you at home? Is Teri with you?" Cirrillo was try-ing to figure out the best course of action, already thinking two steps ahead.

"By your blatant refusal to answer my question or to deny what I just told you, you leave me no other choice but to believe that what I just said is the truth. I'm very disappoint-ed in you, friend." Knight spit out the last word as if it was poisonous.

"John, shut the fuck up and calm down," Cirrillo said. He had raised his voice for the second time that evening. The last thing in the world he needed was some emotional individual running off at the mouth about something he knew little of, if anything. He needed to get to John and talk some sense into him. Find out what the hell had happened and when Teri had talked to him. She was supposed to be in New York. Dammit. "Look, John, there were reasons why you weren't involved in those decisions. But I simply do not wish to go through them over the phone."

John was quiet.

Good, thought Cirrillo. Now he had regained the edge in this little outburst. John Knight had to be reminded who ran this show.

"Now, John, if you wish to ask me questions and have them answered, I suggest you calm down, find some place nice and cozy, get yourself a drink, and wait for me to arrive. Do I make myself clear?"

"Fine. I'll meet you at the Four Seasons. Thirty minutes, Al---thirty fucking minutes, that's all. And, Al, if you are one minute late, I swear to God I'll start raising all kind of hell. And if you try to bullshit me, I'll get my answers from some other place. Don't forget that I'm meeting with Director Rogers tomorrow. You hear me, Al? Don't fuck with me!"

"I'll be there," was all Cirrillo was able to utter before he heard the dial tone on the other end. That son-of-a-bitch,

John Knight, had hung up on him. That would be the last time that ever happened.

———◦———

Cirrillo walked into the kitchen, removed another coffee mug from the cabinet. He poured himself a cup. Tonight would be a black coffee night after all. He leaned against the counter and developed his strategy for the knock-down, drag-out that was about to come. It crossed his mind to call his grandson, but Jeff didn't need to know anything right now. And hopefully, John wasn't stupid enough to talk to anyone else before he got a chance to talk to him. Instead, Cirrillo picked up the phone and called one of his men. On the second ring, the call was answered.

"Correct me if I'm wrong," Cirrillo began, "but did you not tell me that all phases, except one, had been completed, successfully?"

"That's correct," Sexton responded. He hated being questioned like he was an amateur, and Cirrillo knew this.

"Then, relay to me what happened with phase one," Cirrillo stated, taking a sip from his mug.

Sexton took a deep breathe before he spoke. It was obvious that Cirrillo had information he didn't, but he would continue to play along. No need in biting the hand that fed him.

"Everything went according to plan. Things got a little rough for a minute, but, as usual, she handled it."

"I see," Cirrillo replied, again taking another sip from his mug.

Sexton continued, "She took some tapes and other items with her, but nothing of significance to us, at least nothing that we don't already have. I personally checked the residence after she left and made sure of it. She left a few items of hers, but nothing major. Nothing that she didn't normally leave and nothing that could identify her. My last report indicates that she was headed for the airport and on her way to New York."

"So she flew?" Cirrillo asked, pouring himself another cup of coffee.

"Not exactly. She used the airport to ditch Casner's SUV and to pick up the car she'd purchased a couple of weeks ago. Anyway, as of yet we haven't received confirmation that she's arrived there, but that's not surprising. She could have gotten a hotel room along the way because of the weather. Look, Mr. Cirrillo, obviously something has happened that you would like for me to be aware of."

"That's correct. I think she's either in D.C. or stopped here. And somehow she's revealed her identity to John. I'm pretty certain she told him about Miami as well. I knew I should have had you tail her to New York. This could get real sticky. Did someone check the car after she changed vehicles?"

There was silence on the other end.

"I take your silence to mean, no. Get that done right now. There's no telling how long before Casner learns the location of that vehicle. And we damn sure don't need Teri to have dropped any piece of paper or anything that will give him any idea where she is, who she is or where she's headed, now do we?"

"Consider it done. But I think she took care of the where she's headed part herself."

"What do you mean?"

"Well, it was sort of a brilliant idea on her part."

"Please indulge me," Cirrillo said, picking up another slice of pizza.

"She booked three flights back to back to back, with a final destination being Brazil. She used Casner's charge card to do it. If Casner is as smart as we think he is, he'll investigate that angle."

"Good for her, but we still have the other problems to contend with."

"I'll dispatch someone to Hartsfield immediately. Kevin is en route back to D.C. as we speak. I'm sure he can handle things in Chevy Chase. You'll need to give him some time though, when I last spoke to him, he said the roads were getting pretty nasty."

"I don't care about that. We need to take care of these little problems, before they become big problems. Call me back when everything is checked at the airport. I'll go talk to Teri myself."

"Will do."

"Good. Now, how are we looking with the final phase? It will be completed soon I hope?"

"In a few hours. Don't worry. I'm personally taking care of this one."

"Good."

"Oh, while I have you on the phone, what do you want me to do about our friends down here in Miami?"

"Send a very noticeable message."

———◦———

Cirrillo walked back to the counter, turned off the pot of coffee. He grabbed another slice of cheese pizza and walked into the family room. Twins had taken up residence beside C.J. on the sofa. Both wore very revealing lingerie. Cirrillo smiled at the two beautiful creatures and allowed himself a second of admiration before he spoke. He also wanted to finish his pizza.

"Good evening," Cirrillo said, smiling at the half-naked women. He looked at C.J. "I have to meet Senator Knight about something important." If C.J. heard, he didn't acknowledge. "Anyway, I like the new wheels *and* the company."

"Thank you," C.J. managed to utter.

"I also brought by some documents for you to sign, but if

it's all right with you, we can do that later, after you are finished here of course," he added, smiling at the twins.

"Whatever," C.J. responded.

"The package is by the door," Cirrillo said, stealing one more glance at the twins. Naughty thoughts danced in his head. "I'll let you guys get back to your party. By the way, happy birthday, kiddo." Cirrillo excused himself, walked out the front door.

C.J. continued to stare at the television. The movie was approaching another one of his favorite scenes. The twins made their way toward the kitchen.

CHAPTER 30

ATLANTA
HARTSFIELD INTERNATIONAL
AIRPORT
12:27 A.M.

GARY SEXTON sat in the passenger seat of the black Yukon as it entered the lot designated for short-term parking. He and the two guys with him had been five miles outside of downtown Atlanta when his brother had instructed them to return to the airport. Before the call, they had undergone thirty-six hours of non-stop work from one of the most lucrative assignments of their careers. The amount of money they had received for that job loudly signified its importance.

Comcor specialized in doing two things -- surveillance and killing. And not necessarily in that order. Over the last few days, they had done everything from kidnapping to breaking and entering, but no killing.

Benito Escada had been severely tortured, but not killed.

They had come very close to killing him, but had stopped just short of completing the task. At the last minute, they had decided to let him die slowly instead. Besides, they hadn't been given the official order to do so, although they knew that it would be just a matter of time. Then his brother, Raymond, would do the honors.

It had actually been very refreshing not to kill Escada, but Gary would never admit that. Doing that would dull the edges, which in his line of business was a definite no-no.

He had just gotten off the flight from Miami when he received the message from his brother, Raymond. He pulled out his two-way pager and read the instructions again. This assignment seemed simple enough, more a temporary inconvenience than anything. He would be in his bed in thirty minutes tops.

Gary yawned, stretched, and cracked his neck. Business was good. Life was good. He never knew where he would be from one day to the next, but that was fine by him. Other than his brother, he didn't have any family; unless he counted the two men with him, whom he had known for well over a decade.

They had all served in the military together and had worked as special operatives. When his brother, who had also been a Navy SEAL, had first brought up the idea of forming Comcor, these two men had been his only choices to join them. Raymond had invited one other person to join and the five-man crew had been running like a well-oiled machine ever since -- five years and counting.

"Sexy, which vehicle are we looking for?" the longhaired blond asked, massaging the back of his neck. Deuce Daley looked like a young rock star. He had donned his preferred look for this job, although that would probably change again shortly. Deuce was like a chameleon, able to adapt to any situation at a moment's notice.

Gary looked at the message again, which wasn't a good sign. That meant he was tired. He yawned before answering. "The silver Land Cruiser," he responded, closing the pager.

A plan of action had been put together on the way back to the airport. Each man had already attached a communication device. Each already knew their role. It was now just a matter of execution.

———◄○►———

Fat Toney sat in the back seat of the cab and thought about the conversation he'd just had with Tish. Something was wrong with her. He could tell that the moment she looked at him. He wondered if she knew.

The cabby was speeding toward the airport, but he didn't mind that. He was late and was just hoping to get to Hartsfield and pick up the SUV before Rick, Spanky, and Stuart arrived back in town. He had procrastinated all evening about going to the airport and then with the peculiar way in which Tish had been acting, things hadn't gone the way he had hoped. Now he had to rush to make up for lost time.

He had gone over to Tish's condo to see if she knew Teri's whereabouts and to see if she wanted to celebrate his newly acquired wealth, although he wouldn't be stupid enough to tell her where the money had come from. That would be a bad idea for several reasons. But by the way Tish had reacted toward him at the mention of Teri's name, he knew that getting her to share any information with him or anyone else about Teri would be a lost cause. Therefore, he had done the appropriate thing and changed the subject.

Even then, Tish had been very short in her answers with him. Her thoughts, clearly on something else. The harder he had tried to talk to her, the more she seemed to withdraw --

that had him worried. They had always had an excellent relationship, but he had never seen that side of her before.

He had only seen her twice since Halloween. He'd been avoiding her on purpose -- just in case she remembered something, anything, about the party. He hadn't heard from her, so he assumed that she hadn't. In fact, on the two occasions that he had seen her since, she had been very pleasant to him. But something had happened since then.

"Where do you go at the airport?" the cabby asked in broken English.

"I don't know; just drive through the parking lots," Fat Toney answered, a little bothered that the cabby had interrupted his thoughts.

"Si, no problema." The cabby smiled.

Fat Toney looked at the meter. He was already up to twenty-five dollars. He looked at his watch. Stuart's chartered flight was scheduled to land at Dekalb-Peachtree Airport in five minutes. He was running out of time. "Circle short-term parking first," he said, leaning forward in his seat. The cabby seemed to get upset at the sudden change in plans.

Junior Taylor walked up to the silver Land Cruiser and looked around the parking lot. It was full of vehicles that travelers had entrusted Hartsfield's finest to protect. What a joke, thought Junior. He took a deep breath and popped the lock on the SUV. The alarm sounded for ten seconds before he disabled it. Junior was upset at himself for taking so long to do it; he was getting rusty.

Junior popped a few uppers in his mouth and took a swig of the bottled water resting on the passenger seat. With the penlight dangling from his mouth, he searched the glove compartment. Nothing unusual found, he inhaled the perfume of the vehicle's last occupant.

He had already started missing Teri's smell and she hadn't been gone twenty-four hours. He had been responsible for tracking her every move for the last year. And it had been one of the few assignments that thrilled him more than killing. He had also started collecting a few items belonging to her. His favorites were the Casner tapes. Casner had gotten her to be a nasty girl. If given the opportunity, he would kill Casner and his friends. He would even do it for free.

Junior continued with his quick inventory of the SUV. If anything of hers had been left, he would notice it immediately. He knew almost everything there was to know about her. There was nothing of hers on the front seats or on the front floorboards.

"Junior, how is it looking?" The question came from the tiny earpiece planted in his left ear.

"Nothing so far." Junior ran his hands underneath the front passenger seat before opening the center console.

"Deuce, how does it look on your end?" Gary asked, as he circled the parking lot in the Yukon, his eyes alertly looking for any sign of a potential problem.

"All clear over here," Deuce sang in his mouthpiece.

Deuce was stationed near the front entrance of the parking lot about halfway to the Land Cruiser. From this position, he had an excellent view of the incoming vehicles. He was also in a position to serve as a decoy if needed.

"Good. Junior, hurry up. I'm ready to get home and no telling how long before we get visitors." Gary rounded another corner of the parking lot.

"Give me two minutes and I'll be finished."

Junior hopped into the back seat to finish his search. He quickly scanned the rear floorboards; nothing. Nothing was on the seat either. He did another once over under the seats, very careful not to miss anything.

The shine from the key caught Junior's eye. It had fallen between where the rear seats met. It looked to be a house key of some sort and was difficult to get to. Junior adjusted the seat back as far as he could and used a switchblade to fish it out. He scooped it up and deposited it in his front pocket. That had been a close one. He only had the cargo area to check.

———◄○►———

The cabby entered the parking lot for short-term parking. Since he hadn't been given any concrete instructions, he did the most logical thing -- he started at the very back of the parking lot. He could make more money that way.

Fat Toney looked out the rear windows just as a light rain began to fall. They had covered a third of the parking lot and hadn't spotted the Land Cruiser yet. He looked at his watch again. The plane carrying Rick, Stuart, and Spanky should have landed three minutes earlier. Rick would be calling soon. "Can you speed it up a little?" he ordered the cabby, who did as instructed.

From his station, Deuce watched the cab enter the parking lot. His gut told him that this could be trouble. He'd relayed that message to Gary. Gary's reply was simple, follow it using his night-vision goggles and keep them abreast of all movements.

Gary could now see the cab. It was heading right toward him and was six cars from the Land Cruiser. He backed the Yukon into an empty parking space, killed the headlights. From where he was, he had a clear view of both the cab and the SUV. Through the rain, he could make out the burly figure in the cab. His heart rate increased just a little. He'd hoped that they wouldn't have to kill anyone tonight. Now, it looked like they would have to kill two people.

"Junior, it looks like you're about to have company. Thirty seconds."

At the sound of Deuce's first warning, Junior hopped into the cargo area. He landed on a rectangular item, heard it crack. He bit his tongue to numb the pain, dropped his penlight in the melee. Other than that, he was cool and calm. And would not hesitate to kill. His first inclination was to exit the vehicle through the cargo door, but the interior lights of the vehicle would come on and illuminate him like a Christmas tree. He would have to wait for another opportunity.

Junior pulled the switchblade from his pocket. He didn't like guns. It didn't take much imagination to subdue someone with a firearm. Even a fool could aim and fire. He was an expert dart thrower from forty feet away. He could kill from this distance with his eyes closed. And that's exactly what he planned to do, if he was discovered.

Fat Toney saw the Land Cruiser. He tossed the cabby forty bucks, told him to wait. Rick would be calling at any moment and he still needed to check the vehicle. Fat Toney removed the keys from his pocket, deactivated the alarm. He climbed in the vehicle and started it up. While the interior lights were still on, he searched the front and rear seats. He picked up the bottle of water Teri had left and took a sip; he was thirsty.

Fat Toney turned on the stereo console, pressed the CD button. Nothing happened. The CD changer was empty, as he'd figured it would be. He grabbed the bag that he'd brought with him and pulled out one of his favorite CDs. While Lenny Kravtiz blared from the speakers, he removed six more CDs from his bag. Once he got his music situated, he would be ready to roll.

By the look of the inside of the vehicle, Teri hadn't left anything. But the vehicle was in their possession now, so he could thoroughly check it later. Fat Toney waved for the cabby to drive off. Everything was all right.

Deuce watched the cab pull off and noticed the couple with the two young children walking in the direction of the vehicle. He relayed what he saw. He really hated killing innocent bystanders, especially when they looked to be so happy. Probably fresh from a vacation of some sort.

Deuce nodded to the couple as they passed by the vehicle. The man gave him an uneasy look, but the toddler was tugging at his sleeve. Smart kid, thought Deuce. Just keep walking folks and everything will be fine, he mumbled to himself. If anything happened and they were anywhere near the Land Cruiser, he would have to kill them, and a part of him hated that.

"Deuce, if anything happens, take out the couple, leave the kids." Gary's voice commanded through the earpiece.

Gary watched the action from the front seat of the Yukon, his mind traveling a hundred miles an hour. Either they were about to be very lucky or very cursed. He had to do something.

Junior clutched the switchblade in his hand; he was ready to toss it between the eyes of his discoverer. He had heard the conversation between Gary and Deuce, but obviously had other things in need of his immediate attention. Junior had become one with the back seats. He made himself as invisible as possible. At times, being of small-build had its advantages.

Junior shifted the switchblade from his right hand to his left. It didn't matter which one he threw from. He was equally proficient with either. He steadied his breathing, shifted his body to the appropriate angle. There would be no room for error with this guy.

Gary watched the guy climb out of the Land Cruiser. He started the Yukon, turned on the headlights. At the same time Deuce watched the female toddler drop the Pooh-Bear. It landed right in front of the Land Cruiser. This was about to get real ugly, real fast. Fat Toney spoke to the family as they walked past. He opened the cargo door. Junior heard the cargo door click, raise slowly.

Everything was happening in slow motion.

Junior felt the bead of sweat on his nose. He could see the leg of the discoverer as the cargo door opened higher. If the guy opened it another foot, he would have to kill him.

The bright lights hit the back of Fat Toney's head like a spotlight. He turned, placed his hands over his eyes to shade the glare. The little girl ran toward her parents.

"Excuse me!" Gary yelled.

Fat Toney looked in the direction of the intruder. "Yes, sir?" he answered.

"How do I get to Georgia 400?" Gary asked, leaning out the window. It was the only thing he could think of, but it appeared to work.

Gary's distraction was all Junior needed to grab his pen-light, roll out of the SUV, and under the neighboring vehicle. Twenty seconds later, he was five cars over. And by the grace of God, everyone had lived.

CHAPTER 31

JOHN KNIGHT was pissed as he parked the car in the underground garage. He couldn't find Fred. He couldn't find Carmellia. He couldn't get in contact with a damn soul.

John held up one of the video tapes and shook his head. Everyone had been lying to him, and now this. He tossed the tape back in the carry bag. Carmellia should have been more careful. How could she have been so fucking stupid? Caught on video, doing God knows what, with Chase Chandler of all people. Fuck, what was she trying to do to him.

This would require some serious damage control. A lot of money would have to exchange hands. Knight scratched his head, looked at his watch. Cirrillo would be arriving shortly, and he would dump it all on his lap. That would teach them about keeping him in the dark. Let them try to squirm there way out of this one. Cirrillo had to know about the rekindling of the relationship between Chandler and Carmellia. How could they have been so careless about it. Knight held up second for the four videotapes with Chandler and Carmellia. He shook his head, tossed them back in the travel bag. He looked at the names on the side of the other tapes. Powerful people, very powerful people. He took a deep sigh, composed his thoughts. Everyone involved had better pray like hell that these were the only tapes.

---◀◦▶---

Edgar Rivera hated the thought of going home, but he had no other choice. How could he face his wife knowing that he had lost most of their money on companies that were now worthless?

For weeks, he'd been borrowing from Peter to pay Paul. But now he had run up a massive amount of debt. Debt that it would take them years to climb out from under. How was he going to face Anna knowing that he had destroyed their lives?

For months, Anna's heart had been set on purchasing a certain yacht. He'd promised it to her as an early Christmas gift. And she had told all of their friends and family. But now that wasn't gonna happen.

Rivera said the words "it's not gonna happen." Their utterance signifying the finality of the situation. He pounded the seat with his fist and let out a loud yell.

Oh, how he wanted to turn back the clock, just fourteen months, that's all he needed. He wished that he could get a do over, but that wasn't gonna happen either. "Anna, Anna, Anna," he cried, pounding his head on the steering wheel.

He had intended to honor his promise to her, but the damn stock market had nose-dived. The fucking bastards. Why had he listened to those guys? Why had he invested so much in their businesses? Businesses that he knew nothing about.

Staring into the rearview mirror, he knew the answer to that question. "It was because you are an arrogant fuck, Edgar."

He was the guy with the golden touch. He could spot a winner a mile away. That's what everyone told him. And he'd started believing them. He had fallen in love with his own press clippings. He should have remembered the first rule of thumb in venture capitalism. ALWAYS READ THE BUSINESS PLANS. And never risk something you are not afraid to lose. But he hadn't, and he did.

He had figured that he could trust these guys. He had gone to school with them and they believed in their product. He'd trusted his legendary gut instinct. "You dumb fuck, Edgar," he yelled in the rearview mirror again.

They had promised him that in less than a year, he would double his money. How could he pass up a deal like that?

He couldn't.

He didn't.

He should've.

How could he have let those guys juke him?

HIM, Edgar Rivera of all people.

Rivera took another sip of the cheap bottle of vodka. He pulled out his wallet, looked at the picture of Anna. She was so beautiful. He kissed the picture, held it against his heart. He didn't deserve her. Deep down he knew it. And worse, her father knew it, too. But Anna had stuck by him because she believed in him. She'd gone against her family's wishes and married him.

HIM, Edgar Rivera.

And he had made her happy. For four years, he had proven that he did deserve her. He had proven them all wrong; everyone except Anna, that is. She had never doubted that he would make it.

He had moved her to a sprawling estate in Potomac, Maryland. They'd invited her family over three times last summer for the weekly Sunday social. Her family had been so impressed with him and what he had accomplished. They, too, were had become believers.

He had been profiled in *The Washington Post*. *Sixty Minutes II* had interviewed him. He'd dined at the White House on numerous occasions. Part of the "new breed of entrepreneurs." "A multicultural role model." One of the "faces of the future." Belonging to the "in crowd." The "man with the Midas Touch." He had been referred to as all these things.

HE, Edgar Rivera, *was* all these things.

But now it was all gone. Everything but a measly two million. How could he and Anna live on two million? Just four years before he'd been worth over two hundred million. How embarrassed he felt now.

Rivera drained the last of the cheap vodka, started the Porsche. His meeting hadn't gone as well as planned. In fact, it hadn't gone at all. His own cousin had stood him up. The prick hadn't even shown him the respect of a phone call. He'd left a message with the concierge.

Chase had been his last hope. He was hoping to get a small margin account -- twenty at most. That would be enough to get in on a couple of hot deals, and maybe get Anna a smaller yacht. He was just having a string of bad luck, that's all. In six months, he would be back on top. But Chase had laughed at him. A credit risk. That's what Chase had called him. The BASTARD.

Rivera cornered the third level of the parking lot, barely

missing an SUV. Chase had embarrassed him through a note. Even the concierge had looked at him with distaste as he passed off the note. How dare a concierge look at him in such a manner? All the money he had greased the concierge's slimy palms with over the last couple of years.

To add injury to insult, the concierge had even refused to accept his tip. How embarrassing. When he made it back on top again, Fenway, the concierge, would be the first one he would offer his ass to kiss.

Rivera cornered the second level of the parking lot. He increased his speed and barely missed an Audi coming up the ramp. This was just a blip on his radar -- nothing more. He just needed some time. He could still call in a few favors. Two million wasn't that bad. Anna and he could live off that. They'd done it before. And downsizing on the yacht wasn't a bad thing. Besides, Anna didn't really like the water all that much. She would understand. She would still believe in him.

"Oh, Anna, Anna, please believe in me."

Rivera cornered the first parking level. The next time out he would be stronger, wiser, better. Many successful people had been in a far worse predicament than he was. The Donald was one. And now look at him. Worth well over a billion dollars. If Donald Trump could do it, so could he.

HE, Edgar Rivera, could do it.

He'd be more conservative next time out. No he wouldn't. Conservative was for old white men. He took risks. That's all he knew. Okay then, maybe he would tone it down a couple of notches. Keep his worth to himself. There wasn't a need to be flashy -- not anymore. Everyone knew who he was. Hell, he was famous. A friend of the president. But what good was fame without fortune?

"Fuck! Fuck!!" He pounded the steering wheel again.

This wasn't supposed to be his life. He was different. He was special.

HE, Edgar Rivera, was special.

Rivera reached for his jacket to retrieve the validated parking ticket. "Fuck! Fuck!" Which pocket had he put the ticket in? He took his hands off the steering wheel to search for the ticket. "There you are," he said, feeling the ticket inside his left front pocket.

He placed the ticket on the passenger seat, down-shifted to third gear. The jerk from the release of the clutch caused his glasses to slide off the seat and onto the floor.

"Fuck!"

He needed his glasses. He wouldn't be able to drive that well without his glasses; especially drunk. Well, he wasn't really quite drunk; at least not too drunk to drive. Besides, he'd driven home in worse shape. This would be a piece of cake. He'd even use two hands and drive below the speed limit. With any luck, he would be home in less than one hour.

Rivera steadied the car with his knees, while he bent down to retrieve his glasses. His eyes were averted for a split second when he felt the car go over the speed bump. The jolt caused his foot to slip off the brakes and hit the accelerator. Rivera sat up, tried to regain control. But it was too late.

"Oh shit!" he yelled, trying to avoid the man getting out of the car carrying the small travel bag. The last thing Edgar Rivera remembered hearing before driving off was the man's loud scream.

———<o>———

John was barely breathing. He was going to die. He could feel it. Why hadn't the man stopped to help? He just wanted to live. Everything was now going according to plan. Teri, Carmellia, his Senate seat, Fred, his legacy. All those things. He really did love and appreciate all those things.

Just hold on, Johnny, someone will come along and help.

Why had the guy left him? The guy looked familiar. He could have sworn that he knew him. But to think about that now would be wasted energy. Conserve your energy, Johnny. You have to be strong. Breathe slow. Keep your eyes open.

The tapes! What about the tapes? Where were the tapes? He wanted to feel around for them, but they weren't that important. He needed to conserve his energy. Concentrate on his breathing.

Breathe slow, Johnny, breathe slow.

Al. Where was Al? Al would be there soon. Al was always on time. Al would save him. NO. They had had an argument. Why had they argued? Why had he threatened Al? Please, God, don't let me die.

John could hear cars passing by. Did no one see him? Was this world so cold that no one cared? Was this how his story would end? Him dying alone on this cold, hard concrete.

Positive thoughts, Johnny. Nothing but positive thoughts. Where was his guardian angel? In the movies, there was always a guardian angel. Who would be his guardian angel? Or would he get an angel of death? Oh, God, no. Where was his mother?

Almost immediately, he could see his mother's face. She was smiling down on him. Momma, tell me what to do. Momma, I can't hear you. She was mouthing words, but he was unable to hear her. Why can't I hear you, Momma? She was pointing to someone else. He couldn't make that person out. Who was his mother pointing to? She was walking away. Why was his mother walking away? Don't leave me, Momma. She kept walking, waving goodbye.

Help me, please, somebody help me, please.

Johnny listen to your heart. That was his father's voice. Listen to your heart, Johnny boy. Let it be your guide. It's on you, Johnny. Hold on, son. Fight, Johnny, fight. Goddammit! I didn't raise no quitter.

He hated his father. From the grave, he was insulting him.

I'm not insulting you, son. I love you. I just want you to do your best, to give your all, Johnny. John Phillip Knight III, be a man. Goddammit! Be a man.

His father's words trailed off in the distance, but their purpose had been served.

He listened to his heart.

CHAPTER 32

STUART'S MIND raced with a hundred and one questions on the walk to Rick's SUV. Ninety-nine of which he couldn't answer. Spanky would be following in another SUV.

He was glad of that, because there were some things that he needed to talk to his cousin about. Privately. Rick's answers would go a long way in determining the future of their relationship -- personal and professional. But before any of that dialogue could take place, he needed to check his messages.

Stuart retrieved his cell phone from his jacket pocket and attempted to turn it on.

Nothing.

He tried again.

Nothing.

He removed the battery pack, replaced it.

Still nothing.

His battery had died.

"Damn!" Stuart yelled, smashing the phone against his knee.

Rick looked in Stuart's direction, kept driving.

"I own a fucking communications company with all kinds of high-tech shit and I can't even check my fucking messages. I'm getting rid of all you so called top-of-the-line fuckers tomorrow. I swear to God I am!"

Rick looked at him again and laughed.

"Man, fuck you," Stuart snapped. He tossed the phone in the back seat of the SUV.

Nothing had gone as he had hoped it would. Even the chartered flight back from Miami had not taken off as scheduled. He hated being off schedule. It was the ultimate sign of unprofessionalism.

Plus, he was highly disappointed in Rick. Rick had done a half-ass job in preparing for the Miami meeting. In one sense, they had been very lucky that the meeting had been postponed for a couple of days. That would give him enough time to answer some of those one hundred and one questions that now nagged him.

The only thing he knew for certain at the moment was that if Rick didn't get serious about the project, it would be off. No further discussion. The business plan that Rick had drawn up had been an embarrassment. A complete fuckup. Nowhere near worthy of having his name associated with it.

But against his better judgment, he had trusted that Rick would do a competent job. Since the Cortez deal had been Rick's idea, Spanky had persuaded him to let Rick head up the initial negotiations and draw up the preliminary business plan. They would ride shotgun and offer technical expertise only. And for once, he had decided to go against his gut instinct and let Rick run the show.

Could that have been a wrong move?

Stuart massaged his forehead. How had he gotten here? How had he allowed himself to be placed in this position? On the cusp of doing business with people he knew were major drug dealers. The kind of people he knew had been responsible, in some way, for the death of his parents.

He stopped massaging his forehead.

He knew the answer to those questions. Because even with all his flaws, Rick was still his family. And like his grandfather had said, family was all he had.

———◁○▷———

"Who are we listening to?" Stuart adjusted the volume on the radio. "And when did you start listening to smooth jazz?"

"Boney James. I'm trying to become more refined like you."

"Yeah, right. The CD probably came with the new ride."

Stuart closed his eyes and allowed the smooth sounds to take him away. In his mind, he was on a deserted island with a special lady. No one else existed.

Rick interrupted his dream.

"How you wanna handle the Miami thing, Stu? Since Benito disappeared, we may not be able to get the information I know you want. I would understand if you wanted to pull out of the deal."

Stuart thought about Rick's comments.

"No, I couldn't do that to you. I know how much you want to do business with these cats. And it's not like you are, excuse me, we are getting involved in any of their other business ventures. It's just telecommunications services we're providing." Stuart looked at Rick for any detection that he might be wrong. There was none. "But Rick, regardless of who the customer is, my reputation is still on the line. That means, you gotta promise me that you won't half step on your preparation and professionalism. That business plan you showed me tonight was unacceptable."

"Yeah, I know, Stu. But I told you about what happened with Teri. Stuart, she took the damn laptop I had the thing stored on, man."

Stuart looked at Rick's bandaged forearm. He wanted to believe his cousin. He needed to believe in his cousin.

"Next time, make sure you have a backup stored someplace safe."

Stuart continued to look for any sign that Rick might be lying. Rick had been very vague about what had happened with Teri, and he hadn't pushed the issue. It was obvious that something physical had happened. He just hoped that Rick hadn't struck Teri. Violence against women, he couldn't condone---not anymore anyway.

"And besides, Rick, you know I never back out of a deal once I've given my word."

"I appreciate that, Stu." Rick smiled at his cousin.

For several minutes, neither said a word. Then Stuart spoke. "What you think about Benito disappearing like that?"

"I can't figure that one out. It definitely sounds a little fishy. I think we need to wait more than a couple of days to see how that situation plays itself out."

Rick looked at Stuart to gauge whether or not he agreed with him.

"It's your call. Whatever you want to do, however you want to handle it. I got your back." Stuart closed his eyes and leaned his seat back.

"Thanks, Stu. It means a lot to me that you still want to do this deal. I don't know too many folks that would have stuck around after all the shit that's gone down today."

"That's because I'm not folks." Stuart adjusted his seat back up and looked over at Rick. "I'm blood. And you know what they say about blood." Stuart smiled.

Rick met Stuart's smile with a smile. That was all he needed to hear.

———◄○►———

Stuart ended his phone call. Something important had come up. There was someone he needed to see. They had stopped at an Amoco gas station for Spanky to fill up and Rick to use the bathroom.

"What did you think of Benito's woman stepping up like that to run the show?" Stuart asked, as Rick pulled back onto Peachtree Street.

"I don't know, Stu. Something about her just doesn't seem right to me. She was almost too aggressive."

Stuart said nothing.

Rick continued, "We may be better off just trying to broker a meeting with the Cortez brothers ourselves."

Stuart shook his head at Rick's suggestion, "I don't think that would be a wise thing to do, Rick. Remember as your lesson from this morning should have taught you," he pointed to Rick's bandaged forearm, "there's nothing worse than a woman scorned.

"And I can guarantee that the Cortez brothers will not do business with us if we dis her. In fact, I think that would be a fatal strategic error on our part to ostracize her. Remember, she's trusted by them, and with Benito out of the picture, she'll have something to prove. Let her run the show. We'll just tag along."

Stuart allowed himself another moment to think about the danger associated with this business venture. Had he weighed all the pros and the cons? His gut was telling him that he hadn't. He dismissed the feeling just as suddenly; he'd given his word. "I think this could be a blessing in disguise," he said, then looked out the window.

"You could be right. I have more luck working with women

anyway. Plus, I need a new main lady."

Stuart shook his head and laughed. "Man, you are pathetic."

"What?"

"Man, your woman left your ass...what?" Stuart looked at his wristwatch, "Almost twenty-four hours ago and you ain't replaced her yet?"

"Come on, Stu. I'm in mourning," Rick replied weakly. Stuart continued to laugh. Rick thought about how pathetic he sounded and laughed, too. "I guess my nose was opened wide for a minute, huh?"

"Shit, wide enough that we could've driven this new Range Rover through it."

"Yeah, but I'm straight now. And as you can see," Rick patted the steering wheel of the Range Rover, "I'm back with a vengeance."

"Yeah, I'm definitely feeling this new ride. But I can't dog you out too much; Teri was fine."

"Who you telling? And man she could." Rick closed his eyes, smiled, and shook his head. "Umh, Umh, Umh. Lawd, Lawd, Lawd."

Stuart looked at his cousin and shook his head, "Man, please. You sounding whipped. I can't believe Teri had you whipped like that. What we need to do is go by Liquids and get your playa card back, especially now that you have this new ride. Pull right up front, just pull two chickenheads right out the club."

Rick indicated that he was up to the challenge. Stuart grabbed Rick's cell phone and dialed Spanky to give him the new plans.

"Spanky, change of plans. We gonna swing by Liquids to see if Rick can earn his self-respect back. Stop at the Publix to park. You can ride with us."

After Stuart finished talking to Spanky, Rick called Fat Toney. While Rick was talking to Fat Toney, Stuart pressed the repeat button on the stereo. Everyone deserved another chance, even his troubled cousin. Stuart closed his eyes and hoped that the lady on the beach was still waiting for him.

CHAPTER 33

THE ATMOSPHERE inside Club Liquids was festive. And exactly what Stuart needed. Even with things not working out the way he would have liked them to in Miami, he was still enjoying the night out with his boys. Rarely did the four of them get the opportunity to just hang out. With him and Spanky now spending a lot of time in D.C. and abroad, it was a wonder that they ever got together at all. The last opportunity had been Rick's annual Halloween Bash, which he and Spanky had missed because of international business. He had heard from several people that it had been Rick's best yet. When he got a chance, maybe he would borrow the video and watch it. Rick always videotaped his events.

Stuart glanced over at Spanky who was sitting in the VIP section. Spanky had been his best friend since childhood -- his right hand man. If he was Batman, then Spanky was his Robin. He trusted Spanky more than he trusted anyone. Spanky was one of the only people he would give his life for, because he knew Spanky would do the same. Aside from his sister, his grandfather, and Rick, Spanky was the only other person he would take a bullet for.

A small and energetic type, Spanky had a chocolate complexion with a babyface. He was also a smooth talker, who possessed a wicked sense of humor and a killer smile. And to top it off, he could charm the panties off almost any woman -- Spanky was that good.

Stuart had started calling him Spanky because of his fixation with *The Little Rascals*; that was when they were ten. Spanky had been born Elvernon Cleaver, but only his mother and Stuart were allowed to call him by his birth name. His mother could do it because she was his mother and Stuart could do it only in case of an extreme emergency, meaning the life and death kind. Stuart had done it once in twenty-five years. And that had been the day he had asked Spanky to be his business partner.

Stuart looked at Spanky hamming it up with the three ladies. Oh, how looks could be deceiving. Who would have thought that Spanky also had a very bad side. In fact, Spanky was one of the coldest men he knew. But none of that mattered to him. What mattered most to him, was that Spanky was loyal to a fault. His fights were Spanky's fights. His problems were Spanky's problems. If he was stuck in a foxhole, Spanky was the one he wanted with him.

Stuart motioned for the bartender to refreshen his pineapple-juice. He also ordered a bottle of Moet to be sent to the VIP section. Spanky and his new friends would know what to do with it.

Stuart walked toward the stairs leading from the dance floor to the VIP. He liked to peer over the rail and out over the dance floor. It gave him a God-like feeling. And more importantly, allowed the greatest visibility in the club. He would be able to spot her from there.

On the dance floor, he could see Fat Toney grinding with a South American cutie. Their movements suggested that their business would continue later.

He smiled at the sight.

Over the last five years, Fat Toney had grown. He could now officially be classified as big and burly. Fat Toney stood six-five, easily weighed two-ninety, and carried a chip on his shoulder. His skin stayed flush year round as if he had just finished running a marathon.

He had been a star offensive tackle at Georgia Tech, but had been busted having sex with the athletic director's high school daughter. It didn't seem to matter that Fat Toney had been nineteen at the time and the young lady had been two weeks shy of eighteen. He had been forced off the team six days after the offense.

Feeling sorry for Fat Toney, Rick had befriended him. Then, as now, Stuart suspected that Rick had done it for selfish reasons -- Rick needed a flunky. And Fat Toney fit the role to a tee. Fat Toney wasn't the cerebral type; he was a bruiser. But Fat Toney had earned Stuart's respect over time and through his actions. Aside from his idolization of Rick, Stuart considered Fat Toney good people.

Stuart looked at Fat Toney sweating profusely on the dance floor. For a big man, Fat Toney was agile. The South American cutie that he was dancing with was giving it to him good. But to his credit, Fat Toney was hanging with her.

Stuart looked at his watch. It was almost 2 a.m. She was late. He walked down to the first floor to see if he had missed her. He had specifically told her to meet him on the stairs nearest the VIP. Maybe she had tried to call him to let him know that she would be late. He reached into his jacket pocket for his cell phone.

"Fuck!" He had forgotten his piece of shit cell phone was in Rick's SUV. Stuart scanned the club. There was no sight of Rick. "Ain't this a bitch," he mumbled. Any other time Rick's ass would be glued to my hip. "Fuck!" he yelled again, this time loud enough for everyone in earshot to hear.

"You okay, Stu?" It was Spanky.

"Naw, man, I'm looking for Rick. You seen him? I need the keys to the Range."

"Yeah, he's up on the roof getting wasted -- too wasted to be driving. I took his keys and gave them to Georgia Tech." Spanky pointed in the direction that he'd last seen Fat Toney.

"Good looking out, Spank. By the way, what was up with them hotties I saw you with?"

"That's why I needed to find you. I'm heading in, unless you have something else we need to take care of?"

"Naw, we straight."

"In that case, I'll give you the keys to the SUV. I think I have a ride home."

Stuart gave Spanky a hug before accepting the keys.

"Don't party too long and hard, Hugh Hefner. Remember we have that lunch meeting tomorrow."

"I'll be sharp as a razor."

The three women walked up happy and fine. Every man's dream.

"Will your friend be joining us?" the Asian one asked.

"Umh, I hope so," the Caucasian one added, licking her pouty lips.

The African-American one didn't say anything. There was no need to, her eyes spoke for her. She was too damn fine, thought Stuart. He thought about going just to fuck her on GP. "Not tonight, sweethearts, maybe next time," he replied, still looking at the African-American bombshell.

"Too bad," whispered the bombshell, before kissing Stuart on the lips.

Stuart had to fight the urge to give in. Spanky gave him the killer smile, another pound, and hug.

"Be safe, partner." Stuart nodded.

"Always," Spanky replied.

—◦—

Stuart walked back up to the second floor of the club and saw Fat Toney in the middle of a fondle. He tapped him on the shoulder to get his attention.

"Fool, what you…I'm sorry, Stu; I didn't know it was you."

"Forget it, man. You look like you handling yours."

"Damn straight. You know how we do. I came to her rescue earlier today and she said she's ready to thank me properly." Fat Toney winked and smiled. "You wanna join us? I think she may be a real freak."

Elana Futora looked at Stuart and smiled. Stuart noticed that she had the same type smile as Spanky. This was a dangerous woman, freaky or not, he thought to himself. Fat Toney would have to be careful with this one.

"Maybe next time. But check it; let me get the keys to the Range. I have some business of my own to take care of."

Stuart gave Fat Toney the you know whatsup look. Fat Toney was pretty slow, but he got the message.

"My man, yeah, yeah. Go head and handle yours, Stu." Fat

Toney reached into his pocket for the keys.

"Thanks, Toney. And don't worry about Rick, I'll make sure he gets home. I wouldn't want you to miss one minute of quality time with your lady friend here," Stuart replied, grabbing the keys.

Before walking away, Stuart took one last look at the cutie with Fat Toney. Something told him that Fat Toney was in for the night of his life. And he didn't begrudge him one bit.

———◆———

Stuart made it to the lobby and saw Rick passed out in a booth off in a corner of the club. Rick could never hold his liquor. For the umpteenth time, he would have to carry Rick's big ass out of a club. But that came along with being family, he guessed.

Stuart pulled the keys out of his pocket, headed for the exit door. He would have to pull the SUV right up front, although for a different reason than he and Rick had talked about earlier.

He had taken three steps toward the door, when he ran into the person he'd been waiting for.

CHAPTER 34

ATLANTA, GA
CLUB LIQUIDS PARKING LOT
1:42 A.M.

STUART WATCHED her ass as it moved in front of him. Gina Bershon's walk made everyone notice, regardless of sexual orientation. It screamed sex. Gina was now a graduate student at Emory University. When Stuart and she met, Gina had been a cheerleader for the Atlanta Hawks basketball team and a full-time model. At one point, they had been an item, but he had ended their relationship when Gina had become obsessed with settling down and having kids. Gina had wanted the house in the suburbs with the white picket fence, the 2.5 kids, and the dog. She also had a big mouth and was very jealous. And in his eyes, that had been the deal breaker.

Four years after their breakup, Gina still had the hots for him and would do whatever he asked. He had taken advantage of this and requested that she look out for Tish while she attended Emory. Gina had been more than happy to do so.

"Hi, Stuart. Were you about to leave?"

"Hello, Gina. No, I was going to check my cell to see if you called."

"Dag, you leave your cell in your car? What if I had an emergency and needed to get in contact with you?" Gina looked disappointed.

"Something tells me you would have found a way, Gina. Why don't we walk outside so you can tell me what's going on?"

Stuart grabbed Gina by the arm, led her out the door. He figured it would be better to talk to her outside. Plus, he didn't have the energy to deal with her inside the club.

As they approached the vehicle, he could feel Gina's brain calculating the cost of Rick's new Range Rover. He decided to tease her a few seconds before telling her that it wasn't his.

"Nice ride, Stuart."

"Yes, it is."

"When did you get this?"

"It's not mine, Gina. It's Rick's." Again Gina looked disappointed.

Stuart leaned against the back door of the passenger side. Gina stood beside the front door. He sensed that Gina was waiting for him to open the passenger door. He hadn't planned on letting her inside the vehicle, even though the outfit she was wearing wasn't conducive to cold weather.

After watching a few seconds of Gina shifting uncomfortably in the cold, he acquiesced and unlocked the passenger side door. However, he still intended to make their conversation as brief as possible. He climbed in the driver's seat.

The new Range Rover was nice. Rick had outdone himself. The leather seats were butter-soft. The interior was handcrafted. The sound system was state of the art. It was a definite head turner.

"This is very nice. I like this," Gina said, scanning the inside of the SUV.

"I'm sure you do, Gina." Stuart shook his head.

"And what's wrong with that, Stuart?"

"Nothing, if you work for it. Look, Gina, I don't feel like getting into it with you tonight. Anyway, what's going on with my sister?"

"Oh, so it's like that now. I get all dressed up to see you and spend some time with you and all you want to know is what's going on with Tish?" Gina folded her arms, started sulking, and looked out the window.

"Gina, you need to stop trippin'. First of all, I told you years ago what was up with us -- nothing. And ain't nothing gonna be up with us as long as you keep trippin'."

"So what you saying is that we still have a chance?" Gina asked with eyes of hope.

"Gina, what's going on with Tish?" She had already exhausted his patience.

"Okay, I'll tell you, but you have to promise me that you won't say anything to her. She trusts me, Stuart, and I feel bad enough telling you about it as is."

"Gina, what's going on with my sister?"

"All right already, damn! Well, I think she might be pregnant."

"What? What the fuck did you just say, Gina?"

"Don't get mad at me, Stuart. I'm just telling you what's going on."

"How in the hell? I thought she was on birth control. Who's the bastard that got her pregnant, Gina?" Stuart could hear himself yelling.

"Why would she be on birth control, Stuart?" Gina said, calmly looking at him.

"What kind of ignorant ass question is that? Why else

would a woman take birth control, Gina? So that shit like this won't happen."

"Stuart, I swear for you to be so bright, you don't know shit about women," Gina replied and folded her arms again.

"Okay then Dr. Ruth, fill my dumbass in then because I'm not understanding this at all."

"Stuart, your little sister and my best friend is a virgin or should I say was a virgin. She's just as confused as I am or you are."

"Wait a minute, Gina. How can Tish be a virgin and get pregnant?"

"I don't know, but we took three of those damn pregnancy tests this afternoon and they all read PREGNANT."

"Gina, you're not making any sense."

"Who you telling?" Gina offered and looked out the window.

"Who's she dating?"

"That's what I'm trying to tell you, Stuart. There has been no dating. Tish has been busy studying. Shit, she hasn't been on a date since last summer. I actually had to drag her behind to Rick's Halloween party."

"Well, Gina, my little sister has been having some powerful dreams."

"Look, you can call it what you want to. I'm just telling you what I know for a fact. And the fact is, your sister was a virgin and is now pregnant."

"So how..."

Gina interrupted. "I don't know, but I'm trying to get her to go visit my doctor. She's ashamed to go to her regular gynecologist. And I'm not gonna let her see any of the doctors down at the Emory clinic. Shit, her business would be all over the campus, before she walked out the damn door.

"Stuart, Tish is scared. She took pride in the fact that she was a virgin. She wanted to save herself for her husband."

Stuart looked at Gina in amazement. He couldn't believe

what he was hearing. He had just assumed that Tish was sexually active. Damn, he had even given her some condoms.

"Gina, you know I have to talk to my sister."

"Stuart, don't; please don't." Gina grabbed Stuart's hand. "Let her deal with it, Stuart. I promise I will keep you in the loop."

"I don't know, Gina. This is serious."

"And you don't think I know that, Stuart! Please, just back off and let us handle this. Right now, Tish is upset with herself and everyone else. Plus, you know how she loves you and cares about what you think."

"I don't know, Gina. I don't like this."

"Stuart, please let me handle this. I love Tish just as much as you do. And I promised you that I would look out for her. Let me do that. Please. If I need your help, I'll call. You just make sure you have your cell phone with you," Gina joked and poked him in the ribs.

Stuart laid his head back on the headrest and thought long and hard. The night had seemed so promising just a short while ago. Now it seemed that two of the people he cared about the most were having problems that he couldn't talk to them about. He hated to admit it, but Gina was right. She was his best option with Tish.

Stuart turned to face Gina. She was looking toward the street, trying to give him space to make his decision. He reached for her hand. Gina turned to face him.

"Okay, Gina. We'll do it your way. And by the way, you look beautiful."

"Thanks, Stuart. It was a Christmas gift from a secret admirer."

Stuart's expression showed surprise. "Is that right?" he managed to save face and ask.

"Don't look so shocked, Stuart. Other men do find me

attractive you know." Gina smiled, opened up her purse, and pulled out a small videocassette.

"I hope that's not you and one of those other men."

"No. It's me and Spanky -- fucking," Gina shot back and laughed. Stuart laughed with her, although a little uneasily.

"I'm kidding, Stuart. It's Rick's tape of the Halloween party. Could you give it back to him for me? I know how finicky he is about people borrowing stuff from him and not returning it when they promised to. I barely had enough time to watch ten minutes of it over a week's time. And with me now studying like crazy for finals, I can't see having the time to watch it any time soon.

"I would really appreciate it if you gave it to him for me. Tell him I'll watch it another time. On second thought, never mind. I think Tish made a copy of it. When I get a chance, I'll watch hers."

Stuart accepted the tape from Gina, placed it in his jacket pocket.

"How is school going for you?"

"Three more exams and I'll be finished, thank God." Gina clapped her hands together as if she was saying a prayer.

"Gina, I know I haven't told you, but I am very proud of you for completing your graduate degree and I appreciate you looking after Tish for me."

"Thank you, Stuart. It means a lot to hear you say that." Gina smiled, the hint of a tear forming in the corner of her eye.

"I should have said so a lot sooner, Gina."

"Thank you, Stuart."

Stuart looked at his watch.

"Maybe I can get you to take me to breakfast sometime to celebrate me graduating?" Gina asked playfully.

"How about if I do one better?"

"Excuse me?" Gina replied nervously, the pit of her stomach turning.

"How about I cook you breakfast?"

Gina nodded that Stuart's suggestion was more than fine by her.

For the first time that night, they smiled at each other.

CHAPTER 35

TISH COULDN'T sleep. How could she be pregnant? She'd never had sex -- not so much as a finger inside. Had only held a real penis in her hands once, and that had been Bobby Dubach's in the fourth grade behind the bleachers.

The tears came down again.

How could this be happening to her? She had been a good girl. Had tried to do the right thing. But what had doing the right thing gotten her? Knocked up, that's what. Even worse, knocked up and confused.

What would Stuart think of her now? Would he think that his little sister was a slut? Someone who gave it up to anyone.

Oh, God, she hoped not. Not Stuart. Please, God, not Stuart. And what about her parents?

"Oh, Mama, Daddy, I'm so sorry to have disappointed you."

Tish fell to the floor, curled up in a ball. She felt sick to her stomach.

"Why me?" she cried. "Oh, God, why me?"

———◄○►———

The rain was falling outside. Tish wondered if it symbolized her parents weeping. She needed to deal with this. She could deal with this. There had to be a logical reason why her tests were all indicating PREGNANT. Scientifically, it didn't make sense.

Tish closed her eyes and tried to remember. She hadn't been on a date in months. She hadn't been close to a man way before then -- not so much as a kiss.

She rubbed her temples, willing the answers to come. What had she done? She couldn't think of anything. Where had she been? She couldn't think of anything. It was no use. She couldn't remember one single thing of relevance.

Tish turned on the television. She needed a distraction. Sometimes it was better to focus on someone else's problem. She didn't feel like a sitcom -- laughter wasn't in her right now. No videos -- too sexual in nature and they would only serve as a reminder. What about a movie? But nothing too sappy. Three minutes later, she was still flipping channels. Nothing was on that she really wanted to watch.

Disappointed, she turned off the television.

What about a book? That might prove to be helpful. She walked to bookshelf and looked at her offerings. Stephen King, no. Sidney Sheldon, no. E. Lynn Harris, no. John Grisham, no. Zadie Smith, why not?

Tish pulled out *White Teeth*, plopped down on the sofa,

She immediately jumped up, let out a yell. Something had stuck her in the butt. She looked down at the videotape she'd recorded of Rick's party.

The sound of someone struggling to open a door, startled Tish. She turned in time to see her grandfather rush from the guest bedroom in his boxers, a wife-beater, and dress socks. She had forgotten about him.

"Peaches? Peaches? You okay?" Pork Chop shouted wielding a baseball bat. He was already swinging wildly, hitting walls, and damaging furniture.

"Chop, I'm fine," Tish said, ducking and trying to avoid an errant swing.

Pork Chop stood in the middle of the room, looking around and breathing hard. He was on high alert status now, eyes darting to every corner of the room.

"Then what's all that yelling about?"

Tish held up the video she'd sat on.

Pork Chop looked confused.

Tish started laughing.

"Girl, you better start explaining yourself. All that yelling and carrying on. Could've given me a heart attack." Pork Chop took a seat at the bar.

"I'm sorry, Chop. Didn't mean to scare you. Just couldn't go to sleep and I went to sit down and...shoot, I'm sorry," she said and went to sit back on the couch.

Pork Chop looked at his granddaughter, then looked at his foot. He had stumped it getting out of the bed. It was hurting like hell and he could feel it bleeding. He grimaced slightly. Tish noticed it.

"Chop, are you all right? Did you hurt your foot? Probably did it coming in here running and swinging like you Barry Bonds."

"Peaches, I'm all right. Take more than a bed post to keep this old dog on the porch," Pork Chop said, trying to hide the bloody sock from his granddaughter. The pain was intense and his grimaced.

"Chop, is your foot all right?"

"Huh?"

"Don't huh me, old man," Tish rose from the sofa, headed toward her grandfather.

Before he could get up off the stool, she reached him, and spotted the bloody sock.

"Ohhh. Oh, God," she said, reaching for her grandfather's foot. The sock was soaked in blood. "Chop, you gotta let me take you to the hospital."

"No."

"But, Granddad!"

"LaTisha, I said. NO! No hospitals."

Tish looked at her grandfather's stubborn face, sighed, and backed away.

"Then at least let me look at it," she said, already cuddling his foot in her hands. "I'm gonna put some ointment on it and dress it up, okay?"

Pork Chop nodded.

———◦———

Tish washed her grandfather's foot, cleaning it and dressing it as best she could. It wasn't as bad as it first seemed. He would limp for a while, but he would be okay. While she had the chance, she also gave him a pedicure and a manicure. She fussed at him about not taking better care of himself. He was her last living grandparent, she reminded him.

Pork Chop fought her the entire time, but deep down he enjoyed attention from his granddaughter. When Tish was younger, she often used him as a doll baby. She would put makeup on him and spend hours brushing and twisting his wavy hair. This usually occurred on Saturdays when he was supposed to be watching her and Stuart, while Grace and

Sheila went shopping. He used the time to catch up on his sleep.

Pork Chop smiled as he thought about those times. Life had been simpler then. His family had been safer then. He looked at his granddaughter, the only one he would have. His two girls had blessed him with three grand babies and he loved them all. They all had issues. But eventually they would find their own way. Discover their own rhythm.

Stuart was right, Peaches was keeping something bottled up. And Pork Chop had no plans to leave until he found out what it was. It was time for him and his granddaughter to have a talk.

ACT FIVE

THE MEASURE OF A MAN...

CHAPTER 36

SPECIAL AGENT Stan Belinda placed the cell phone back in his pocket, surveyed the scene. It was the seventh time he'd done so in the thirty-two minutes he had been there. A fucking zoo was how he would classify it. It was actually sort of comedic, too, but he wouldn't dare let anyone see him laughing. Director Rogers had just made this his case. Today was his lucky day.

It was by coincidence that he was actually there. He had been considering staying the weekend at the Four Seasons with a new lady friend visiting from California. Having her stay at his place was out of question; especially since he hadn't exactly gotten around to finding a place yet. Something like that usually took him at least six months. He had at least two more weeks to go. But what the hell, his lady friend didn't need to know that. Besides, he had already started with the foundation of his lie. The things men did for a piece of tail, thought Belinda.

He usually stayed in new hotels alone first; at least for one night. This was his way of getting the lay of the land so to speak. If at all possible, he tried to do it for free. He had a hookup back in New York at most top-of-the-line hotels. The Four Seasons happened to be a recent addition. The only catch to some of his hookups was sometimes he had to pay market price during high demand. It was just his luck that the East Coast was currently being hit with a severe storm.

Belinda looked at the growing madness around him; at least he would be getting one free night out of the deal. He'd get another hookup tomorrow. Over the next couple of days, the Four Seasons would not be ideal for a romantic interlude. Yes, thought Belinda, as the Channel 4 news van drove into the parking garage, it would make perfect sense for him to find other accommodations; especially now that he knew he would be dropping a shit load of money for them. Who said God didn't have a sense of humor?

Belinda crushed his cigarette, tossed a mint in his mouth. He took a deep breath, and surveyed the scene again.

---◄○►---

Nosy hotel guests and the media had already started arriving. They would find out very shortly who had been involved in the accident. Then, they would want to know the answer to the most basic question -- who had committed this gruesome act? And Special Agent Stan Belinda wouldn't be able to answer it. Not until he'd had a chance to view the tape from parking lot surveillance, which they were now in the process of securing.

But the media wouldn't be satisfied with that response. More questions would spring forth; more rumors would get started. And then it would be impossible for him to control the situation.

"Stan, you may want to look at these."

Belinda turned in the direction of Special Agent Atkins. "What are they?" He ashed out another cigarette, accepted the travel bag.

"It appears that Senator Knight planned to do some tape watching."

Belinda stopped himself from making the smart comment that had parked itself on the tip of his tongue. Instead, he read the strips on the side of the tapes. The titles immediately got his attention.

"You shittin' me, right?"

"Afraid not. The woman that found him, found these. She gathered them up, didn't know if they would be important or not. Figured they might be. If you want to talk to her, she's over there."

Belinda glanced in the direction Atkins was pointing. He noticed the redhead leaning against the black Suburban. The way she leaned against the hood, sipped coffee, with the nervousness on her face, he wondered what she was hiding.

Belinda nodded at her; she nodded back.

"Put her in the SUV. Get Ortez to keep her company until I can talk t her."

"We haven't checked the tapes yet to verify their contents. You want me to see if we can use one of the hotel's VCRs?" asked Atkins.

Belinda looked around at the growing crowd.It was almost Showtime.

"No. If what's on the strip is actually on the tape, we need to keep this very quiet. Matter of fact, why don't you take these down to HQ. Have the lab boys look at them. They need to be authenticated. And I want to know the minute they have something. And Atkins, don't tell anyone about these. I mean, NO ONE."

Belinda cold-eyed Agent Atkins in the eye to signify the seriousness of his last statement.

"I see," replied Agent Atkins. "You want me to do that now?"

"Yes."

As Atkins headed toward the SUV, Belinda looked over at the redhead. She was still staring, still looking nervous. He was interested in the why.

———◄○►———

Al Cirrillo finished his phone call. The person who had murdered Paul would be dead very soon. A family never forgets. He took a drink of the bottled water in his hand, tossed the empty bottle in a trash receptacle, and walked toward the FBI agent. He'd met Special Agent Stan Belinda before, though briefly. With a forlorn look on his face, Cirrillo tapped the FBI agent on the shoulder to speak to him privately.

"Do you need anything else from me, Special Agent Belinda?"

"Not right now, Mr. Cirrillo. I think that what you gave us should do, for now. Obviously, if we have any more questions, we'll be in contact."

"Of course."

Cirrillo looked over at the sight of the bashed in BMW which John had been found lying next to, barely breathing.

"What's gonna happen to the coward that did this when you find him, Agent Belinda?"

"Assuming it's a him," Belinda interjected. "That all depends on whether Senator Knight lives or not."

Belinda saw the look in Cirrillo's eyes when he made the statement. The man was miles away, thinking about other things. Belinda was positive that some of them were illegal. He let it pass, chalked it up to emotions.

"How's he doing?"

"They took him into surgery at Georgetown Medical Center. It doesn't look good. In fact, if you are finished with me, that's where I'm headed."

Cirrillo looked at his watch.

"I'm sorry to hear that. My prayers are with him."

"Thank you."

Belinda looked over Cirrillo's shoulder, saw the reporter heading their way. It was Showtime.

"Find the person who did this, Agent Belinda," said Cirrillo, before he walked away.

Belinda smiled. He didn't need to hear from Cirrillo how to do his job. Truth was, he'd lost someone very important to him because of a hit and run. And as far as he was concerned, people who committed hit and runs, ranked just above rapists, murderers, and drug dealers.

CHAPTER 37

TERI TURNED up the heat in the truck. This was crazy and she knew it. Here she was sitting out front of her ex-boyfriend's house in a snow storm. She took another sip of the 7-Eleven coffee. She had already been up to the apartment twice, and gotten no response. She was debating whether she should do it again. Well, she wasn't really debating because she knew that she would do it again.

The sounds of WHUR filled the cab, and she had the urge to dance. She laughed at her own silliness and stepped out of the truck. In spite of how it had begun, the last twenty-four hours had turned out okay. John had agreed to help her and she was back in the city she loved.

Teri stretched and smiled as a college couple passed by holding hands and throwing snowballs. By the way they were looking at each other, it was obvious that they had been doing more than studying. Seth and she used to play similar games.

Teri massaged the back of her neck and looked at how much the neighborhood had changed. She had forgotten how close this street was to Howard's campus, and suddenly remembered the University's plan to buy up the abandoned neighborhood buildings and renovate them. Apparently, that's what was happening. Every other car seemed to have an HU bumper sticker or parking decal. She smiled at the progress and stepped back inside Big Shirley.

She missed the city and its edginess. D.C. always made her feel that at any moment a party or story would break. The only other city that caused her to feel that way was Miami. Nervous energy, she called it.

Teri looked at her watch again, either Seth or his roommate, Wayne, would be arriving at any moment. Though it was late, this was something that she had to do, while she had the courage. Maybe everything would work out just fine after all, she thought.

As she was reaching for the coffee cup again, in the rearview mirror she saw a familiar walk. She pulled up the lapels of her jacket and pulled down her baseball cap. She took a deep breath and waited for him to get closer. Once he was less than twenty feet away, she stepped out of the truck.

"Hey you," she said

CHAPTER 38

C.J. LOOKED over at the twins resting comfortably in his bed. They were good girls, a little misguided, but good nonetheless. He reached into his desk and pulled out the lock box. He entered the combination, opened the box, and removed the videocassettes -- his family videos.

He grabbed the videocassettes and walked down the hall to the guestroom. He closed the door and locked it, just in case one of the girls decided to wake up and start looking for him. He didn't want anyone else in on this secret.

C.J. inserted one of the cassettes into the VCR and waited for the images to appear. The same ritual had been performed for five years now. These tapes had answered so many questions for him. Things that as a child growing up, seemed normal, but in retrospect weren't. Erin, the woman he thought to be his mother, had never shown the love and affection that one would expect a mother to show. Many times, his friends had commented that they couldn't believe she was his mother. He had been ashamed to admit that he felt the same way.

C.J. forwarded the tape to the part where Erin bares her soul to Rick Casner. He listens intently as she tells Rick that she regrets not having given birth to a child. Rick is a little shocked by her confession, but she explains in a fifteen-minute soliloquy why she chose to pretend to be C.J.'s mother. How she believes that his biological father didn't want him or his mother, and how Paul was connected to it all.

C.J. ejected the tape, inserted another one. This one of a different woman, his real mother. He smiled, then ejected it. He still couldn't bring himself to view it in its entirety yet. Maybe next year, he decided.

The tape of his mother was replaced with the tape he had taken from Al. *The Happy Family Tape*, he'd titled it. Paul, Teri, and Helen. His grandfather, his aunt, and the woman who should have been his grandfather's wife.

He'd met his Aunt Teri once, at her mother's funeral. They had looked at each other very strangely that day, but at the time he was too young to realize why. He wondered if maybe she had sensed something as well.

After watching *The Happy Family Tape* for a few minutes, he put in the all-important tape -- the tape that would bring his father and him face to face. C.J. watched five minutes of it, just enough for him to get the inspiration he would need. Satisfied, he pulled out pen and paper.

———◦———

Hi friend,

I hope you are enjoying the show. Now that we both have showed our palms, we can get down to business. I know you're probably second guessing your decison to wire the deposit. If it's any consolation, know that you really didn't have a choice. At least not if you wanted to continue living your dream life. Now, I wanted you to enjoy the pictures before you heard from me. Our girl is quite a performer don't you think? But I'm sure you already knew this; maybe that's why you're marrying her. Anyway, being the visual creature you are, I knew that the pictures would only please you so much, you voyeur you. And since I am the consummate team player, I have included a DVD. Think of it as an instructional video. You should remember those from your days of playing in the Major Leagues. When you view it, you'll know what I mean. Seriously, it's quite entertaining, although a little dated. Still though, as you will see, the lead actress was giving Oscar worthy performances, even then. I also included a disk that will provide you with a clue as to why your future wife may have chosen her line of work. I thought this information made for one hell of a story. And I must admit I was tempted to sell to the highest bidder. In fact, I'd already contacted someone, but luckily your deposit came through. I knew there was a reason why I'm still a fan of yours, probably your number one fan. Anyway, you are an inspiration to entrepreneurs everywhere. It's people like you who make this country great. You are truly my hero. And don't worry, the money has been well spent. I did something worthwhile with it. I must go now. Duty calls.

P.S. Once you've read this letter, and reviewed the contents of everything esle included in the package, please wire the balance. I kept my word, I expect you to do the same. And don't worry, this is the end of our -- partnership. There will not be any future transactions. This was a special offer, available for a limited time.

Plus, blackmail is really not my style. It's sort of tawdry -- low rent really. I just figured you would appreciate the information I had to sell, especially when it pertains to family or in this case, future family. So, if anything else comes up that I think may be of interest to you, I will give you a call. You have my word. And as you now know, I am a man of my word. Tell your fiancee I said hello. Thanks, Partner.

P.S.S. Please don't piss me off by trying to discover my identity. You won't find me -- trust me on that. Besides, I think we both know that there are people out there who would take great pleasure in watching you bleed a slow death. Remember, I know where the bones are buried, so why would you want to make me an enemy? That wouldn't be using good business sense.

Sincerely,
KOS

C.J. folded the letter and placed it in a plain envelope. A copy of it would be kept in the lock box. The original would be delivered tomorrow morning by a courier service. The packet of pictures had been dropped in the inter-office mail the day before. Thanks to Rick Casner and his videotapes, businessman, Chase Chandler, who had donated so much to Carmellia's YMCA project, was a few dollars poorer now. Chandler had already wired a ten million dollar deposit. That had since been moved to several different banks, in several different countries. He'd lied in the letter; the money hadn't been spent yet, but it would be in a few hours.

C.J. sat back in his chair and smiled. Everything was going according to plan. For a few thousand dollars, he had been able to buy the complete Casner library from Junior Taylor. Junior was a druggie and he needed money to score a fix. Several months ago, C.J. had started dropping hints to Al about his suspicions concerning one of his "workers." Al had pretended as if he knew not of what C.J. spoke, but C.J. knew otherwise. He knew that once a seed was planted in Al's head, the least he would do was investigate. C.J. suspected that Junior's days as a Barrett employee would soon come to an end.

C.J. placed the videos back in their lock box. He placed the lock box back in his desk. He rechecked the wiring instructions for tomorrow's transaction. He placed everything back in the top drawer, locked it. C.J. walked over to the window and looked out over the lawn. So far it had been a beautiful morning and he had no reason to think that the day would offer anything different.

CHAPTER 39

THE ROLLING credits woke Pork Chop. He looked at his granddaughter lying peacefully on the sofa and wondered what it was that was bothering her. She hadn't confided in him yet. He would try a different approach in the morning.

Before they had dosed off, they had spent forty-five minutes talking about RJ and Teri, then Stuart and Gina. He teased her about the midnight visit from RJ's friend, Fat Toney. But even a blind man could see that his granddaughter wasn't interested. In fact, she seemed downright repulsed, and he didn't blame her. Fat Toney really wasn't in his granddaughter's league.

Pork Chop removed Peaches' feet from his lap, careful not to wake her. He stood and stretched, covered her with a throw. He bent down and picked up the stuffed teddy-bear that had fallen on the floor. Peaches had been cuddling it during their conversation. Anyone who knew her, knew Peaches only did that when she was afraid of something. She had been doing that all her life.

Pork Chop tried to place the stuffed animal back in his granddaughter's arms, but she moaned and rolled over. Instead, he tucked it under his right arm and smiled.

He stood for a few minutes and grazed over her. She really did look at lot like Sheila, although Peaches wasn't as feisty. But physically, their hair had the same reddish tent and their face, the same freckles. Sheila and Peaches even had the same body size. Not to mention their smiles.

Pork Chop bent down to kiss his granddaughter on the forehead. Again, she moaned and rolled over. He smiled again. His granddaughter would be all right.

Pork Chop turned off the television and picked up the items Peaches had used to clean and bandage his foot. He placed them back in the First-Aid kit and made his way toward Peaches' bedroom.

He smiled at the assortment of stuffed Teddy Bears assembled. Peaches had been receiving bears from the day she was born. In his basement alone, there were several boxes and bins. He placed the one under his arm and a few that had fallen on the floor, neatly on the bed and made his way to the bathroom. Those damn imported beers were calling again.

CHAPTER 40

THE BODY lay on the kitchen tile, and showed no signs of life. The person was dead. And naked.

Elana Futora held Fat Toney's house key in her hand. Once she locked the door and started the drive toward the airport, she would toss it out the window. She gathered everything she'd marked "important" from earlier visits, placed the items in a blue carry bag, and threw the bag over her shoulder. She did not feel sorry for the deceased. Toney Pruit had gotten what had been coming to him.

Elana picked up her baseball cap and slipped it on her head. Her hair was another color now. And except for the smile, everything else was different. She pulled on her leather jacket and performed a quick search of the deceased's home. Satisfied that no evidence existed that she'd been there, Elana smiled. Everything was now complete.

After she had met Toney at the club, he had given her a key to his place. He had something that he needed to take care of and would meet her there shortly. His openness had surprised her. When men thought with their small head instead of their large one, they tended to be very careless.

On the drive over to Toney's, she'd placed a call to Al Cirrillo. She was instructed to go to the bedroom and play coy. She had also been instructed to leave the back door unlocked. She knew from earlier visits, that Toney did not have an alarm. He was invincible.

Cirrillo had told her to do whatever it took to get Toney naked and into the kitchen. That proved to be a rather easy feat. Apparently, Toney had decided to strip before he made it to the bedroom. Thus, all she had to do was ask him to bring her a glass of water, which she was certain she would never receive. She was to remain in the bedroom, until she received a call from Cirrillo. Under no circumstances, was she to witness what took place. In case anything went wrong, she would have complete deniability.

For a few minutes, Elana stood and watched the lifeless body lying at her feet. She then flashed back to the night when her brother and the girl had been killed. She had driven the limousine that transported the young lady to the abortion clinic. She had tried to console the young lady by telling her that everything was gonna be all right. Even though she had seen in the girl's eyes, that it would never be. At least not for her anyway.

As much as she wanted to, Elana couldn't get those images out of her mind. She had spent hours talking to Carol. Trying to make her see what she was doing was for the best. Trying to make her see the idealistic view that she possessed of the world didn't really exist. She knew that better than anyone.

That had been the last time she'd seen Paul alive. He would be dead less than thirty minutes later. Killed by the man now resting at her feet, naked as the day he had entered into the world.

She hadn't left the clinic that evening. Instead, she had circled back and parked the limousine four streets over. Then she had cried.

She had cried for the babies that she would never have and the pain that one man had inflicted on so many lives. She had cried for her mother whose love had been unconditional and a father whose lust had been all consuming. But most of all, she'd cried for Carol. She had wanted to be there for her, which was why she had gone back.

She had arrived back at the clinic in time to watch Toney Pruit press the button that would kill Paul and Carol. She had been standing less than thirty feet away, frozen in fear. Unsure of what to do.

She remembered the pleasure that Toney Pruit's face had exhibited that evening, in spite of the act he was committing. That face had lulled her to sleep many a night. That one could get so much joy out of another's pain, she would never understand -- nor did she necessarily want to. But this guy had deserved to die for all the pain he'd inflicted -- all the lives he had destroyed. And unlike the night when Paul and Carol had been murdered, there would be no tears.

That she was sure of.

CHAPTER 41

ALPHARETTA, GA
545 WINDLAND CLOSE
4:27 A.M.

DEUCE AND Gary watched Elana walk out the front door and lock it. They waited for her to get into the rented Mercedes and drive off. They waited a few more minutes, then entered the premises. They did not check the guy in the kitchen because they knew he was dead. Junior was a thorough killer.

While Gary created the crime scene, Deuce wiped down all the places that Elana may have touched. Although she had been instructed to go into the bedroom only, they knew that often times curiosity got the better of the average person.

Fifteen minutes later, both men stood in the kitchen. One more look around and they were satisfied. When Toney Pruit's body was discovered, the police would know that it had been a burglary.

Five miles away, Raymond put out the last of the cigarette, making sure that he placed the butt in the pocket of his jeans. With his penlight, he circled the vehicle, searching for any neglected evidence. A few items that could be identified as belonging to Toney Pruit had been tossed nearby. Satisfied, Sexton picked up the container of gasoline and doused it on the hood, completely soaking the vehicle from front to center. When the container was empty, Sexton tossed it into the front seat. He picked up another container, duplicated the act. This time starting at the rear and working toward the center. With a quarter of the container remaining, he doused the remaining on the figure in the front seat.

Their eyes met and Raymond turned away. He understood what needed to be done, he just didn't like doing it, not like this. He pulled the gun from his holster, attached the silencer and fired one shot, striking Junior in the center of the forehead. He then reached in the car and closed his eye lids.

Sexton placed the gun back in his holster, said a prayer, and fought back the tears forming in his eyes. At times, he really didn't like his job.

From his jacket pocket he removed a Marlboro, stuck it in his mouth, and struck a match. He allowed the match to burn low enough that it now tinged his fingers. He slowly placed it to the cigarette, then tossed it on the vehicle. Within seconds, the vehicle was immersed in flames.

Sexton removed the cigarette from his mouth, exhaling the smoke slowly. He took in the Georgia air, inhaling deeply. When he could see the containers melting away on the front seat, he turned and walked away. Phase Three was now complete.

CHAPTER 42

WASHINGTON, DC
THE J. EDGAR HOOVER
BUILDING
5:19 A.M.

BELINDA FOLLOWED Kip as they hurried down the corridor toward the Strategic Operations Center. SIOC was a specially designed suite from which the FBI directed major operations. Belinda had never been in the SIOC, but he had heard about it. He had heard that entering SIOC was like going through submarine decompression.

Kip had been summoned to headquarters around 3 a.m. And looked as if he would implode at any moment. For the last hour, his phone had been ringing non-stop. And it probably would continue to do so.

At the moment, Belinda felt very sorry for Director Rogers.

They stopped long enough for Kip to enter the special code and turn the special lock on the vault door, which was marked with a red Restricted Access sign. While Kip entered the code, Belinda noted the sliding sign labeled IN USE, and the name, Operations Center. He also noted the television camera positioned on the entrance.

Belinda had to stop himself from asking questions. This was not a guided tour and he doubted Kip would find his request amusing.

When the vaulted door opened, they stepped onto a raised floor. Belinda remembered being told that the purpose was so technicians could examine its underside for electronic bugs. He hadn't believed it then; he did now.

Kip stood in the middle of the room and tried not to be overwhelmed by everything that had happened in the last six hours.

"Agent Kim, bring up those photos for me."

Kim quickly did as he was told.

Kip looked at the photos of Benito Escada. Or at least what was left of the man. Belinda grimaced at the human carcass on the photo. Everything but the man's face had been mutilated. Whoever did this was trying to send a message.

The photos had been faxed in from the Miami field office, less than thirty-minutes earlier. Benito Escada's body had been placed at the back door of the Bureau's Miami field office, which was one of the many reasons Kip was ready to lose it.

Kip massaged his temples. Someone had murdered Benito Escada, and at the moment the list of probable suspects was a mile long. But the surprises hadn't stopped there. The lifeless body of the salon manager where Benito Escada had been abducted, was found at a sex club in Miami. Preliminary investigations suggested suffocation. Two dead bodies. A blind man could see this connection.

"Agent Ford, what do you have?"

"Give me a second, sir, and I'll bring it up on the big monitor for you. You're gonna be surprised who it was."

Agent Ford punched in numbers on his keyboard. He had captured the man's image from several hotel monitors. Before the image appeared on the monitor, the vaulted door opened and in walked Deputy Attorney General Fordham.

Kip didn't acknowledge his existence. Instead, he raised his eyebrows, stroked his chin, and looked at Belinda.

"Okay, we're ready," Agent Ford said, as the image of Edgar Rivera came on the screen.

Fordham had seen enough; he exited the room.

Kip cursed. His morning had gotten worse.

CHAPTER 43

AL CIRRILLO climbed inside the limo and hit speed dial on his phone. John was out of surgery and now everything was touch and go. He hated calling the old fellow at this time of morning, but he had no other choice. These developments he would want to hear about.

"We have good news and bad news," Cirrillo said when he heard the deep baritone voice.

"I figured as much with you calling me so early, Alphonso. Give me the bad news first. It has something to do with my granddaughter I take it?" C. Preston Barrett sighed.

"Not exactly. There has been an accident and it doesn't look good."

"Is Teri all right?" C. Preston asked with a hint of concern.

"Yes, she is fine. This is not about Teri, Preston."

"Then whom are you talking about, Alphonso? Really, it is too early for these mental gymnastics."

"John. He was involved in a hit and run at the Four Seasons in Georgetown."

"Did he get hit or did he run? And why was he at the Four Seasons anyway? Wait a second before you answer that, Alphonso. I was just getting ready to take my medication."

C. Preston Barrett popped two pills in his mouth and washed them down with the glass of water sitting next to his recliner. Before the call, he had been wide-awake, flipping the channels on the television -- all three hundred plus of them. When the phone rang, he had been contemplating ordering a new George Foreman something or other. He would not admit it, but he was a QVC junkie.

Ironically, he had been anticipating a call from someone about something. He had always had a sixth sense about certain things. Thus, he had always made provisions for most things. That way, any problem could be solved at a moment's notice.

Preparation had always been one of his strong points. Even as a little boy growing up in Atlanta, Georgia. He'd always been prepared for anything. Sort of like the large Oak tree that had help define much of his childhood and listened to so many of his secrets.

Growing up in the South, C. Preston had been an only child. His parents had decided that one would be sufficient. So for companionship, he had befriended the large Oak tree that separated his family's land from the neighbors. As he had grown, so had the Oak tree. Only the Oak tree had outlasted many generations and it would one day outlast him.

But he didn't have a problem with that because the large Oak tree had earned that right. It had survived tornadoes, hurricanes, droughts and fires. Lost limbs and still, it had grown.

It had listened to his dreams and at times, had guided him home. It was the birthplace of so many of his greatest ideas -- always a source of inspiration. Other than God, it had been the only thing C. Preston Barrett had ever considered more powerful than he.

C. Preston cleared his throat, then spoke.

"All right, go ahead, Alphonso."

"I'm afraid John was hit, Preston. And he's not looking too good. He just got out of surgery and it's wait and see. John was at the Four Seasons for a meeting." Cirrillo chose not to elaborate.

"Umh, I see."

C. Preston's mind was racing a mile a minute. Obviously, he was concerned about John Knight, but he always looked at the bigger picture. The Greater Good, he called it. He paid others very well to worry about the minutia. John Knight would receive the best care possible; he would personally see to that.

In the meantime however, this little incident could prove quite rewarding. He had always thought that John made a better chief of staff than senator, which was why he'd waited until the last minute to tell the calvary whom to back in the last election. There were other candidates whom he liked better, but he was still developing those relationships and making sure that they were team players. C. Preston believed in team players.

C. Preston closed his eyes and said a silent prayer for John. "Alphonso, make provisions to get the best medical care possible for John. Where is he?"

"Georgetown Medical Center."

"Then, it is quite serious," C. Preston mumbled.

Cirrillo knew to be silent, see what his orders would be.

"What are his chances for survival, Alphonso?"

"Slim to none ten minutes ago."

"Okay. I'm surprised that the media hasn't broken this story."

C. Preston flipped the television to CNN Headline News.

"I called in a couple of favors, made them sit on it," Cirrillo responded.

"Good, Alphonso. Very good. Now make sure no comment comes out of our camp until you have a chance to get everyone together and on the same page. Where's the wife?"

"Last I heard, she was still in Atlanta. Fred is trying to locate her."

"Tell him to try the Westin Hotel in Dunwoody. She is there with the mayor's press secretary. Really, Alphonso, we have to talk to her soon."

Cirrillo wasn't surprised that C. Preston Barrett knew this. The man had spies everywhere. We having to talk to her, meant that he would be entrusted with the honor.

"Do we know the person who hit John?" C. Preston asked.

"Not yet."

"Who's heading up the investigation?"

"Special Agent Stan Belinda."

"Isn't that the same agent who's heading up the D.C. end of that CASTEL investigation?"

"Yes, it is."

"Where's he from again?"

"New York."

"And what's our working relationship like with him?"

"We don't have one."

"Well, I'm sure that will change very soon," C. Preston said before coughing. "Speaking of New York, has Teri arrived there safely?"

Cirrillo hesitated before he answered. He still hadn't decided whether he wanted to tell C. Preston about the phone call from John prior to the accident. At the moment, he could see no benefit in doing so. He would keep the information to himself for the time being.

"Alphonso, are you there?"

"Yes, Preston. Teri was still en route last I checked."

"Good. And everything with her house is secure. You already have a security team looking after the property, right?"

"Yes, we do, Preston," Cirrillo lied.

He was not planning to hire security to look after Teri's new place. She was a grown woman and it was high time that they started treating her as such. If any of the Barrett clan deserved to be treated with dignity and respect, Teri did. Teri had given no indication that she would damage the all-important family image that C. Preston Barrett had spent over six decades of his life building. Even though in theory, she had the biggest gripe of any of them, including C.J.

"Good, Alphonso, you know how important it is for us to know that Teri is safe and out of harm's way. She is my favorite grandchild you know. Although, I guess she should be considering everything I've done to her. All that I have taken from her..."

Cirrillo heard the sadness and regret in C. Preston's voice. Teri was the only grandchild that had that effect on him, which was probably why C. Preston went to such great lengths to make sure she was protected, as he did now for all his children and grandchildren.

C. Preston believed that the measure of a man was in how well he took care of his family. He had always taken care of his family -- always. But regardless of what he did for Teri from now until the rest of his natural life, he would never be able to give her one-tenth the value of the things he had taken from her. Even C. Preston knew that.

Cirrillo changed the subject. "Speaking of your grandchildren, I saw your great-grandchild tonight."

The utterance of C.J.'s name perked C. Preston up. "Christopher James, really? And how was he?"

"Just as nonchalant as ever, if you can imagine. I swear, the chip on that boy's shoulder gets bigger every fucking day."

C. Preston was laughing on the other end.

"That's my boy," he said proudly. "I tell you, Alphonso, he's gonna be the best of us all. He has it all I tell you. C.J. is the complete goddamn package."

"I believe you, Preston."

"So, what did he get this year?" C. Preston asked excitedly.

"A Cadillac Escalade."

"I tell you that boy is a car junkie just like I was. As a matter of fact, he's worse than I was, don't you think, Alphonso? I think I'll take that Porsche that I purchased of his for a spin tomorrow. Yes, that's exactly what I'll do."

"Yes, I do, Preston. And if you do that, could you please try to drive under eighty miles an hour. I hate dealing with the Palm Beach police force. They've threatened to revoke your driver's license the next time they clock you speeding."

"Fuck 'em, Alphonso. I'm gonna break the speed limit just for the hell of it. And I'll give any son-of-a-bitch trying to stop me a race for his money."

Cirrillo knew better than to try to talk C. Preston out of his inevitable attempt to break the law. He made a mental note to call the Palm Beach police captain to give him a head's up. That way, C. Preston could break the law with supervision.

Cirrillo was thinking of a way to end the phone call; otherwise, C. Preston would talk another hour or so.

C. Preston was thinking of other things -- more important things. Things for the Greater Good.

"Look, Alphonso, I know you need to take care of some things, so I won't hold you up. Call me if anything changes with John's condition."

"You know I will, Preston."

"Alphonso, don't worry, John will be fine. One way or another, John will be fine."

"I hope you're right, Preston."

"Oh, Alphonso, I know I'm right. Now what was the good news?"

"It's done, Preston. Paul's killer is dead."

"Thank you, Alphonso. Thank you."

"I told you it would be taken care of, Preston."

"Yes, you did, Alphonso. Yes, you did. Goodbye, Alphonso."

C. Preston ended the call without giving Cirrillo a chance to say goodbye. Before the phone hit the cradle, the tears began to flow.

—◄○►—

Cirrillo stuffed the phone in his jacket pocket and looked out on the snow-covered lawns. He was surprised that C. Preston hadn't mentioned a possible replacement for John in the Senate yet. Although he was sure that a short list had been compiled. He would give him twenty-four hours to mention it.

Cirrillo rolled down the back window of the limo as it traveled down Connecticut Avenue heading toward Chevy Chase. It had been confirmed that Teri was in D.C., but she had stepped out to visit an old boyfriend. He would wait for her to return and then they would talk. He would tell her everything she needed to know about that night and hope that she would understand why they had chosen to do things a certain way.

In every war there are casualties, and some hurt more than others. He knew that better than anyone. But he didn't regret any thing that he had done that night or many other nights since. Paul had always been special to him, which is why he went to such great lengths to protect him.

Paul wasn't supposed to be in Miami. C. Preston had

wanted him to take Carol to get the abortion, but at the last minute Paul and Elana had talked him out of it. This was one time that they felt responsible for cleaning up their father's mess. And that one time had cost Paul his life.

Cirillo allowed the snow to fall into the car. The coolness and cleanness of it was so refreshing. He stuck his head out the window and did something that he hadn't done since he was a kid -- Cirillo opened his mouth and allowed the snow to melt on his tongue. Life's simple pleasures were more appreciated in times like these.

CHAPTER 44

TERI SAT up in the daybed and looked around. She had fallen asleep, and someone had covered her with a throw. Someone had also given her a nice, big pillow. She wondered if it had been Seth. Probably not, she figured. More than likely it had been Wayne.

The look on Wayne's face when she had spoken to him had been priceless. He had actually dropped the carryout bag he'd been holding. He had definitely lost cool points for that one.

Wayne had invited her in. He had also filled her in. No, Seth wasn't seeing anyone -- not seriously anyway. Yes, he still worked at the club. In fact, that's where he was just coming from. Seth had written a book and he was scheduled to have lunch with an editor from a major publishing house the next day.

Seth would get home rather late as he was going to Kinko's to make copies. No, Seth wouldn't be offended that she had just popped up. He still thought that she and Seth made the cutest couple. No, Seth wasn't angry about her leaving. For what it was worth, in his opinion, it had been the best thing for both of them. Their ending would be more romantic that way.

Teri grabbed the pillow and hugged it tightly. The last twenty-four hours had been very strange. She'd gone from one man who she really didn't know, to another one who really didn't know her, not yet anyway.

Teri looked at her watch. It was a few minutes past 5:30. She stood up again and stretched. She remembered there being a bathroom in each bedroom. That was one of the things she had always liked about this apartment. If she remembered correctly, the bathroom in this room was off to the right.

Teri walked to the bathroom and smiled. Someone laid out a brand new toothbrush, toothpaste, sponge, and towel for her. That same someone had also laid out a Howard University cotton sweatsuit. Teri held the clothes up to her nose and inhaled the scent. Seth still wore the same cologne. Oh, how she missed his scent. He had always smelled like fresh lemons. And she had a thing for citrus fragrances.

Teri finished drying her hair and slipped into the sweat-suit. The twenty-minute shower had been just what the doctor ordered. She hoped that he wouldn't be mad that she had taken such a long shower. She had just gotten so used to being able to, after being at Rick's. But that part of her life was now over. A diversionary tactic at best.

This was where she had always belonged. She knew that

now.

Teri pulled her hair back into a bun, slipped on the pair of wool socks that had been left for her. She suspected that Seth would be waiting for her on the other side of the door. In the past, the morning following an argument, he had always offered her breakfast. That had been his olive branch.

Teri closed her eyes, said a silent prayer, and opened the door.

———◄○►———

Seth Fisher heard the door open, even though the cartoon was playing in the background. He opened his eyes and took in the sight. The soft light from the television was the only light in the room. The shades were drawn and the sun had yet to make its appearance. Yet and still, her beauty illuminated the room.

He had watched her sleep hours earlier. Her chest rising and falling with each breath. He had wanted to wake her, to touch her face, but just in case it was a dream, he decided against it. He had forgiven her long ago for leaving like she had. He understood. Time and maturity had made him. He was just glad that she was safe and secure -- that's all he had ever wanted -- for her to be safe and secure.

He already knew most of what she had to tell him and some more things about who she was. Carol had told him everything days before she died. He had wanted to tell Teri, but the time never seemed right. That's why he had written, *Feet of Clay*. He had written the book for Teri & Carol.

He hadn't been able to help Carol, but he could make sure that her memory was honored. The truth deserved to be told, regardless of the consequences.

He would be there for Teri during the coming ordeal. In the book, he had tried to tell Carol's story honestly. In doing that, many worlds would be shattered, but he was all right with that. He had given everyone involved enough time to do the right thing. Five years later, they still hadn't.

Seth stood from the sofa. Teri stood in the doorway. Two old friends staring at each other, wanting to say the right thing, not exactly knowing what that right thing was. Teri smiled first, not knowing what else to do, still unsure of what to say. Seth returned the smile, then spoke.

"Pancakes or waffles?"

E pilogue

FEET OF CLAY

Haley's **Department** Store was located on the corner of Cedar and Main Streets. It served as the main shopping hub for the city of Richmond, Virginia. Saturdays were usually the busiest day, so Sam chose it as the perfect day for him to go shopping. He had traveled to Richmond on several occasions; thus, he knew exactly what to expect.

As Sam had imagined, Haley's Department Store was busy. There were mothers shopping with daughters. Fathers shopping for wives. Teenagers were trying on the latest fashions from up North. If he could succeed at pulling this off, the world as Sam knew it would be forever changed. But if he failed, Virginia had very strict laws for this type of crime.

It was a risk that Sam was willing to take.

As the sales clerk approached, Sam's palms began to sweat and his mouth became dry.

"May I help you, young man?" the clerk asked.

"Yes, you may," Sam replied nervously.

Sam could feel the sweat forming on his forehead. His knees began to get weak. Many years later, he would tell his best friend how it felt like he was standing for judgment day. Sam cleared his throat. "I am interested in purchasing one of your fedoras," he said.

"Is there any particular type you have in mind? Any particular color?" the sales clerk asked with a smile.

"Black will be fine I suppose. On second thought, what's fashionable?"

"I take it this will be your first hat purchase?"

"Yes, it will be. So, if you don't mind, I will defer to your recommendation."

"Excellent then. Let me see. I would venture to say that you are a size 7."

While the sales clerk pondered which hat would best fit, Sam began to feel more at ease. So far, so good, he thought. If the sales clerk suspected anything, he didn't let on.

"Ah, ha. I think I have just the one," said the clerk enthusiastically. "We just received this new bunch in yesterday and I think one might be perfect for you. Wait here; I'll be right back." The sales clerk hurried away to retrieve the fedora. Sam let out a long sigh of relief. He knew that he had passed. The white sales clerk had not noticed that he was black. From that moment on, Samuel Chase began to keep a secret.

———◀◦▶———

Theodore Chase, Sr. made his fortune as the owner of funeral parlors in Atlanta during the mid-nineteenth century. He amassed enough wealth to become one of the five richest blacks in Atlanta. He utilized that wealth to establish a powerful presence among the city's elite. He exploited that presence to marry the daughter of another prominent Atlanta businessman.

This combined financial and political clout was parlayed into seats on committees and purchases of land. Through committee seats, Theodore Chase, Sr. helped form banks and insurance companies. Through land donation, he guaranteed free education for his heirs.

When Theodore Chase, Jr. was born, he had the best nanny available. When Junior and his sister, Teresa, were old enough, they attended private elementary schools formed by Theodore Sr. and other prominent black families in the community. When the Chase children socialized, it was with other children of prominent black families.

Ted Jr. attended Morehouse College and then, Meharry Medical School. Teresa attended Spellman College. The Chase children were instructed to marry people of similar social standing. Theodore Chase, Jr. married the daughter of a prominent barbershop owner. This exclusive barbershop catered to an affluent white clientele only. Samuel Chase was the only child of Ted Jr. and Carolyn Chandler, and often worked at his grandfather's barbershop.

Carolyn Chandler was born with a very light-complexion. On several occasions, she had been mistaken for a white woman. And from time to time, she availed herself of those opportunities. Samuel Chase looked exactly like his mother and was with her on many of these occasions.

In most people's eyes, Sam grew up with a privileged childhood. Being the only child afforded him many opportunities. Working in his grandfather's barbershop gave Sam first hand experience with how whites were treated. He would listen as the patrons would relay exciting stories of trips and adventures. He would listen as the businessmen talked about deals and women. In his grandfather's barbershop, Sam Chase learned how to think like a white man and act like a white man. He began to study the inflections in voices and the mannerisms in body language.

Whereas previous generations of Chase's had attended predominately Black Colleges and Universities, Sam attended the University of North Carolina. While a student at UNC, Sam distanced himself from other black students and developed associations with white students only. During his freshman and sophomore years, Sam made excuses for not visiting home more often. The summer following Sam's sophomore year, Theodore Jr. and Carolyn Chase died in a racially motivated house fire. This experience changed Sam Chase forever.

The day before their funeral, Sam had made the trip to Haley's Department store. Their funeral would be the last time that Sam Chase would return to Atlanta. Following his parents' death, Sam dropped out of UNC and moved to Europe where he officially recreated his life.

After two years in England, Sam was accepted into Cambridge University where he graduated three years later. Years later, while giving a guest lecture at Oxford, Sam met the woman who would later bear his second and last child. To decrease the likelihood of being exposed, Sam decided to never, under any circumstances, father any more children. Anything or anyone who threatened that, became expendable.

———<o>———

C. Preston and his friend sat in the room laughing and reminiscing. They had both lived full lives. Between them, they had amassed tens of millions, legally and illegally. Both had sacrificed a lot to get it.

The friend was battling the flu and had been sentenced to bed rest, which was why C. Preston was there. They had met sixty years before at a bar in Chicago. The friend was there selling, C. Preston there buying.

They had been through fire and hell, and considered each other brothers, which meant they trusted each other explicitly. From time to time, they did special favors for one another.

Their only rule -- never to question those favors.

When a favor had been carried out, it was written down on a napkin, then burned. No evidence. No discussion.

While his friend coughed profusely, C. Preston pulled a napkin from his pocket. His friend removed a pen from the nightstand and handed it to him.

C. Preston scribbled out the note. As usual, his penmanship was superb. He handed the napkin to his friend, who read it, then burned it.

Once again, C. Preston had come through for him. The only man who could link him to the Hastings murders was now dead.

The two old friends spent the next forty plus minutes discussing replacement candidates for John Knight's Senate seat. Over the next three hours, all the necessary people would be informed, and by mid-afternoon, the leaks would begin.

C. Preston Barrett kissed his friend and bid him good day.

They would meet again tomorrow. Same time, same place.

The sun was shining, a nice crispness in the air. C. Preston walked to the Porsche and sat behind the wheel. The last twenty-four hours had been exhilarating, but he had enjoyed it. Once again, his family was safe. Once again, it all had been done for *The Greater Good*.